RANSOM

RANSOM

by

Robert Kimmel Smith

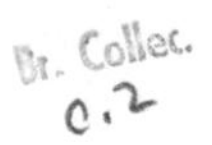

David McKay Company, Inc.
New York

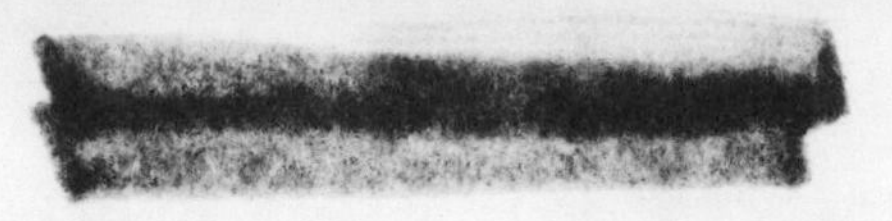

RANSOM

Design by C. R. Bloodgood

LIBRARY OF CONGRESS CATALOG CARD NUMBER: 72-152281

MANUFACTURED IN THE UNITED STATES OF AMERICA

FOR CLAIRE WITH LOVE AND JOY

So I returned, and considered all the oppressions that are done under the sun: and behold the tears of such as were oppressed, and they had no comforter; and on the side of their oppressors there was power; but they had no comforter.

—*Ecclesiastes 4:1*

The price of hating other human beings is loving oneself less.

—Eldridge Cleaver, *Soul on Ice*

RANSOM

PART I

The Children

THURSDAY

6:40 A.M.

Carmine Mancuso's hand kept wanting to reach out to the sugar bowl on the back of the counter, but his conscience said no. At forty-six he was much too heavy to continue to indulge his sweet tooth. You got heart attacks that way, from pasta in the gut, and he wasn't going to dig his grave with a fork the way his father had.

And so he sipped his coffee black, hating it, while trying to ignore the plates of sugar doughnuts and danish pastries crowding the shelves.

"That all you're having this morning?" Mae asked, using a wet rag to wipe away an imaginary stain from the spotless counter of the diner. "Why don't you try a fresh muffin? Frank baked some just an hour ago."

"Nope," Carmine said, "no muffins."

"How about a half?"

Carmine sighed. "You sound like my wife," he said. "Just a little linguine, and a little veal parmigiana, and a little ice cream. And little by little I'm getting to look like a balloon. Thanks, Mae, but I'll just stick to the coffee. Besides, I'm on the late side this morning."

Ace Limousine Service, the business wholly owned by Carmine Mancuso, had grown with the County. Twenty years ago he had started it in his home. With his wife Rose manning the telephone, he drove the County's roads in his polished black Oldsmobile, hustling for a dollar. As the population grew his service flourished. People needed to get to the city airports and terminals. With bus service between towns minimal at best, Carmine picked up customers willing to be transported hither and yon, and well off enough to want to be taken in style. Style was of great importance in the County. It was the reason he now operated a whole fleet of shiny air-conditioned Cadillac limousines. Style demanded that his chauffeurs (for he no longer did any driving himself) be outfitted in uniforms and caps. The same style had demanded that, as he could afford it, he improve his own circumstances.

His home cost fifty thousand dollars in 1965. It was a fantastic contrast to the frame shack in which he had grown up. He drove a silver-gray Lincoln, traded new each second year. His son Roland would soon be graduated from the upper form of the Sloane School. The fact that his son would have not just an education, but the very best education money could provide, symbolized the success Carmine had made of his life. For of all the private schools in the County, the Sloane School was the most august and revered. Acceptance was the goal of *nouveau riche* and blue-blooded WASP alike.

It had not been easy, getting his son into Sloane. First, he had outbid several other limousine services for the exclusive right to convoy Sloane students to and from the school. Once he had his limousines in the doorway, he bore down hard. Complaints were handled with great dispatch. Extra services were provided at cut rates for teachers and staff. Soon he was courting the good graces of the school's upper echelon. After two years, the moment came. In a rare open moment Dr. Charles Carew, the school's stiffly correct headmaster, had complimented him on the services he was performing. Taking a deep breath, Carmine confided how he had come to love Sloane, which epitomized his dream of American success. His secret ambition, he confessed, was to see his son enrolled at the school.

It had worked. In the fall Roland entered the second form, vouched for by the headmaster himself, who took the opportunity of asking Carmine to provide an automobile, gratis, for use in the school's driver education program. Carmine gave it willingly.

Slipping a quarter under the edge of his saucer, he took a final sip of coffee and, waving goodbye to Mae, went out the door.

6:42 A.M.

Richardson Greer swung the old black Chevvy off the parkway onto Waring Avenue. Slowing a little, he checked the rear-view mirror to make sure Joyboy was following. There he was, the dented gray Volkswagen crabbing sidewise on its broken front spring.

"He there?" Sparrow asked.

Greer nodded, the eyes in his mahogany face fully focused on the road, seen only dimly through the misted, rain-dotted windshield. Greer began to pick up speed again, slowly, so the Volks could stay with him through the many turnoffs ahead.

"Goddamn rain," Sparrow said, his high voice contrasting with the low whir of spray under the tires. "Maybe we better turn around."

"Uh-uh," Greer said easily. He shifted his tall frame to glance at the small man beside him.

Sparrow put a smile on his face. "Only jokin'," he chirped as Greer looked back to the road. "Hell," he added, "maybe the rain'll change our luck. What's this, the fourth time we comin' up here to try it?"

"The third," Greer said.

Uncomfortable, Sparrow shifted to look at Greer. The lean planes of Greer's face were set, his eyes fixed on the road ahead. He looks like a high school teacher, Sparrow thought, so thin and straight. Until you see his face up close you wouldn't guess he was only nineteen. And when he sticks those eyes into you, you'd swear he was thirty. Idly, Sparrow let his hand drift to the space between the seat cushion and the back of the seat. The revolver was cold to the touch.

"Leave it alone," Greer said without looking.

Sparrow moved his hand away. "I was only touching it, man."

"Well, don't," Greer commanded. He looked at Sparrow and grinned. "Never mess with a gun," he said, "unless you're fixing to use it."

Sparrow chuckled. "All right," he said. "Okay."

Whistling to accompany the Nina Simone record on the radio, Greer put his foot down enough to bring the Chevvy to a steady forty miles an hour.

6:45 A.M.

He looked at his face in the mirror for a long moment and then, as if disappointed with what he saw, Maxwell Barnett plunged his head under the cold-water tap. The shock opened his eyes wide, as it did every morning. He let the cold rush of water cascade through his hair and down his face until he felt fully awake. Drying himself with the fluffy green towel, he felt courageous enough to take another look in the mirror.

His dark brown eyes, which seemed to recede farther into his face and grow smaller with each passing year, were red-rimmed and bloodshot. The delicate tracery of small veins on his nose looked red. Redder than last week? he wondered. Or last year? He was drinking too much, he knew that. And working too hard. And not spending enough time with Shirl and Kathy. He was not much of a husband and a father these days, but when you were head man on the Tickee Toys account your time was not your own. There was a hard spring and summer ahead, preparing the big Christmas ad push. And the fall would be spent in buying and checking spot TV time. "And holding Chris Menakis' hand," he said aloud. Yes, he would spend most of his time doing that. And arranging parties, and playing golf with Chris, saying "Yes, Chris baby" and "No, Chris baby" and making sure that the eight million dollars' worth of billing, which yearly returned one million, five hundred thousand dollars to the agency (and put eighty-five thousand in his pocket), did not fly away to some other shop. None of it was fun any more. It had not been for a long time.

When he had finished shaving he heard stirrings through the open bathroom door. They meant that Kathy, his daughter, was up and beginning to get dressed. He smiled. He and Kathy were still all right. At sixteen Kathy was beautiful, like Shirl had been when they married. Boys were beginning to flock around the house these days, but with their long hair and strange clothes Barnett thought they looked soft, not really like boys at all.

Now don't get started on *that*, he told himself as he stepped into the shower. There's pain enough in this world without going out of your way to look for it.

He dressed quietly in the mirrored alcove off the bedroom, looking at Shirl from time to time to see if she was still asleep. When he had finished lacing his shoes he walked to the edge of the bed. Even in sleep, it seemed to him, her face was not relaxed. Reaching down, he put a gentle hand on her cheek.

Shirley Barnett smiled even before she opened her eyes. "Max?" she said, her voice husky with sleep. She stretched and began to sit up.

"Would you like breakfast?" she asked. "I mean—a real breakfast?"

"Just coffee, baby. I'm on the run again. So you just stay put and grab some more sleep."

"Oh," she said. She reached for a tissue on the night table and blew her nose. In a quiet voice she said: "What time did you get home last night?"

"Two . . . three o'clock, I'm not sure. I didn't look to see what time it was. Anyway, it was too late to wake you." Max turned away and walked to the window. It looked like another drizzly, depressing April day.

"Crazy Chris?" she asked.

"Crazy Chris." He turned to look at her. "Some big toy buyers were in town. We saw a show, had dinner . . . then we all went back to Chris's place for some drinks and coffee."

She dabbed the tip of her nose gently with the tissue. "And what else?"

Christ, he thought, she's at it again. As if it wasn't difficult enough, playing nursemaid to a neurotic thirty-year-old swinger of a client, he had to come home and be faced with accusations of infidelity. Well, his conscience was clear. "Some very boring conversation, that's what else," he said more sharply than he wanted to. "Like this one." He headed for the door.

"Max!" she called as he reached the top of the stairs, but he didn't answer. She heard his footsteps receding down the curved, carpeted stairs. She sat up and lit a cigarette. Beautiful, Shirl, she said to herself, you've done it again. Now you won't see him for a week.

She thought of the last time they made love. God, how long ago was it? A month? More. It was the Saturday night of the Ambersons' party. They had come home after two o'clock, Max was a little high from too many scotches. He had reached out to rub her shoulder after they had settled in bed. She wasn't in the mood—was she ever in the mood?—but had turned to him anyway, smelling his whiskey breath and tasting the liquor on his darting tongue. He had moved all over her then, in a frenzy of rubbing and feeling and licking that heightened his passion but only served to cool hers. It revolted her. It almost always did. In the early days of their marriage she had been eager to learn the ways of sex. But then, as her feelings grew and grew, only to be abruptly cut off as he spewed into her and sank back with a sigh, she began to take a cooler view of their love-making. There was no release in it for her. What began with the promise of fulfillment ended always in the same way. With Max a dead weight on her breast, sometimes falling asleep, sometimes murmuring a quiet apology for his haste and her failure.

And now he's getting it somewhere else, she thought as she stubbed out the cigarette and settled back under the covers. I wonder who she is, and if she likes it any better than me?

Maxwell Barnett poured a cup of coffee and took it into the breakfast nook. Seating himself, he opened the morning paper to the business section and found Stephen Phillips' column, "Adland." When he read the small item tucked away at the end of Phillips' column he put his coffee down hastily. "*Rumor hath it that Tickee Toys,*" it read, "*is unhappy with the latest crop of TV commercials produced by current agency. All fun and games and not enough sell is the trouble, although Christopher Menakis, Tickee prexy, was unavailable for comment.*"

Barnett swallowed hard and read the item again, thinking furiously. This little item could ruin him. How the hell did Phillips get his hands on it? Who planted it?

Barnett knew well enough about the uproar the item would soon produce. Like a pack of marauding wolves, the ever-hungry agencies in the city would be fighting to get appointments with Chris Menakis. Chris's phone would be ringing nonstop this morning. There would be telegrams, messengers, cute gimmicks, and crazy items coming to his door. Agencies would be stumbling over each other in the rush to grab Menakis and get a chance to pitch the account.

Barnett pushed his cup away and lit a cigarette. When Kathy came down to breakfast and sat across the table he hardly noticed. He had to think very clearly now. There were four commercials in the can, ready for air. He had sold every one to Chris, gotten his approval, and mothered them from casting and shooting right through to final prints. Now someone at Tickee Toys apparently doesn't like them, and that someone blabbed to Steve Phillips. Who could it be? Think.

Across the breakfast table, Kathy Barnett brushed her blond hair aside and gazed at her father. He was off somewhere. She could see his jaws working, his thousand-yard stare. She started to interrupt him, then thought better of it. He didn't look receptive and what she had to tell him was painful. Something was terribly wrong with her mother, of that she was sure. Some kind of depression that was tearing her up, sending her into crying jags when Dad was at the office and she was at school. It was something between the two of them, Mom and Dad, but whatever it was it had to be brought out into the open.

Maybe tonight, she thought, I can speak to him. That is, if he comes home.

6:50 A.M.

"Mommee," the voice said. She felt a small cold hand on her shoulder. Maybe if I ignore it she'll go away,

Emma Porter thought. She snuggled deeper under the bed clothes and pretended sleep.

"Mommee, guess what Paulie's doing in the bathroom?" the voice said, a little louder this time.

Groaning, Emma raised her head and focused a half-opened eye on the clock.

"You'd better come and look. He's making a mess," Heidi Porter said.

Emma struggled out from under the covers and sat up, blinking. "Where's Letty?" she croaked, and before Heidi could reply Emma remembered that her housekeeper had taken Thursday as her day off instead of the usual Wednesday. "What's Paulie doing?" she asked.

"You'll see," Heidi sang and skipped out of the room.

Emma slowly swung her legs off the bed and in bare feet followed her daughter. There was a hissing noise coming from the bathroom. As she looked through the door, she saw what it was. A can of her hair spray. In the hands of her three-year-old. Who had already sprayed the twin sinks and the mirror with a thin shiny film and was now concentrating on making interesting-looking designs on the wallpaper.

I won't hit him, Emma said to herself. You're damned right I'll hit him, she thought, and her hand flew out and smacked Paulie square on his padded bottom. "Out!" she shrieked in a voice that startled even herself. Paulie dropped the can of hair spray on the floor and scooted out of the room.

"I told you he was making a mess," Heidi gloated.

"You didn't try to stop him, I suppose?"

"Are you going to punish him, Mom?" Heidi grinned. "Will you hit him again?"

"Go wash your face and brush your teeth," Emma

replied. “No, wait,” she added hastily. “Let me wash up in your bathroom first. I certainly can’t do it in here.” Taking her toothbrush and a towel, Emma padded down the hall to Heidi’s bathroom.

And it’s not even seven o’clock, she thought, as she splashed cold water on her face.

6:55 A.M.

Tom Seaver spun through the air and landed face up on the thick blue carpet.

“A winner!” cried Henry Taylor Jr. as he reached down to scoop up the baseball card.

“We had fun last night, didn’t we, Junior?” Mike Schwartz said.

A wide grin split Henry’s *café au lait* face. “Your mother wasn’t mad, was she?” he asked.

Mike finished buttoning his shirt. “Nah. She wasn’t mad.” He thought about how many times his mother had poked her head in the door as the two boys lay talking and giggling in the dark. Finally she turned the light on and informed them it was the very last time she would come up and tell them to go to sleep. It had been after eleven o’clock. “When she’s really mad she doesn’t talk, she yells.”

As they came downstairs to breakfast, Mrs. Schwartz was already in the dining room, pouring orange juice. Henry was impressed by her. He knew Mrs. Schwartz had been a model—that’s how she met my dad, Mike had told him—and the slow, graceful way she moved looked like the girls you saw in the TV commercials.

“Good morning, boys,” she said pleasantly. “Did you sleep well? Or should I say, did you sleep at all?” Then she smiled and took their breakfast orders to relay to the cook.

7:00 A.M.

Dr. Henry Taylor rinsed his coffee cup in the sink and glanced up at the clock. He would be waking Junior now, he thought, if Junior were home. He walked to the front closet and found his raincoat, listening for a moment at the foot of the stairs for a sound that might tell him Mildred was out of bed. Hearing none, he opened the front door and closed it quietly behind him, then jogged through the light rain on the flagstone path to the garage.

Because he was in no hurry he let the Oldsmobile warm up for a time before he pulled out into the driveway. He was not due at the clinic in the city until nine o'clock. As was his custom, however, he would arrive shortly after eight. In the hour before patients were admitted he would consult with the other doctors on the staff. This hour of coffee and conversation was a happy and exciting time. To rub shoulders with these dedicated black doctors filled him with pleasure.

Years before, with the help of some Northside businessmen, Dr. Taylor had established the Garvey Clinic. It was not much more than a storefront with only the most rudimentary equipment. But it was a beginning. He gave the clinic all his time, then, and had seen it grow in size and scope. A Lasky Foundation grant had helped build the clinic's present facility. Ten years ago the city had assumed partial responsibility, recognizing that this essentially private health station was taking on part of the load of its already overcrowded hospitals.

Henry and Mildred Taylor had moved to the County

just after Henry Jr. was born. Henry's private practice, divided almost equally between the poor black community in Rochdale and the wealthy blacks of Houghton, had burgeoned. "A million-dollar ghetto," Mildred had called Houghton, and Dr. Taylor agreed. As lush and fair as any community in the County, Houghton was a hideaway against the city for the black businessman or executive who had achieved success. Which is why, when he and Mildred had moved out of the city, they had chosen to live in South Rochdale instead of Houghton. Reverse segregation was snobbery, he thought, and worse, a more subtle, but just as reprehensible, kind of racism.

It had not been easy. Although no crosses were burned on his lawn, the dark looks and coldness shown by his neighbors had been bad enough. But time and his own sunny personality had helped.

Being a doctor helped, too. He remembered when the Fantinos' little boy fell out of the tree. His arm was broken. Henry could see the bone protruding through the boy's flesh as he came running from across the street. Amid his mother's screams and the boy's sobs, he picked Bobby up and, followed by the crowd of neighbors who had collected in the street, carried the boy into his house for treatment. It was the first time any of his neighbors had seen the inside of his home. Or had spoken to his wife. Or had met his son.

It had been a beginning.

They had been accepted on that day, and, better, had made a number of acquaintances who became their friends. Some of these neighbors became patients, and now his practice was about 10 percent white. Friends first, then friends of friends, then others who had heard about him began making appointments.

Sometimes, in the quiet moments just before sleep, Dr. Taylor wondered how long it would have taken to become an accepted citizen of South Rochdale if Bobby Fantino had not fallen from that tree. Or if he would ever have been accepted at all.

But that was the past, and Henry Taylor believed in today. The clinic occupied his mind as he backed the big Oldsmobile into the driveway. Today was the one day of the week he could spend there. One day out of seven, devoted entirely and without pay to the people and problems of the Northside ghetto. It was, in his mind, a tithe he gave for his good fortune; a link forged between his good life in the County and the dark, dirty streets of the city he had left behind. And though it had been many years since he had lived in Northside, each week, as he drove to the clinic, he felt he was coming home.

Awakened by the sound of an automobile engine turning over, Mildred Taylor reached the bedroom window just in time to see her husband's car turn out of sight at the end of the driveway. She gazed briefly at the drizzly spring morning, then washed and dressed. Downstairs, she smoked and sipped coffee at the white Formica table and listened to the silence. Strangely, it made her feel sad.

She wondered how Junior was getting on over at the Schwartzes' house, and how he and Mike had behaved. Chiding herself for worrying, she smiled, thinking about the two boys. They were almost like brothers, Henry sometimes said, black and white versions of each other. Each boy was an only child, and they had become inseparable after meeting at the Sloane School. Both were passionate about sports, idolizing the local baseball and football teams and their heroes, in season and out. With Junior pitching and Mike catching they formed the first-string battery of the Hawks in the Rochdale Little League. In school they were alike, too. Doing well in math, science, and French, just scraping by in English and social studies.

Why don't you call Irene . . . just to see how they're doing?

Mike had been Junior's overnight guest before, and vice versa, but always on the weekend. This was the first time Junior had spent a night out of the house on a school day. It had been Irene's idea. Knowing that Dr. Taylor and Mildred had to attend the annual dinner dance of the County Medical Society, she had suggested that instead of the usual babysitter Junior spend the night at her house with Mike and she'd see them off to school in the morning.

How handsome Henry had looked last night, Mildred thought, so tall and distinguished. In his dinner jacket and ruffled blue shirt he looked like the young, intense man she had met eighteen years ago. The man who had vowed to spend years working his way through medical school, interneship, and residency to become a doctor. And I will be your nurse, she had told herself in that dewy Baltimore garden, although she didn't bother telling the young man for many months afterward.

And now I don't have to be your nurse. And you don't have to be out and moving at seven in the morning on five hours' sleep, except that you're still wrapped up in medicine, and people, and helping, and you'll probably never change.

I'll call Irene later, after they're off to school in the limousine.

The limousine, she thought. She should tell them Junior would be riding in Mike Schwartz's limousine today, and not to send the regular car. Mildred looked up at the clock on the pastel wall. There was plenty of time. One more cup of coffee and then she'd call Mr. Mancuso at the limousine service.

7:05 A.M.

The low fieldstone wall guarding the Melton estate loomed up on his right as Greer pulled to a stop at the traffic light. When the light changed to green both he and Joyboy cut left across the intersection. He shot a glance at his watch. They were right on schedule, a little ahead of it, in fact.

What if something happens? said a voice inside his head.

Ain't nothing going to go wrong, he reassured himself. What can happen? If there's traffic too close to the limo, we forget it. Like the other days we tried and backed off. If the kids act up I shoot one of them. That ought to make the others behave.

"We're gonna make it today," he said aloud.

Sparrow looked at him. "Cool," he said.

Greer allowed himself a small smile. "I got a feelin', baby chick, and when I get a feelin' . . . watch out!"

Sparrow laughed and thumped the seat.

Well, man, Greer thought, you got him believing it. Pull this off and everyone'll be believing it. The cat who snatched six white kids from the goddamn best school in the County and made their folks sweat a bucket of bread to get them back. The cat pulls that one off is going a long way. There'll be a lot of feet marching behind that cat, that's for sure.

"We gettin' there," said Sparrow.

"Not much longer now," Greer said. "Not much longer at all."

7:06 A.M.

The doughnut was greasy. The doughnut was always greasy. Ben Carter took another small bite and set it down on the shelf, then went back to his textbook.

"Hey, Carter!" one of the men in the group of drivers clustered about the coffee machine called. "We're getting up a pool on the Derby. You want in?"

Ben shook his head negatively. There was a lot on his mind this morning. The calculus exam was no more than a week away, and it promised to be a stiff one. And if you wanted to become an engineer, as he did, you had to get calculus down cold.

As the oldest sophomore at City University, and a black one at that, Ben Carter's road was a difficult one. A night student, he felt strangely out of touch with the youngsters surrounding him. The clothes they wore, their attitudes and behavior, sometimes made him feel as if a whole generation had landed fully grown from some distant planet. Carter was twenty-seven, a veteran of Vietnam who had planned to make the army his career. But while in the service he began to change. Amid idleness and inefficiency, he worked smoothly and well. What others did carelessly, through sloth or boredom, he did efficiently. It was then that he began to sense that he had set his goals too low. That he could be more than a respected twenty-year man.

His math instructor at the university called him a

late bloomer. (It always made him smile and think of a departed pair of panties.) He was that, though, and when he felt confident enough to come back to civilian life he had completed his final two years of high school in six months. Taking the biggest load of credits the school allowed, he enrolled in the night division of the university. To help support his mother and sister, now that the army wasn't, Carter went to work driving a limousine for Carmine Mancuso. And the G.I. Bill helped a bit, too, though not enough.

Ben lifted his eyes from the textbook and looked out into the parking yard for a moment. The rain was pelting down on the rows of parked limousines. In another twenty minutes or so he would start his run, picking up the six children on his morning trip to the Sloane School. He stared at the doughnut he had laid aside, thought better of it, and went back to his reading.

7:10 A.M.

The girl with the long golden hair was running her tongue across his chest. Laughing, she threw back her head and pushed herself astride him, her short dress rising up to reveal a stretch of smooth, tanned thighs. He reached out and stroked her, working up those thighs until he reached the soft, curly center of her passion. Moist. Hot. He slipped a finger inside and began to stroke. "Oh, God," she said. "God . . . don't stop . . . oh baby . . . oh . . . oh . . . oh let's fuck it. Hard, baby, come in and fuck me hard. . . . Oh!" He thrust upward, reaching out with both hands to melt her to him. Hands reaching out, reaching . . .

"Get away!" Martha said sharply. "Get your goddamn hands off me!"

He awakened.

"What?" he said, his erection already beginning to subside.

"Damn sex maniac. At seven in the morning!"

Ernest Flood looked at his wife. The curlers made her look older and somehow cruel. He retrieved his errant hand and used it to rub his eyes. "What time is it?" he asked.

"Time for you to get up."

"Seven?"

"A little after, I think. I shut off the alarm a while back."

"Aren't you getting up?" he said. He thought of his ten-year-old boys.

Martha Flood snuggled deeper under the blanket. "Uh-uh," she said, yawning. "Mary will get the boys off to school. She's done it before."

"You think that's right?" he asked. But she didn't answer.

He pulled himself out of bed and walked slowly into their bathroom. He wet his dry mouth with a tumbler of cold water, drinking very slowly and thinking about Mary. Yes, the *au pair* girl from England could certainly feed the boys and see them off to the limousine. But shouldn't Martha be there?

Frowning, he stripped off his silk pajamas and stepped into the shower. As he soaped his genitals he realized something. That golden-haired girl in his dream; it was the *au pair* girl, Mary Gowers.

One floor below, Mary set the breakfast tray on the dining room table. "All right then," she said, smiling at the two redheaded boys. It was as if she were staring into a fun-house mirror, they were so identical. "Peter, you asked for hot cereal, didn't you?"

The boys exchanged sly glances. "I'm Peter," they said in unison.

Not again, Mary thought, as the boys dissolved into giggles. She leaned to the twin sitting nearest her and grasped his wrist. Turning his wrist over she glanced at the name engraved on the silver bracelet he wore. "No more foolishness," she said, "*you're* Peter."

The boy looked up, his blue eyes serious. "Oh, no," he said, "I'm Ralph. We just switched bracelets."

7:15 A.M.

Heidi had chewed her vitamin pill and washed it down with a full glass of orange juice. She had destroyed a bowl of Rice Krispies with sliced bananas. She had finished her glass of milk with a brownie left over from the night before. Now she was asking for a peanut butter and jelly sandwich.

"How about a half, dear?" Emma Porter said. Heidi was an eater, like her late father, and she was developing a well-rounded paunch just below the belt. I thought kids were supposed to burn up all that food, Emma thought as she went into the kitchen to make the sandwich. Baby fat, and all that. Well, if Heidi wasn't watched closely she'd have baby fat the rest of her life.

Where was the peanut butter? Yesterday there had been at least a quarter of a jar on the shelf.

"Heidi!" Emma called through the louvered door that separated kitchen and dining room. "Did you see the peanut butter?"

She heard a high-pitched giggle. "I had a snack after school," Heidi called.

"And you finished it?"

More giggles.

Emma Porter felt betrayed. They had a rule about after-school snacks. It was to be fruit or milk or nothing at all.

Very determined, she stomped back to the dining room. "Well, then," she said as she looked as sternly as possible into that round pigtailed face with the large green eyes, "no peanut butter, no sandwich."

"Okay," Heidi said, "make it cream cheese and jelly."

7:20 A.M.

Willie Franklin, sometimes called Joyboy, swung the Volks through the turn and down-shifted into second. The Chevvy was too far in front of him. He pushed the little car up to forty, still in second, then slipped the shift lever into third. He noticed Greer was slowing down, helping him to catch up.

That Greer, he don't let nothing go by. Got eyes in the back of his head. *So what you afraid of?* said a persistent voice inside his head. *What can go wrong?*

He knew, even without thinking about it, what could go wrong. Plenty. Well, he had given up his life already, what more could he lose?

Greer had all their lives. He held them pledged to that great-day plan he had spoon-fed each of them. Joyboy had been a stoned-out junkie. He would have either died of an overdose or been gunned down by some cop. It was just a matter of time.

And then Greer . . .

Joyboy hadn't even known where he was when he woke up, he was so spaced out. The thirst was there, as it always was, and he must have downed a quart of water. The cat watching him said his name was Greer.

"You're here to kick it," he told Joyboy. "You're locked up here where no one's gonna find you, and you either gonna kick it or I'm gonna kill you." Greer had touched his gun. "And when you kick it, your ass is gonna belong to me." Just like that, without a flicker of a doubt.

And Joyboy had kicked it. Three days of hollering and screaming and yelling for a fix. Three days of rolling on the floor and shivering and crying as the chills and fever took turns running through his body. Greer had given him water and washed him and wrapped him in blankets, letting him touch nothing but water and sweet chocolate candy. And he was through with it. Half dead, maybe, but clean.

The Chevvy turned right at Oakmont Lane, and Joyboy followed.

First he got my body, and then he took my soul. We're gonna make a revolution, he said. We're gonna hit Whitey and hit him again and keep hittin' him until we get what we gotta have. Make up your mind, Joyboy, you just became a soldier.

They only stole when it was necessary. They shaved every day and dressed in clean clothes. They ate good, plain food. There were five of them now, he and Sparrow, and the little kid, Jimmy. And Loretta Jo, Greer's girl. She and Greer took turns educating them. They had dozens of books to read. Hard books, filled with the stories of blacks in America. They filled him with a new kind of pride, and for the first time he began to have a sense of who he was.

What can go wrong?

Greer can go wrong, or you can go wrong on Greer. Just like he showed you the gun once, you can do the same sometime. So far he's been right all the time. But what happens when he's not? Can anybody ever tell Greer he's making a mistake?

As he swung the Volks through a turn, Joyboy rolled the window down and spit into the rain.

7:25 A.M.

The only trouble with a diet, Carmine Mancuso was thinking, was that it kept you in a perpetual state of hunger. He watched his secretary, Brenda, sipping her coffee and licked his lips. A roll would be nice right now. With butter. "Brenda," he said, discipline returning, "how about you go across to the diner and bring me back a container of coffee. Black."

"Anything else?"

Before Carmine had a chance to face this new moral crisis, the phone rang. He picked it up, waving Brenda on her way. Another "no show," the Cable boy. Wasn't that on Ben Carter's route? He put the phone down and scribbled a note. As he finished the phone rang once more. It was a North Rochdale call, an airport trip. "County Airport?" he asked.

"City Airport. I'm making a twelve-thirty plane."

"Right. We'll pick you up at nine-forty then." At that hour, with the normal tide of slow-moving, late city-bound traffic, the trip would take almost two hours.

Carmine wrote out the address and destination on a trip ticket. A nine-thirty or ten o'clock call was an almost perfect trip. He could send one of the school limos, normally deadheading back to the office at that time. What's more, the car would be back from the airport, even the one in the city, in plenty of time to make the three o'clock pickup at Sloane.

When Brenda came back, Carmine picked up his

coffee container and the two notes he had made, and walked out of the office into the yard, feeling the drizzle on his neck. He weaved his way through the parked limousines and stumped over to the shed where Ben Carter was sitting by himself, reading.

"What's up?" Carter asked, closing the book.

"Business, business. The Cable kid's sick, so don't bother picking him up. And I've got an airport trip for you, up in North Rochdale. It's a nine-forty pickup, so you can go up there after you get through with the Sloane run."

Carter nodded and took the trip slips.

"How's school coming?" Carmine asked. "They make you a professor yet?"

"That's next week, didn't you hear?"

Carmine smiled. "Oh. Okay. You have any trouble down there, tell them I'll come down and beat the shit out of them."

"Sure, sure." Carter grinned.

He put his peaked cap on and got into the big front seat of the limousine. *"Nil sine magno labore,"* he said.

"Right," said Carmine. "What's that?"

"The motto of City U. Meaning you got to bust a gut to get somewhere." He turned the key and started the engine.

"Jesus, just what I need. A driver who talks Latin." Carmine rapped his knuckles on the rear deck as the big Caddy pulled out of the shed. That's you, kid, he thought. Steady Eddie. Another couple of years and you won't be driving a car for a living.

As he watched Carter turn south on Edgemont Road, heading for his first pickup, Carmine took a sip of coffee. Wincing at the bitter taste, he glanced idly at the place where Carter had been sitting. Carter had left a doughnut, with just a small bite gone. Carmine hesitated for no more than a second, then decided it was a sign from heaven. The doughnut was gone in two bites.

7:35 A.M.

Norman Schwartz shifted his compact frame and, pulling Irene's pillow behind him on top of his own, sat up in bed. He switched on the bedside lamp and took his reading glasses from the night table. He would give himself the pure luxury of reading the morning paper in bed today. There was no need to rush. His business was in good hands, things were going well. The new line of sportswear, product of six months of backbreaking effort, had been accepted and judged worthy by buyers from the country's largest department stores. Now it was a matter of shipping the goods and waiting for the reorders to come in. And he had enough good people working for him to be confident that all would go smoothly.

Besides, he was a man with an imperfect heart. Wasn't that the way his good friend, Henry Taylor, had put it? He remembered the scene in Dr. Taylor's office six months ago. All those black squiggles and scratches on the electrocardiogram. "You're not the man you were, Norman," Henry had said seriously. "That's what you have to keep remembering. You've had a minor heart attack . . . you're not going to kick off tomorrow or next week, or even next year. But . . . it's not a good heart either. So you've got to be careful. No more smoking. Lose ten pounds. But most important, stop being a work horse. Let up. Take it easy."

"How bad is it?" he had asked.

"Not bad. Let's just say imperfect." A slow grin creased Henry's face as he rolled the long cardiogram into a tube. "Don't worry, Norm, we'll be playing golf together in a couple of months. You're my pigeon, remember? I can't let you get away from me."

Schwartz opened the *City Tribune* across his knees and scanned the front page, then turned to the sports pages.

A few moments later, his wife came in. "They're off to school," she said. She sat down at her dressing table and began to brush her hair. When the phone rang, Irene smiled and picked up the Princess phone. "It's Mildred," she said to her husband, "bet."

Norman Schwartz looked over the newspaper on his knees and smiled. Looking at Irene was one of the great pleasures in his life.

Irene put the phone to her ear and said: "Good morning, Mildred."

"Oh, my," Mildred Taylor said, "am I that predictable? How did you know it was me?"

"How did I know. Who else would it be, calling me at this unlikely hour of the morning?"

Mildred laughed again. "Sorry, Irene, but—"

"But you figured the house burned down, we've all got smallpox, and Junior fell into a manhole getting into the limousine, right?"

"Am I that bad?"

"I keep telling you, Mildred, you're a Jewish mother. Black, maybe, but a Jewish mother." Her friend laughed. "Listen, they ate like horses, stayed up half the night giggling, and left for school not ten minutes ago."

"No trouble?"

"Trouble? From who, Junior? Never. You know that."

Norman put his paper aside and swung his legs off the bed. As he passed his wife, Norman leaned down and planted a kiss on the nape of her neck. How can she smell so good so early in the morning, he thought. He stroked her hair for a moment, feeling its softness under his hand. Then he left the two women to their conversation and strode into the bathroom to shave.

7:42 A.M.

Ben Carter pushed the big black limousine up to thirty miles an hour as he came off Wyckoff traffic circle and headed up Maple Avenue on the way to pick up Heidi Porter. He looked into the rear-view mirror and checked the two boys in the back seat. So that's the Doc's boy, he thought, looking at young Henry Taylor. He had never met Dr. Taylor but knew he was a famous figure in the County, especially among the black community. There was even talk that one day the doctor would go into politics.

Ben turned off Maple Avenue and rolled slowly up Murray Drive. The trees, dripping in the morning rain, formed a green arch over the macadam street. It was quiet and peaceful, with beautifully landscaped houses set wide apart and separated by high and neatly trimmed hedgerows. In the middle of the street he swung onto the Porters' driveway.

"This is Heidi Porter's house," he heard Mike

Schwartz say to the Taylor boy, "and she's always late."

"Not always, Mike," Carter said over his shoulder as he brought the car to a stop.

"She's always eating, that's why," Mike said.

Ben grinned. It was true. The little girl never failed to have something hidden in her school bag. And as the other kids talked and joked on the way to and from school, Heidi would be sharing candy and cookies and not speaking much because her mouth was always too busy chewing to talk.

He was about to honk the horn when she came skipping down the front steps and opened the rear door. It looked like they were going to be early today.

7:45 A.M.

Greer approached the corner where the Sloane limousine would have to stop. Ten yards short of the road sign he pulled onto the shoulder of the narrow road and cut the engine. Looking into the rear-view mirror, he watched Joyboy pull up behind him in the Volks. They were smack on schedule.

"We're here," Sparrow said, his face expressionless.

"On the money, baby chick," Greer said. He smiled thinly at the little man sitting beside him. Rolling down the window, he waved at Joyboy to leave the Volks and join them. The rain was pouring down now and when he brought his arm back inside it was soaked.

Joyboy jogged the few steps to the Chevvy and quickly got into the back seat. "Beautiful mornin', ain't it?"

Greer turned sideways to look at him. "How you feel?" he asked.

"Fine, fine," Joyboy said quickly.

Jumpy as a cat, Greer thought. "All right now," he said, speaking slowly to control his excitement. "We're gonna go over it one more time, okay? You first, Joyboy. You gonna take the Volks and pull up just around the corner. Then you sit there, motor running, and wait. Until you hear what?"

"Two beeps."

"Right. Two beeps. Like this." Greer hit the horn ring twice and the sound echoed through the surrounding woods. "What does that mean?"

"The car is in sight . . . I get ready to move if I have to."

"Right again," said Greer. "And if anyone drives down that cross street you pull out and block them so they don't see me when I'm flagging down the Caddy. You just pull across the road like you was making a U turn. Take your time and make 'em wait. You got that straight?"

"Yeah."

He's scared, but he's all right, Greer decided. "You got the note?"

"In the glove compartment," Joyboy said. "And after I see you come around the corner drivin' the Caddy I just drive on up to the school, real easy, and wait. When the cop leaves, just before nine, I pull up to the front gate and drop the note over the wall by that bush we picked out. And then I head for home."

"Three things," Greer said. "Drive nice and slow. We don't want no speeding tickets this morning. Two, when you drop the note. Take your time, ain't nobody gonna be lookin' at you or suspecting nothing. So just make sure it falls behind that bush and next to the wall where we said. If they don't find that note . . ." He laughed without smiling.

"What's the third thing?" Joyboy said.

Greer reached over and opened the glove compartment in the Chevvy. He took out a pair of black leather gloves. "These here. That note is clean now and it going to stay that way." He handed the gloves to Joyboy and watched as he drew them on his large and bony hands. "Okay. Now you sit here while I take Sparrow up to his post. Anybody comes along, why you just get a road map out and look like you're checkin' something. Don't worry, nobody gonna bother you."

Greer opened his door and stepped out. "Let's go, baby chick. We got work to do."

7:48 A.M.

Shirl Barnett decided, finally, to face the day. She turned onto her back and opened her eyes, trying very hard to think of nothing. It was something she had become expert at, the practice of blanking out her thoughts and feelings, mostly feelings about herself, her husband, and the quality of their life in this perilous year before she turned forty. But the day was with her, the last harsh words Max had said still hung in the quiet room. She sat up and swung her legs off the bed, searching with her toes until the mules were under her feet.

Somewhere along the way they had lost it, she thought. Somewhere in the past few years it had been lost among the late nights and early mornings and long, dull hours spent waiting for him to come home; and when he arrived it was gone. Was it the whiskey on his breath? The rumpled look of his clothes? Or was it only the suspicion that gnawed deep in her brain?

She pulled her cotton nightgown over her head and turned to the full-length mirror on the bathroom door. Your waist is gone, she thought, pinching the roll of fat that hung between the bottom of her ribs and her hips. Turning, she looked at the rounded curve of belly and behind, accentuated by the smallness of her breasts. You're shaped like a light bulb, she thought without amusement. She went into the bathroom and began to brush her teeth.

Did I begin to shut him out, or did he change first? It was like the question of the chicken and the egg. But the important thing was what would finally happen to them. Divorce? No, not that. They'd stay together, as much for Kathy as anything. Inertia would keep them together because to face the problem would be to end it. And that was something she could not face.

She took the little vial from the medicine cabinet, removed a green capsule, and swallowed her first Equanil of the day.

7:50 A.M.

Many years ago it had been known as the Elmer Garage, but now it was not known at all. Above the double-width door that retracted twenty feet up above the sidewalk was a sign. Paint-flaked now and badly in need of cleaning, it said merely:

ELME G RA E

It was just another abandoned business, flanked by empty tenements in the middle of the Northside ghetto. Once the street had teemed with life, and local people would bring their autos to be serviced by the Packer brothers, Elmer and Sidney. But that was long ago, and the brothers, both dead now, had moved away along with their trade. There had never been any thought of selling the property; who would want such a useless building in the worst area of the city? The brothers' heirs had put a padlock upon the tall front door, the appropriate utilities had been notified to cease service, and the property had been forgotten.

Elmer's son would have been surprised to find that for the past six months five people had been living in the abandoned garage. The padlock had been removed from the front door. A thick wire snaked out the back door and ran several hundred feet down the block, bringing electric current into the building. Extension wires ran spaghettilike along baseboards and up walls, providing a feeble illumination by means of bare bulbs, hanging in socket outlets from the cracked plaster ceilings.

On the third floor, in what had once been a storage area, a number of ruined mattresses lay near the door. Toward the rear of this room, a warren of dusty wooden shelves stretched from floor to ceiling. A small Sony television set was plugged in to an outlet near the door.

One floor below, a rickety card table and three rusted bridge chairs stood directly beneath a hanging bulb in what had been an office. A hotplate was plugged into a socket near the cracked sink, and an ancient though still serviceable refrigerator groaned through its cycle next to a cupboard in which an assortment of chipped plates, cups, and saucers were stacked. By the door leading to the stairs, a bookcase had been constructed of old boards and bricks, and it held a number of paperback books.

The people of the neighborhood were unaware of the

tenants of the garage. Or if they knew, they took no notice. From outside, the decaying building looked the same as ever. Rusted metal plates covered the spaces which used to be windows, and no hint of light showed through in the night. From time to time an old black Chevrolet sedan and a battered gray Volkswagen came and went. The retractable front door opened and closed so fast that you would have to be waiting and watching to spot them. And even if you did, what of it? In the Northside ghetto, you looked the other way. It was better not to see the pushers and the junkies, the numbers runners and petty hoodlums, the thousand and one gyps and rackets and hustles that went on unchecked by the police. For if there was law in the ghetto it was one of survival. And to survive you kept your eyes on your own business and your mouth firmly shut.

7:55 A.M.

On top of the hill overlooking the crossroad, Greer and Sparrow stood in the rain, checking the road.

"That's where they'll be coming from," said Greer, pointing a finger at a black slash in the rolling hills about half a mile away.

"I been up here four-five times already. I *know* that's the fuckin' road," said Sparrow. He turned his face away.

"Easy." Greer put his hand out and patted Sparrow on the shoulder. "One step at a time, then we get it right. Okay?"

Sparrow nodded.

Dumb bastard, Greer thought, I got to lay it all out for you or you'll screw up for sure. He caught Sparrow's eyes and smiled at him very slowly. "Now then. I'm down there below on the edge of the road, right? And I'm watching you. You look through them glasses, where the road cuts through that hill and when you see that Caddy, start counting."

"Twenty-five seconds."

"Right. That's what I need. And if no other car shows up behind them in that time, you wave your handkerchief and I'll know it's safe to make my play. Twenty-five seconds is all I need." He paused to look once again at the road. "Then, as soon as I move, you hustle your ass down the hill and follow me in the Chevvy. Make it quick, man. I ain't gonna be waitin'. Once I'm in that limo, I'm gone."

"Don't worry," Sparrow said, "I ain't gonna be standin' around." He turned his head away.

Too hard, Greer thought, you're coming down too hard on him. He reached for the little guy's wrist and lined up Sparrow's watch with his own. "Gentlemen," Greer said in a phony way, "simonize your watches."

Sparrow grinned. "Like a goddamn war movie, ain't it?" he said.

8:00 A.M.

Carter checked his watch as the long black Cadillac rolled to a stop at the Flood house. Yes, they were early all right.

"The wild men of Borneo live here," Mike Schwartz was telling Junior in the back seat. "The Flood twins, Ralph and Peter. You can't tell them apart, really. They're identical."

Heidi Porter stopped munching a chocolate cream sandwich cookie long enough to add: "Who'd want to tell them apart, anyway?"

Carter was just about to tap the horn lightly when the front door of the house swung open. The two boys, in yellow rain slickers, came running down the front steps. There was someone—not Mrs. Flood, Carter saw—standing in the doorway. He recognized Mary Gowers, the Floods' governess, and flashed her a grin.

The twins came barreling into the car, bounced off the closed rear door, and one of them fell to the ground. Laughing, he picked himself up and punched his brother on the forearm, opened the rear door and tumbled in. It was Mike Schwartz who got them sorted out, using his husky frame as a wedge to separate them on the jump seats.

Carter slowly turned onto Spruce Street. With the Cable stop canceled today, they were a full fifteen minutes ahead of schedule.

When she felt the hand on her shoulder, Mary Gowers jumped with alarm. Before she could whirl around she heard Mr. Flood's voice. "Did I startle you, Mary? I'm sorry. I wanted to see the boys off to school." He reached across her body and closed the front door. There was something in his voice, she thought, he sounds different.

"You just missed them by a tick," she said. "They're off . . . in the usual rush. Can I get your breakfast, then?" she added.

Ernest Flood felt an impulse to reach out and clasp her to him. She smelled faintly of lilac, and her long fall of silky blond hair swung about her face. He felt his heart beating under his shirt. Between his legs, a maleness was growing. He nodded, not trusting himself to speak, and followed her down the hallway to the dining room, trying not to look at the curve of her body as she moved under the loose yellow silk housecoat.

At the long table, he took off his glasses and polished them with his handkerchief. He imagined her coming back through the door, the housecoat open so he could see her breasts. Now stop it, he said, almost aloud. You don't make a grab for your sons' governess . . . with your wife asleep upstairs . . . in the middle of a Thursday morning. How do you do it, then? *Away from the house*. But where?

When the girl came in with his breakfast, he smiled. "Sit down, Mary," he began, "there's something I'd like to discuss with you."

8:10 A.M.

Mildred Taylor had once dubbed it "the inspirational hour," but to Dr. Taylor this morning's bull session was proving to be as bitter as the coffee growing cold in his paper cup. Roy Hart was holding the floor, and the stringbean-tall ex-basketball All-American from Southern Illinois turned internist via Meharry Medical College and New York's Bellevue Hospital, was visibly angry. "We are not doing enough," he was insisting, "not half enough. We are treating the symptoms and not the disease, and that, Doctor, is bad medicine."

"All right, Roy," Dr. Taylor said, "I agree. We are not doing enough. No man ever can do enough. The Northside needs ten . . . twenty more clinics like ours. We need buildings. Equipment. Staff. All that and more."

"And it still wouldn't be enough," Freeman Johnson said.

"Now that's what I'm talking about," Hart said, his even teeth flashing white in a thin smile. "That's the old medicine. The old approach. But more doctors and more clinics are not going to cure a disease that is endemic. I'm talking about ignorance. Poverty. Sanitation. The fact that half of our people don't even know that proper medical attention is a basic human right."

"Oh, God, Roy," Dr. Johnson groaned, "not politics again."

"Let him speak, Freeman," Henry Taylor said. He tamped a fingerful of tobacco into his brier pipe and slowly lit up. "So far, he's making sense."

"You bet I am," Roy Hart said. "Here's what I mean. Old Mrs. Simpson was in again this week. Three rat bites on her leg. What did we do? We treated the rat bites and sent her home." He paused and looked closely at the two older men. "Now here's what I'm saying. It's not enough for us to treat a patient for rat bites and send her home to be bitten again. What we have to do is *get rid of the rats!*"

Freeman Johnson looked at Henry Taylor and winked. "You ready for the rat business, Henry?"

Roy Hart was on his feet now, dwarfing the small staff room. "We treat pneumonia patients every winter . . . and send them home to unheated apartments. We get diphtheria deaths every year. Diphtheria! Because no one ever told the babies' mothers to get their children inoculated, or checked up to make sure they did. Lead poisoning from children eating paint chips." The young doctor's voice rose sharply.

"Easy, Roy, easy," said Henry.

"Tuberculosis deaths among our people are four times the white average," Roy Hart was saying. "Infant mortality, one and a half times as great. Life expectancy is seven years less than whites. Now that's a disease that's called being black and poor and ignorant and living—if you can call it living—in Northside."

"The conditions that prevail, Doctor," said Johnson. "Our average patient works until he's about to fall down. Because he's got to bring in the money to live. Trouble is, when we get hold of him, he's already on his last legs."

"Exactly," Roy Hart said. "We can't go on just treating patients when what's really sick is the ghetto. . . . And to cure it, we have to start making ourselves heard."

The three men looked at the floor for a moment, avoiding each others' eyes. Slowly, Henry Taylor said, "You realize, of course, that half of our funding comes from the city. And if we start making ourselves heard, we could be running the risk of antagonizing the very people who vote through our appropriations?"

Roy Hart's eyes were glittering. "Yes," he said coolly, "I realize it. But do you?"

8:15 A.M.

Mildred Taylor took her husband's blue cotton pajamas from the hook behind the bathroom door and, folding them neatly, placed them in the bottom drawer of his bureau. Moving to the oversize double bed, she straightened the sheets and carefully worked the black and white tapestry bedspread into position. Her movements were practiced and sure, without waste motion. Ten years of nursing experience, of making hospital corners and hauling bedpans, of moving swiftly through long marble corridors and wards filled with people in pain, had given her an almost machinelike efficiency.

As she dusted the top of her dresser, she straightened

the antique silver frame that held three photographs. On the left her mother smiled uncertainly, the silver-framed eyeglasses toning down the strong face. At the right, she and Henry peered through the smoky haze of La Zaragozana, the nightclub they had visited on their honeymoon in Puerto Rico. The central, and largest photo, was of Henry Jr., a photograph taken when the boy was six. Two teeth missing in his smile, he held a striped bass in his hand, caught on an early-morning tide at Montauk Point on Long Island.

It had taken many years for the Taylors to have Junior, and if not for Freeman Johnson, their friend and Mildred's gynecologist, they might never have had him at all. They had been trying for three years, after having waited eight for Henry to finish training and establish his practice. Mildred had stopped working then. She would be a mother. But nature did not cooperate. It was not until she had had two miscarriages and seen countless specialists that Dr. Johnson took her on as a patient. She remembered how he made her chart her fertility cycles for six months, and then had given her a new experimental drug. She had taken her temperature religiously, finally calling Henry home at three in the afternoon to laugh and roll with her on that small bed in the apartment on Decatur Street, making a baby to order. During her pregnancy Dr. Johnson had kept her in bed for six months. Six long and boring months of inactivity. But look at what she had produced: Junior, the image of his father and the cornerstone of their life.

Mildred moved down the hall to the boy's room. His bed, unslept in last night, was as neat as she had left it yesterday. Still, there were a few books on the shelf near the window that could use some dusting. She parted the curtains and wiped the windowsill, looking for a moment at the gray and misty morning. Suddenly, she felt a chill. As she walked back to her room to find a sweater, she wondered if it was only the weather that gave her a feeling of loneliness and dread.

8:17 A.M.

As his car topped the rise and turned onto School Avenue, Philip Stuart caught sight of the Sloane School, its tall turreted bell tower half hidden by the low-hanging gray mist. Turning slowly through the entrance gate set in a high fieldstone wall, he brought the car up the winding drive and parked behind the main building in a space reserved for him under the sign: Dean of Boys.

Pauline DeBusschere, the headmaster's secretary, was typing as he walked through her adjoining office on the way to his own. "Is that for the catalogue copy?" he asked, after they had exchanged greetings.

"That's finished," she said without looking up. "I'm doing the other thing you gave me."

Stuart walked into his office and put away his raincoat and briefcase, then came back. He took the newly typed sheaf of catalogue copy over to the window and looked it through. Stuart was writing a new and expanded version of the yearly catalogue, one that hopefully would help raise large contributions from alumni and present parents of Sloane students. Next year would mark the school's one hundredth anniversary, and although Sloane was amply endowed, it was its policy to finance building and expansion schemes without touching that endowment. The new Science Building, now only an excavation alongside the football field, would cost over two million dollars to complete. The chemistry laboratory alone would be three hundred thousand dollars.

Mrs. DeBusschere stopped typing for a moment and snickered. She swiveled her chair to face Stuart. "Wow," she said. "I'm just reading this proposal through."

"Yes?"

She picked up the notes he had given her to type and read from them. "'. . . that these full tuition scholarships be extended to disadvantaged black students in the County, and that we seek gifted black children from as far away as Northside and provide round-trip transportation daily to enable them to attend Sloane.'" She rolled her eyes toward the ceiling. "Phil," she said, "you're out of your gourd."

Stuart laughed. "Thanks," he said.

"Letting poor black kids into Sloane? From the ghetto? When Dr. Carew sees this proposal he'll go through the roof."

Philip Stuart looked out the window at the drizzle falling on the wide green playing field. "Do you know exactly how many black students Sloane has?" he asked softly. "Twenty-five. Out of an enrollment of six hundred students. And every one of those special twenty-five come from well-to-do homes."

"So?" she said. "Look—you weren't here five years ago, when we had no black students at all. What a struggle that was, getting the board to admit them."

"Half a loaf," he shrugged. "We've got to open it up all the way. It would be terrific to have some really poor black kids up here. I think it would be good for them, and good for Sloane, too."

Pauline sighed. "You want me to finish typing this, then?"

"Yes," he said, "and leave it on my desk." He walked to the hall door.

"It's your funeral," she muttered as he walked out into the hallway.

The tempo of the school was beginning to quicken. Already, teachers and a few early-arriving students were coming in through the ornate double-doored entranceway. Stuart walked toward them, pausing for a moment to look at the huge portrait of the school's founder that hung near the front door. The artist had posed him in the stiff "captain of industry" manner of the late nineteenth century, his head thrown back, one hand tucked into his watch pocket, just above the rounded sweep of his ample stomach. Behind him, a panorama of the West showed cowboys and Indians, settlers and wagon trains, and a long curving stretch of railroad track. Commodore Endicott Fleetwood Sloane, Stuart thought, not for the first time, the exploiter and the land he ravaged. Our founder and patron saint, who built an empire on the backs of the heathen Chinese and Irish immigrants, dispossessing—or killing—the people who stood in the way of his railroad's progress to California and the sea. Commodore Sloane: the best of men and the worst rolled into one.

Stuart walked to the door and looked outside. Way off, down the curving drive by the front gate, the first limousine rolled onto the school grounds.

8:20 A.M.

"It's time, baby, let's get started," Greer said.

Joyboy stubbed out his cigarette in the ashtray. He

reached across the front seat and clasped Greer's right hand with both of his own.

"Good luck."

"Um-gah-wah," Greer said, grinning. He watched as Joyboy left the Chevvy and walked to the Volkswagen. After Joyboy swung the little car around the corner and out of sight, Greer started the engine and moved the Chevvy across the road, directly opposite the stop sign. He pulled the .38 Police Positive out from the crack in the seat cushion and for the last time opened the revolver and checked the action. Satisfied, he tucked the revolver in the waistband of his black trousers. He looked again at the front of the car. The keys were in the ignition. The engine was off. The road map was on the seat, the window open. All right then. He got out and began walking down the grassy shoulder, taking up a position just inside the tree line at the base of the hill. Looking up he could see Sparrow, binoculars to his eyes, searching the road that led back to Rochdale. Just a few minutes more, Greer was thinking, just a little while more.

The rain had changed to a fine drizzle.

8:25 A.M.

Sparrow shivered in the chilly wet wind and for the third time in the last ten minutes thought about unzipping his fly and relieving himself. But the car was due any minute now and Greer was watching. He kept the binoculars firmly fixed to his eyes. If he missed the car, if he failed to give warning when it came into sight . . . he shivered again. He knew what Greer would do. There was no mistake possible today. He couldn't face that smile again, or that knife. Three thin slices had been cut into the underside of his right arm, the last one barely healed. The ritual cut. Each one reflecting a mistake he had made.

The last cut had come after the dynamite heist from the construction shack. He remembered running full speed across the embankment, the shouts and footsteps of the watchman coming up behind him. In the darkness he could not see the hole that had caught his foot and sent him tumbling and sliding. He had scrambled back to pick up the explosives and then run for the fence. It had been close. And in the mad rush to get away he lost one of the five sticks of dynamite they had stolen from the shed.

How had Greer known? He recalled Greer's piercing eyes as he questioned him in the second floor office above the garage. He couldn't hold anything back from Greer. None of them could. And later . . . Greer's hand in the dim light with the knife slowly coming across, leaving a thin wake of bright red against his coffee skin.

Sparrow raised the binoculars and swept the hill a half mile away where the road came into sight. Twice before he had stood on this hill, glasses raised to his eyes, but both times there had been too many cars near the limousine for Greer to take a chance. Maybe this morning they would really pull it off. A spray of fine mist, whipped by the wind, dotted the front lenses. "Motherfucking weather," Sparrow muttered as he wiped it away, his eyes still fixed on the narrow road, shiny in the early spring rain.

8:30 A.M.

There is something about kids when it rains, Ben Carter was thinking as he held the big Cadillac to a steady thirty miles an hour. He checked the rear view to see who was causing the commotion now. In the mirror he saw the twins wrestling with each other in the space between the jump seats. "Hey now!" He flipped the switch, lowering the glass partition behind him a few inches. "You quit that now, hear?" Two pairs of blue eyes sparkled at him in the rear-view mirror. He raised the glass again. Lord Almighty, it was a good thing he had all the controls up front in the car. If those two could raise or lower the windows, or open either rear door . . . Why they would most likely be riding on the roof.

He flicked his eyes down again as the curve came up. Babying the big car against the slick road, he came across the narrow bridge and put his foot down harder as the road began to climb. On the straightaway he checked the mirror once more and swiveled his head to see Kathy. She was quiet this morning, not helping to keep order in the back as she usually did. Must have something on her mind. With those parents of hers she could have plenty to think about. He remembered the scene in her driveway before last Christmas vacation. The round blond woman with the envelope in her hand, trying to give it to him without actually touching him. And the pinch-faced man in the loud sports coat, Kathy's father, right behind her. "How do you know he's the regular driver, Shirl? How can you tell them apart?" He was swaying so much Ben thought he might fall. He was drunk, very drunk, or maybe that was the way he always acted at eight-thirty in the morning. And Kathy, red-faced, her lips drawn in a thin line, had gotten into the back seat trying not to look at him. Her mother had firmly handed him the envelope and he had thanked her politely, hating himself for it.

Carter pulled himself back to the present and concentrated on the road. They were approaching the School Avenue crossroad.

8:32 A.M.

Here we go, Sparrow thought, his heart beginning to pump fast as he saw the limousine. He began counting the seconds the way Greer had told him, one thousand, two thousand. There was no traffic in front of the car, none at all. And it looked like none behind. He kept counting to ten, then twenty. Goddamn, they were going to make it! At twenty-five he dropped the binoculars onto his chest and reached into his raincoat pocket for the white handkerchief.

Greer jogged along the grassy bank, one hand holding the gun close to his waist. There was plenty of time, it had all been planned out so he didn't have to hurry. On the pavement he went to the open window of the car, reached in, and smacked the horn twice. The *beep-beep* echoed loudly. Around the tree-crowded corner he heard the little engine of the Volkswagen cough and then come to life. He took the road map from the seat and straightened up.

Carter brought the big car around the last turn, slowing down for the stop sign ahead. One right turn and they would be on School Avenue. As he started to look at his watch, his eyes picked up a shape ahead. A black Chevvy and a guy with a map. He began to brake for the stop sign.

Greer raised his eyes from the map and looked down the road. Here it was. He took a small step into the road. The limousine was no more than thirty feet away now and rolling slowly. Smiling, he walked to the white line that divided the road and waved his hand.

Carter pulled up short of the corner. The guy wanted directions. He put his finger on the switch and lowered the window half way.

"I'm lost," Greer said, looking at the window. It's not down far enough, he thought.

"Where are you headed?"

"Fillmore," said Greer. It was the first word that popped into his head.

"Fillmore?"

"It's supposed to be near Rochdale." Greer brought the map up. "They told me it was right near . . ."

Carter put his finger on the switch and rolled the window down. "Lemme see," he said, reaching for the map. Greer pulled it away. Pivoting on the ball of his left foot he drove his right arm forward. The butt side of the revolver struck Carter just above the right eye.

Clubbing the gun, Greer slugged him again and still again. The car started to roll. Greer sidestepped with it and pulled open the door. Flinging himself inside, he began groping for the brake. The driver's body was in the way. He pushed it across the seat and pulled the emergency brake. The car jerked to a stop. Behind the partition the kids were screaming. Greer dropped his gun and pushed Carter completely off the seat, forcing the crumpled body into the space under the dashboard. One foot stayed up and Greer forced it down, bending the knee. Then he reached down and picked up the driver's hat and put it on his head. The screaming behind him was getting louder.

He swiveled in the seat and looked at the kids. A blond-haired girl was looking right into his eyes. Picking up the gun he found the switch marked "G" on the door panel. He pushed it and let the partition roll down about six inches. A wave of noise assaulted him. Raising the gun so they could see it, he shouted, "Shut up, shut your goddamn mouths." It was then he spotted Henry Taylor's frightened dark face. "What the fuck are you doing here?"

The boy blinked once, twice, his face set. How the hell did he get in here? The kids were quieter. The blonde was moaning and the little fat girl was crying, but they were quieter. "Ain't gonna hurt you if you behave," he said, his voice pitched low. "Just gonna take a little ride and then get you home. Now you can go quiet or you can go dead. I'll shoot the first one that makes trouble."

He turned around and put the gun down on the seat. Releasing the emergency brake lever, he drove up to the corner. School Avenue was clear, in both directions. He made a neat left turn and beeped twice at the parked Volkswagen. Joyboy was staring at him with wide-open eyes.

Sparrow broke out of the woods and looked to the corner. The limousine was moving! Greer had the car and the kids and everything was going to work. He started running to the Chevvy, the binoculars bouncing against his chest. Then, hearing a car approach, he slowed to a walk, turning his face away as a green station wagon passed by. His legs felt funny and he could taste the coffee and toast he'd had for breakfast. Oh God, he thought, they wouldn't get away with it. They would be caught. An image of a barred cell flashed in his head. Pigs with nightsticks beating him. . . . He leaned against the car, his head on his arm, and fought the wave of nausea. Doubling over, he heaved hard and spewed his breakfast on the grass.

When he straightened up, the limousine was out of

sight. He would have to hurry. As he was getting in the car he spotted the map flapping in the middle of the road. He ran to it and stuffed it in his raincoat pocket. Then he went back to the car and started the engine. At the corner, he saw the Volkswagen still parked on the shoulder. Joyboy honked as he passed, but Sparrow's eyes were looking straight ahead, searching for the limousine he could not see.

PART II

The School

THURSDAY

8:45 A.M.

The first panic had passed and Kathy was thinking now about survival. She cradled Heidi's head and rocked the little girl in her arms. It had all happened so fast. When the car stopped and the man was standing on the road, she had not been watching, occupied with her own problems. And then that thin, hard face in the front seat. Where was he taking them? What was he going to do?

They were trapped in the back of the car, that much was certain. As long as the controls were in his hands they couldn't open a window or door. And what if they could? At the speed they were traveling they couldn't jump out anyway. No, there had to be some way . . . something they could do.

Slowly, a thought came. She was forgetting about

herself now, about the heavy feeling of dread, the panic in her stomach, the trembling in her legs. There must be something they could do to attract attention, to let people know that they were being kidnaped. *Kidnaped!* The word registered for the first time. They were heading toward the city, or some hideout on the way, to be held captive . . . why? The answer came as she thought of the question. For money. Oh, God, what would happen to them!

She quieted herself and tried to think. What would happen at school when they didn't arrive? She looked at her watch and noted the time. She would be in her math class now, sitting in the middle of the third row, going over her homework with Mrs. Day.

But the teacher would just think she was sick. They were all in different classes, except, perhaps, for the twins. And unless someone noticed that the limousine had not arrived, the chances were that they would not be missed. As far as she knew, no one at Sloane checked the cars in and out. Which meant no one would miss them. And if they weren't missed no one would search for them.

There must be something she could do. Rocking back and forth, smoothing Heidi's hair, she tried to think as the big limousine sped toward the parkway.

8:50 A.M.

On the train, Maxwell Barnett was looking at the Northside ghetto. How the hell could people live there? The train swayed and rocked on the elevated tracks, passing through mile after mile of tenements, six-story brick, most of them, built at the turn of the century or shortly thereafter. Garbage and broken glass dotted the streets. Empty lots and alleys and backyards were strewn with litter. You have to be an animal to live in a jungle like that, he thought. Why the hell didn't they keep their own streets clean? How can you have any respect for people who throw garbage out of windows?

He looked down at the crossword puzzle again, but his mind was not on it. Should he call Steve Phillips as soon as he reached the office and find out who planted that story with him? No, that would only be adding fuel to the fire. Phillips would probably get more out of him, pumping for information in that sharp muckraking way he had, than he would ever get from Phillips. Still, the man was all right and good at what he did. A straight shooter. Damn trouble was you couldn't get him to print what you wanted. There was always an extra angle that Phillips brought to any story, usually an angle with a cutting edge. The guy probably hates advertising . . . but who didn't?

But who had planted the item in Phillips' column? And how do you handle Chris Menakis?

Go right at him, was his first thought. Read the article to him over the phone, if he hasn't already seen it, and tell him it was a hell of a way to run a railroad. No. You can't panic. Don't show the white feather, even if it's sticking out of your ears. Cool it. Yes, that's the approach. Laugh it off. Like, maybe the opposition planted the piece just to get us upset, but you and me, Chris, we're not going to let it bother us.

Exactly right. I'll keep it a routine day. Lunch, maybe, if Chris can make it. A few drinks and we'll be making a joke out of the whole thing.

He felt calmer now, with a plan of action laid out. He'd finesse this crisis, the way he'd finessed others in the past. Hell, that was what the agency was paying him eighty-five thousand a year for in the first place. Coolness under fire.

One thought intruded: What if it was Chris himself who had given Phillips the item?

He couldn't think about that.

8:52 A.M.

Joyboy drove the Volkswagen along School Avenue, keeping the little car at a steady and legal thirty miles an hour. The school cop had his car parked almost in the exact spot where he was supposed to dump the note. The son of a bitch was sitting on his ass, smoking. Joyboy drove on past. He was almost a half mile down the road when he saw the cruiser pull out and start heading back toward Rochdale. His stomach tightened.

He made a left-hand turn and headed down a cross street. At the first corner he swung over and came back.

There was very little traffic as he approached the school again. He turned left as if he were going to enter the school grounds, but once he had crossed the road he swung left again and drew to a stop where the police cruiser had been parked. Putting the car into neutral, he set the hand brake and waited, looking ahead and in the mirror to watch the traffic.

He could still quit now. Right this very minute he could just say fuck it and head out for parts unknown. Why didn't he, he wondered, knowing the answer even as he played with it in his mind. It was the money, wasn't it? Nothing but the money. Not black power. Not revolution. Nothing like that. The money. A hundred grand a kid. Six hundred thousand dollars. One hundred and fifty thousand for me alone.

What would he do with it? Oh baby, what a problem. What a goddamn delicious problem. He'd head for Canada, first off. Just cool his heels in some great hotel for a while, living the life. Pick up some clothes. Five or six suits, maybe. Slacks and some of those groovy-looking knitted shirts. And then what?

Paris. With a hundred and fifty Gs in the kick. You could live a long time in Paris on that kind of loot. MacNeil had been there. Charlie MacNeil, the drummer he'd known in the old days. MacNeil had spent three years there, on the Left Bank. Oh man, they do love us colored people in Paris, Charlie had always said. You could really jive in Paris.

But what about Greer? He wasn't going to split up the cash. That was for the revolution. Guns, grenades, and ammo to put the brothers on top. But the only brother Joyboy cared about was Joyboy himself. And one way or another he was going to get his share of the loot and split.

He took the envelope from the glove compartment. The road was almost clear. He got out and walked around the back of the car, looking at the tires. A lonely Oldsmobile was approaching from the north. When it disappeared over the edge of the hill, he turned and went quickly to the wall. The bush was to his left. The school grounds were deserted.

He tossed the envelope over the wall and watched it flutter to the ground, exactly where it was supposed to be.

Back in the car, he swung across the empty avenue and began heading toward the city.

9:00 A.M.

Where the fuck was Greer? Sparrow pushed the Chevvy up to fifty-five, his eyes searching the two-lane road ahead. The limo was all the way to hell and gone. And he was late. Oh shit, what would Greer do when he got back to the garage?

Was he supposed to wait for me, Sparrow wondered, or was I supposed to catch up with him? Either way, his job was to fall in line behind Greer and keep other traffic away. In case the kids pulled something, or some other driver spotted something wrong.

But where the hell was the Caddy? I took too long to get started, he thought. Maybe something had gone wrong. Maybe the police had already stopped Greer.

I've got to catch up and see, Sparrow thought. Greer had to be somewhere up ahead, on the road that led to the parkway. He pressed down on the gas pedal and watched the needle climb to sixty.

9:05 A.M.

"Very good, Phil, very good indeed." Dr. Charles Payson Carew removed his pince-nez and stuffed them gently into his breast pocket. The headmaster was a spare, rangy man in his late fifties, almost completely bald, with shaggy white eyebrows that dominated a strong, well-defined face. "The catalogue is coming along wonderfully well, don't you think?"

"Yes, sir." Philip Stuart nodded. He sat back in the heavy club chair that flanked the headmaster's antique desk.

"I particularly like the statement of principles you've outlined." Carew took up the top sheet of catalogue copy and read from it. ". . . 'that Sloane students may be responsible, cooperative, creative members of society and self-reliant individuals with inner resources that give enjoyment and meaning to life' . . ." He gestured with the paper, wagging a thin finger. "Responsible . . . self-reliant . . . creative. A very good capsule analysis of the qualities we aim to inculcate in our students."

"I'm happy you think so much of it, sir," Stuart said. "Shall I send it on to the printer, then?"

Carew brought his hand down slowly. And in that brief pause, Philip Stuart knew what was coming. The catalogue copy was acceptable, but now Carew would put his own stamp on it.

"Ah, not just yet, Phil," the headmaster said, his voice pitched low. "I'd like to look it over for a day or so, to live with it for a while. I'm sure it will be fine," he added.

"Very good," Stuart said. He looked at the leather-bound volumes lining the elegant office, at the glass-enclosed clock on the nineteenth-century mantelpiece. Get on with it, he told himself, as he took the black scholarship proposal from his coat pocket.

Now, Stuart thought, so it can be tied in with the anniversary fund-raising drive. If all those funds were earmarked for other purposes, there could be no black scholarship program. "There is something I'd like to take up with you, sir," he began. "It's been a pet idea of mine for some time, and I've put it into words." He laid the proposal before the headmaster.

Carew took up the paper, and finding his pince-nez, swiveled his chair toward the window to read.

Stuart looked out the window past the headmaster. Across a broad expanse of green lawn he saw the brown scar where the foundation for the new Science Building was being excavated.

As Dr. Carew looked through Stuart's brief outline, his expression clouded. A black scholarship program, indeed! Free tuition and transportation that would cost several hundred thousand dollars over the next few years! The idea of bringing ghetto blacks up from the city to rub shoulders with Sloane students was not only distasteful, it was out of the question.

He thought back to the board meeting when the idea of admitting black students to Sloane was first discussed. It had been heavy going, but in the end they *had* agreed to admit some qualified black students. Blacks who tested well.

They had proven to be the children of Negro upper-middle-class parents who could afford Sloane's costs. These children, because of their backgrounds, had at least some hope of matching the social and intellectual levels of the average student.

But this was not what Stuart was suggesting. He was demanding that Sloane open its doors and its pocketbook to an incursion of ghetto blacks, as crude and unpolished as the dirty streets they sprang from.

Carew laid the proposal down on his desk. "An interesting suggestion," he said at last. "Quite interesting, actually."

"Interesting how?" Stuart asked. "Interesting yes . . . to be raised with the board? Or interesting no . . . to be further discussed?"

Carew smiled. His young dean was certainly aggressive. "Aren't you getting rather ahead of yourself, Phil? Until I read your proposal I'd never given the matter any thought at all."

"Precisely," Stuart said. He sat on the arm of the club chair. "Think of what it would mean for us to announce a program to bring ghetto children up here, sir. What a magnificent gesture it would be . . ."

"Now wait a moment," the headmaster interrupted. "Sloane happens to be an educational institution, Phil. Not some government-sponsored sociology clinic."

"Of course. But still, we're in a position of leadership. People follow us. Think of what a blow we could strike against cynicism and prejudice."

Carew shook his head slowly. "We are in the business of educating young minds, period. The best minds, I might add."

Now we're getting to it, Stuart thought. The best minds had to be white, of course. They couldn't possibly exist under a black skin or come from a ghetto. "Granted," he said. "We want only bright students. But certainly, down in Northside, there must be at least a few such students who could flourish up here."

"It's possible," Carew agreed, "to the same extent that anything is possible. But one can't help harboring doubts about how much these students—even if we could find them—could hope to contribute to Sloane."

"That's part of my point," Stuart said, his voice rising. "I think these black kids could actually do more for Sloane than you realize. They'd be very good for us, if only because we'd have to rethink some very basic attitudes. They'd force us to be more relevant, for one thing."

"I can't agree," Carew said flatly. "I don't see how you could possibly think such children would be at all comfortable up here."

"Perhaps not at first," Stuart said quickly. "It would take time."

"It would be a disaster," Carew said. "For them as well as for Sloane."

"I don't think we can know that unless we try it, sir."

"Indeed," Carew said, his nostrils flaring. "Try it at whose expense?"

Carew sighed and looked away. When he spoke again, his voice was calm. "I think you need to learn some history," he said. "You've been with us how long . . . three years? I don't think you appreciate how slowly Sloane moves. Or why. Look at the desk I sit behind," he went on. "For one hundred years the headmaster of Sloane has sat here, Phil. Think of it. Only six men before me have occupied this seat. Only six men have borne the responsibility for the good name and reputation of the school. It's a high honor, and it bespeaks a certain trust. A Sloane headmaster finds his first responsibility is to uphold and maintain the school's character. Experimentation has never been paramount here. There are other values. . . ."

He's beginning a speech, Stuart realized with horror. He sank into the club chair and found his cigarettes. A lecture, he thought, as he lit up and listened. And at the rate the old man is going, it could take all morning.

9:07 A.M.

"More tea, darling?" Irene smiled.

Norman Schwartz looked up from his newspaper and into his wife's shining eyes. He shook his head, no, realizing once again how much the heart attack had changed his life. Tea instead of coffee. A poor substitute. Tea was something you drank when you were ill. Coffee was what God intended you to have in the morning, three or four cups, hot and strong, to get you started. And when you got to the office, more coffee. And coffee with lunch, in the afternoon, and just about the entire evening through. Coffee and cigarettes. God, that had been hard, giving up smoking. He used to smoke two, sometimes three packs a day, leaving a trail of stubs and ashes wherever he went. It was a difficult habit to break, but he had done it. He hadn't had a cigarette now in . . . how long was it? Four and a half months. And I miss them every day, he thought, especially now.

He pushed his teacup away and walked to the window. The drizzle had stopped and the skies were definitely brightening. "I'd better get started," he said without enthusiasm.

"Do you really have to?"

"Yes, I really have to. It's expected. Sometime during the day the boss is expected to be in the office, even if it's only to look around." He walked behind Irene's chair and put a hand on her shoulder.

"Call Jerry," she said, "and tell him that you're taking the day off. Come on."

"In the middle of a Thursday?" he said. "My God, it's positively decadent."

"Come on, honey," she said, "take the day off. We can just laze around this morning, and after lunch, if the weather clears, maybe we can play some golf. What do you say?"

He kissed the top of her head. "I could be persuaded . . ."

"Good. Then it's settled."

"But maybe I have a better idea." He sat down in the chair beside her. Was this the time to spring it on her, he thought, the dream he had been playing with for the past few months? Why not? "I've been thinking, darling," he began slowly, "maybe it's time to make a break with the past. To work, and not work . . . to operate a business and yet not really do it fully, well, it's not like me." He held up a hand to stay her protest. "Yes, I know, I've got to take it easy. I'm not proposing to go back to a full time schedule. No, there's something else I have in mind."

Here it comes, Irene thought. She took a slow sip of her coffee, her eyes fixed on her husband. Here comes the result of all those vacant stares and long silences.

"What I'd like to do," he said quietly, "is sell the business and begin a whole new life." He looked at her, his eyes grave.

"All right," Irene said, "go on." She felt an urge to busy her hands and reached for her pack of Marlboros. "Do you mind?" she asked, holding up the pack.

"Yes, but go ahead anyway." As the smoke curled up about her hair, he continued: "All those weeks, flat on my back, it makes you think. You start to measure yourself, adding up your life. And what I came up with was this: a good wife, a loving son . . . nice home . . . all that."

"Not a bad scorecard, I'd say."

"No. I suppose most people would settle for it. But then you read the newspapers and you see what kind of shape the country's in and you begin to question it. I mean . . ." He searched for the words. "I don't want to wave the flag, but have I done anything for other people . . . that wasn't connected with making more money for myself?"

"Yes, you have. Lots of things."

"Name one."

"Charity. You've given a lot of money to charity, Norman."

He waved his hand as if to brush away a fly. "All tax-deductible. Very neat. But you see, honey, I haven't been involved. I haven't given one thought to things I could do to help people . . . or the country."

He grinned. "My God, I sound like a nut. Or some kind of egomaniac."

"There's an insight," Irene said. "Take helping others seriously and you begin to think there's something wrong with you."

Norman nodded. "Anyway," he continued, "I'd been talking to a group about selling the business for some time." He mentioned the name of a well-known textile conglomerate. "In the last few weeks they've firmed up their offer. What do you think the business is worth to them?"

"I have no idea." It was true, she had never thought of Norman's business in those terms. To her it was only a provider, although a very good one.

"Take a guess."

She paused. "Half a million dollars?"

Delight shone in Norman's eyes. "Would you believe a million and a half? About half in cash, and the rest in stock. All that for a name. My name. Isn't that ridiculous?"

"Nothing you do is ridiculous, darling."

"Spoken like a good wife. What it means, Irene, is

that I'll never have to work again. With what we already have, and the way they'll buy me out . . . incidentally, I can't sell any of their stock for a year, but I don't think that makes any difference."

Irene shivered. What was important was that Norman be happy and involved in something that would not tax his heart. The money wasn't all that important.

"So here's what I figure we'll do," he was saying. "We'll wrap up the deal as quickly as possible. Say by June, when Mike gets out of school. Then we'll lock up the house and spend the summer in Europe with Mike. In the fall we can send him to a school in Geneva—I've already made inquiries. And you and me, we'll see the world while I do some thinking. You know, it's crazy. My father was a tailor. Never had a dime. Came over here in 1904 from Kremenchug, in the Ukraine. I'd kind of like to go there, to see what he came from. And then, after six months or so, maybe I'll have a better idea of what I'd like to do with the rest of my life." He looked closely at her. "What do you think, honey?"

She looked into his dark eyes and felt a rush of warmth. "I think," she said, her mouth twisting, "I think I'm going to cry."

9:09 A.M.

Jimmy Little crushed his cigarette in the coffee-can lid they all used for an ashtray and immediately lit another. "What do you think's happening?" he asked for the third time in the past half hour.

Loretta Jo looked at Jimmy's soft face and smiled. "You nervous?"

"Shit, yeah. Aren't you?"

The thin black girl shrugged and stretched her arms, sitting back in the rickety chair. "Either they pulled it off, or they didn't. By this time they're most likely on the way back . . . or on the run. . . ." She let it hang in the air between them, the third alternative she didn't want to talk about. Greer taken by the police, or maybe worse. Shot and on the way to a hospital, or even dead.

"Jesus, you're a cold fish," Jimmy said. He stood up and began to pace the room, his small body casting large shadows in the dim light of the single, hanging bulb.

"Worrying is not going to get us anywhere, Jimmy. There's nothing we can do to help them now. They're on their own. And all we can do is wait . . . and keep listening to the radio. . . ." She focused her attention on the tiny transistor. The all-news station they were tuned to droned on. There were no urgent flashes, no interruptions. If the plan had failed, if Greer was hurt or dead, they didn't know about it on the radio.

She followed Jimmy with her eyes. The boy was so nervous he was beginning to upset her. She looked at the gold bracelet watch that Greer had given her to seal their relationship. We're together now, that watch had meant, and whatever the road ahead, we are going down it together. She would have followed him even without the watch. That tall, lean, hard-faced guy with the fire in his belly was hers forever, to hold and to comfort, to lean on and help support, even if they had no future. It was as close to a marriage ceremony as they would ever get, she supposed, and the fact that Greer had lifted the watch from an old woman whose purse he'd snatched made no difference. He didn't have to give her anything, they both knew that. It was a token, a keepsake that formalized her break with her family and marked the beginning of something else. It could lead to prison, or the grave. Or, if what Greer was planning came true, a hard and violent struggle that would go on for many years.

Jimmy was still pacing. She looked at the boy and thought back to the evening Greer had brought him in. He was thirteen years old and had been on his own for three years after running away from home. Home for Jimmy was Harrisburg, Pennsylvania, where he had shared his bed with two older brothers and the room with four sisters, his mother, her boyfriend, and a couple of assorted aunts and uncles. Home was grubbing for something to eat when the older people were through, dressing in hand-me-downs that were already patched and worn when they were secondhand, before he was given them. Home was dreaming through schooldays, not hearing or caring about what the teacher was saying, but thinking about taking off and going someplace better. One day Jimmy had simply cut out and thumbed a ride, thinking he probably wouldn't be missed.

"Jimmy?"

The boy turned to her.

"Why don't you go on upstairs and lay down for a while? Maybe watch television. If there's anything doing, I'll call you. Okay?"

With a thin smile the boy was gone, taking the steps two at a time. He was Jimmy the Hustler when Greer had picked him up, after the boy had tried to sell him a hot television set. When Greer questioned him, the boy's story came out. He was living with a group of teenage junkies, running errands and helping sell the merchandise they stole, and on the side he worked deals of his own. He steered for a bordello on Ninety-fifth Street, waiting outside the bars on Lenard Avenue to accost white or black johns. He also helped an older man handle his numbers route, visiting the old women and sick people who couldn't manage to get down to the candy store to place their combinations in person. And once in a while, when he was flat, Jimmy would sub for one of the three pushers who worked the neighborhood, selling two-dollar bags of smack inside the local junior high school.

Greer had insisted they take him in. "He's going to be a child of the revolution," Greer said, "the first one besides ourselves. This child, this gutter animal, is what it's all about. A society that can produce him, and hundreds of thousands more, deserves to be torn down. What have they ever done for this kid except keep him down, and hungry? Jimmy stays with us. In this system he became a hustler to get by. In another life, with his drive, why there's no telling what he might be. And maybe, if things don't work out for us, Jimmy'll be the one to keep the revolution going."

The revolutionist in question switched on the television set and lay down on one of the mattresses that lined the floor. When the picture came on he accepted *Leave It to Beaver* for what it was—something taking place in another country.

9:14 A.M.

Patrolman Michael Bradie of the 14th Motorcycle Platoon took his post on the south-bound side of the parkway overpass, where he couldn't be seen by the drivers still streaming toward the city. The traffic had peaked some forty minutes before, and now there were long clear spots between cars. For the first time in hours, motorists had a chance to exceed the posted speed limit.

Bradie gunned the motorcycle and let it fall back to idle, watching the flow of traffic. When he saw the black Chevvy come barreling along the inside lane, he didn't hesitate. The Chevvy was doing at least sixty-five, but he decided to tail the guy for a quarter of a mile just to make sure. He settled back in his seat and began to watch the speedometer.

9:15 A.M.

Three miles ahead the limousine sped on at a carefully controlled fifty miles per hour. No one was looking for them—of that Kathy was certain. If they were going to find help they would have to act on their own. The driver had a gun. And from the look on his face when he had pointed it at them, he probably wouldn't hesitate to use it. But still . . .

"Listen to me, kids," she said, keeping her voice down and her eyes on the driver. "We're being kidnaped." She cradled the quietly sobbing Heidi and turned to look at the other children. "I want you all to listen to me and do what I say. This man"—she flicked her eyes toward the driver—"he looks desperate . . . and mean. If we don't do what he says . . ." She paused. No, she thought, don't get them any more terrified than they already are. "We have to be smart. And careful. And not let him hurt us. And we've got to stick together, do you understand that?"

"Soon as we stop," one of the twins said, grinning, "I'm going to run."

"No!" Kathy said. This was exactly what she feared.

"When I get moving, nobody can catch me."

"Twinny, listen to me. You don't understand what's happening. That man up there has a gun. Nobody can run away from a gun. You won't run anywhere unless I tell you to. Do you understand that? No running unless I say so. It's our only chance. What we do, we do together. Okay?"

Ralph Flood was obviously disappointed. "Aw, gee, Kathy—"

"Listen, you blockhead," Mike Schwartz said, "you're not old enough to escape. You listen to Kathy. We stick together. And you're gonna do what Kathy says or so help me, when we get out of this, I'm gonna knock your stupid head off."

"Easy, boys," Kathy soothed, "take it easy. Okay. Let's not give that man up there any reason to hurt us, if we can help it." She turned to the black boy sitting quietly beside her. "I'm Kathy Barnett, who are you?"

"Henry Taylor, Junior," the boy said.

The name registered. "Is your father a doctor?"

"Yes," the boy smiled. "Do you know him?"

"Sure," she said. "What are you doing here with us?"

"Just lucky, I guess. I slept over at Mike's house last night."

The doctor's son, she thought. Was there some connection between his presence in the car today and what had happened? Had they been taken only because the man driving wanted to get the doctor's son? In spite of himself, she wished it were so, and that she and the other children would be released. But even as the thought crossed her mind she knew it was not so, and that they were all in the same fire.

"Michael," she said, "I want to do something. Do you think you can help?"

She saw the boy nod, his jaw set.

"Good. Now all of you sit quietly. She smiled to break the tension. "Do you have a pen, Michael? Good. Now open your notebook. Slowly, that's it."

Now what message could be written large enough to attract the attention of a passing car?

"As big as you can, Michael, print this: Kidnap . . . Police . . . Help. . . ." She watched the boy's hand printing the words in thin capital letters. "Make them darker, go over them a few times. That's it."

Where could they put the note? Not the back window. The driver would see it immediately. It had to be the side window then, facing the middle lane, directly behind the driver. She looked into the rear-view mirror and jumped as her eyes met his. She saw him sit up high in his seat, using the mirror to see all of them. Her leg began to tremble. Now the glass was sliding down.

"Hand it over," he said, reaching out a hand. "Come on, *move!*" he added when they didn't respond.

Michael was looking at her.

The glass partition was fully down. "Give it to me, bitch, or this one gets it." The gun was no more than six inches from the twin's head.

"Let him have it, Michael," Kathy said, her voice flat. Now she was certain. The man would kill them all without any hesitation. His face was twisted and hard, and there was no pity in his eyes.

She watched Michael tear off the page and pass it through the partition. The driver looked briefly at the note, crumpled it, and closed the partition.

His voice came over the speaking tube behind Kathy's head. "I can hear every word you say back there . . . so don't try any more tricks."

Kathy closed her eyes, trying to hold back the tears.

9:17 A.M.

Sparrow was passing cars, switching from lane to lane, when he heard the siren. His eyes jumped to the side-view mirror and he saw the helmeted cop bearing down on him.

Oh shit, he thought, they're after me! He put his foot down hard but the Chevvy was already almost on top of the panel truck in front of him. He pushed the horn and held it down, shouting, although he did not know it. Then he saw an opening in the right-hand lane and cut over, narrowly missing the right rear fender of the truck. He had some room now, not much, maybe fifty yards until the next car. He looked at the mirror again. The cop was riding the white line between the lanes and coming up on his tail. Sparrow edged the car over, letting the left wheel ride in the center lane. He looked at the truck driver, whose mouth had dropped open. There wasn't more than a couple of inches between the two vehicles.

The cop was coming around the other side. Sparrow swung back over into the lane and headed for the shoulder.

Crazy son of a bitch, Patrolman Bradie thought as he fell behind the Chevvy again, narrowly missing being swept off the road. He leaned down hard on the siren and began to creep up around the left, edging in between the panel truck and the Chevvy.

Sparrow watched him coming up alongside in the mirror. Right where I want you, he was thinking. He swung left, trying to cut sharply in front of the panel truck and catch the motorcycle on his door. But the cop had anticipated his move, braking sharply. Sparrow braked too but an instant too late. The panel truck hit his left front fender, jerking the steering wheel out of his hands. His head snapped back and the car was skidding, riding backward off the road. Then its tail hit the curb and the car flipped over and Sparrow descended into the dark.

9:20 A.M.

While Mrs. Wade was getting dressed, Dr. Taylor took the time to return to his desk and make some notations on her card. As he waited for the woman to join him he wrote down the results of his examination. Major organs appeared to be functioning well; heart, blood pressure, respiration, were normal. He paused as he noted her height and weight: 5′3″, 98 pounds. Age, 26. Children, 4. "Seems like I ain't got any strength at all hardly," she'd said. "And my legs are just awful painful."

He made out a pink blood-test slip for Mrs. Wade, already fairly certain of the results, for in her eyes he had seen the telltale corkscrew blood vessels. Anemia, most likely, sickle-cell anemia, a cursed inheritance of her African ancestry that was destroying the red cells in her blood. Ghetto medicine, he thought, you can make the diagnosis without even seeing the patient.

"I'd like to ask you some questions about your diet," he said. She looked so pathetic he ventured a smile.

"Ain't on no diet, doctor. My trouble is gainin' weight, not losin' it."

"I mean what you eat, ordinarily. Your daily diet, Mrs. Wade. Do you eat things like liver? Red meat? Fish?"

"Hamburger, usually, that's mostly what we eat for meat. You see, doctor, we're on the welfare. And what meat we gets I mainly let the children eat." She looked at him levelly.

Henry felt a stirring of pity. He wouldn't tell her what he suspected. Not yet. It would be better to wait until the tests confirmed his diagnosis. But he would start the treatment. He took the prescription pad from the top drawer of his desk and wrote out a specification for B-group complex vitamin tablets, and another for folic acid. He handed them to her, along with the pink testing form. "You give this pink slip to the nurse," he explained, "and she'll take a blood sample for testing. And have these prescriptions filled. You're a little thin and run-down, we'll have to start building you up."

Again that direct look. "These medicines, Doctor, they gonna cost a lot of money?"

Money, he thought, it always comes down to money. You have to pay to stay alive in this country. The rule was, if the patients could pay for medication (or even for treatment), let them pay. If they requested assistance, then the city would make the payment. But they had to ask for help before it could be given.

"You tell the druggist to send the bill here—to the clinic—and we'll take care of it. And when you finish with the blood test, make another appointment. I want to see you again next week." He rose and led her out of the room, handing her over to the nurse in charge.

"Got a minute?" Roy Hart asked. Henry watched the young giant duck his head as he went through the doorway, and followed him back into the office. The next patient was already waiting. Hart drew him into a corner. "Will you have some time later, say around ten-thirty?" he asked in a low voice.

"I suppose so. If it's important. What's up?"

"I was just speaking to Colley Watson on the phone. I asked him to drop by and see us."

Colley Watson. The Minister of Defense of the Young Simbas, a militant black power group that was gaining recognition in the community. They were currently conducting a campaign against a local church, trying to get church authorities to permit them to use the church's basement for a pre-school children's breakfast program. A few weeks before, they had occupied the church for five days until the police had come in and forced them out. Three Simbas had been injured in the ensuing melee, as well as a policeman, and the newspapers and television had had a field day covering the trouble. Colley Watson, Henry thought, he was about as controversial a figure as you could find.

He turned and asked his patient if she would mind waiting outside, then closed the door behind her. Colley Watson. He picked up his cold pipe and sucked on it to calm himself. There was no use in showing Roy how upset he was.

"I promised to call him back in five minutes," Hart said. "He's probably waiting."

Henry sat down behind his desk. Hart stood, waiting,

looking down at him. "Colley Watson," Henry said. He drummed his fingers on the desk.

"Yes. I assume you know who he is."

Easy, Roy, Henry thought, don't push too much. "I've heard of him," he grunted.

"Well?"

"Well what?" Henry snapped. "I don't recall saying anything about Colley Watson. Or the Simbas. Or anything like that. Just where did you get the authority to invite the head of the Simbas into this clinic?"

Hart seated himself in the visitor's chair, crossing his long legs. "Well . . . I just assumed, after the conversation we had this morning, that—"

"What do we have to gain by getting involved with an organization like the Simbas, Roy? Just how do you think that's going to sit with the administration downtown?"

Hart's natural ebullience faded. "What was all that this morning, Henry? A lot of crap? I thought you wanted to do something. We were going to begin to treat the ghetto, weren't we, as well as the patients? Or was all that just talk? A line you were handing out to get me off your back?"

"Now just a minute, Roy. Let's keep invective out of this conversation. Why don't you first tell me what we have to gain by having the Simbas in to tea?"

"Manpower," Hart said. "People trying to do something about this stinking ghetto. They could help us, and come to think of it, we could help them. Right now, they're trying to get a square meal into a hundred kids before they go off to school in the morning. That's not exactly a revolutionary aim, is it? And yet, from the reaction they're getting you'd think they were about to burn down City Hall."

"Isn't that next on the program, though, Roy? Isn't that what we'd be hooking up with? Militants who will stop at nothing to get what they want?"

Hart turned and looked at the old man for a long minute. "You've been up in the County a long time, Doctor." The way he snapped out the word "doctor" made it an epithet. "People are dying down here, or haven't you noticed? And finally—finally—there's a group that's speaking up, standing their ground. Saying, Clean it up, we insist. Don't sweep us under the rug the way you've been doing for a hundred years. And they're right, Doctor, damn right. And what's more, you know in your heart they're right."

"Calmly and rationally," Henry said, keeping his voice and emotions under close control. "Sit down, Roy." He waited while the young man did. When he spoke, his voice sounded tired. "I started this place, Roy. When you were in diapers, a long time ago." He held up a hand to prevent the outburst he could see on Hart's lips. "No, I'm not going to give you an old man's speech of how I've been there before. You know all of it, anyway, and it serves nothing. But I don't want to hear revolutionary speeches from you, Roy. That won't get us anywhere, either.

"There are only seven thousand of us black doctors in the country, Roy. And two of them are in this room now. We can't afford to waste our energy by beating up on each other."

"Agreed."

"Now what happens," Henry went on, "if we join forces with the Simbas and they begin to use us? What kind of a name will it give to the clinic—to black medicine—if the newspapers and television start featuring us with Watson's revolutionaries?"

"We can direct the Simbas, I think. They'd work for us, because our aims are alike. Suppose they fanned out through the Northside, rounding up the babies who haven't had their diphtheria shots? That couldn't hurt us, could it? Suppose we got up a pamphlet on sanitation, proper disposal of garbage, the right kinds of things to feed the children. I don't see how that could do anything but good. Suppose they helped us zero in on one block, say, as an example of what could be done. And we clean it up, and start an intensive-care program with the Simbas making sure the people come for regular checkups."

"They'd probably drag them in here kicking and screaming."

"Would that matter?" Hart said. "The thing is, they have the troops and we don't. What I've just said is only a beginning. If they'd join forces with us I'm sure there are dozens of ways we can work effectively together."

"While they get lots of publicity as good samaritans."

Hart smiled. "Are you so sure they aren't, Henry? And does it really matter?"

"No. I suppose not. And maybe if they aren't, we can help make them that." He stood up and looked at his watch. "You're converting me, Roy. Or should I say, subverting me?" He thrust out his arm and shook hands with the younger man.

"Listen, Henry," Hart smiled, "I once heard you say that you would make a pact with the devil himself if you thought it could save lives. All I'm asking is that you meet with Colley Watson, to see if we can do some good together."

It was Henry Taylor's turn to smile. "Tell the devil I'm waiting. And let's hope when he gets here that we end up with his soul, not the other way around."

9:25 A.M.

When the intercom buzzed, Maxwell Barnett interrupted his thoughts and put the telephone to his ear. "I spoke to his secretary," Sally Clarke said, "and she said they expected Mr. Menakis at any minute."

"Well, try him again in ten minutes," he said. "No, scratch that. Come on in here for a minute, Sally." He sat back in his swivel chair and waited. She knocked at the door, then entered, steno pad in hand. She was wearing a yellow loose-knit "poor boy" sweater that clung, showing her high, firm breasts to good advantage. A fall of dark, shoulder-length hair outlined a round face remarkable for its high color.

"I suppose you read Phillips' column this morning," he began. She nodded. "Hell of a thing, Sally. A piece like that . . . why it could start a lot of trouble, as I'm sure you know. What I'd like to find out is, how did Phillips get hold of that quote?"

"It didn't come from me, Max," she said.

Her face was so serious he had to smile. Damn right it didn't come from her. She'd probably cut off her arm before she did anything to hurt me, he thought. "I know," he said. "But I'm not so sure of some of the other people around here."

"You mean . . . people here would actually work against the agency?"

He shook his head ruefully. "It's been known to happen more than once. I've done a good job with that account. Management is happy—grateful, maybe. In a few months, I'm due to move up, some things have already been mentioned. Management supervisor . . . maybe. I'm not naming names, but there are quite a few other guys who'd like to get that spot for themselves."

"And you think one of them planted the story in Phillips' column?"

"Not think. That's too strong. Let's just say I wouldn't be very surprised if one of them did. So what I'd like you to do, Sally, is keep your ear to the ground. See what some of the other girls are talking about, okay?"

"I'm on my way," she said, turning and heading for the door. As soon as the door was fully closed behind her he picked up his phone and dialed Chris Menakis' unlisted home number.

He was surprised when the phone rang only once before it was picked up. He was still more surprised to hear the voice on the other end of the wire. "Who's this?" he asked smoothly, the upset he felt not showing in his voice.

"Who's this?"

It was Eli Bernstein. What the hell was an agency art director doing in Chris Menakis' apartment at this hour of the morning?

"Is that you, Eli?" he said.

"Definitely. Who am I talking to?"

"Max Barnett, that's who. What are you doing down there?"

There was a pregnant pause. "That's a long story, Max. Maybe I should better tell you another time."

I'll bet it's a long story, he thought. "Let me speak to Chris."

"He's kinda tied up at the moment, Max. . . . And I don't think you're his favorite person right now, either."

"Suppose you let me be the judge of that, Eli?"

"Sorry."

The son of a bitch wasn't giving anything away. "How come you're down there, Eli?"

"Look—I gotta run now, I'll talk to you later."

Barnett heard the click as Bernstein hung up. As he put his receiver back in its place, a swarm of possibilities—all of them distressing—flooded through his mind.

9:35 A.M.

It was one of those traffic jams that seem to have no end. All Ernest Flood could see ahead was three solid lanes of cars. Cars jerking forward at low speed, stopping abruptly when the space to move closed up, long lines of tail lights winking suddenly red as progress came to a halt. Trapped, he crept the Mercury forward in the right-hand lane, fuming at the delay.

You acted very badly this morning, he told himself, making a pass at the *au pair* girl. It was a damned silly thing to do. Again, the thought occurred, the one overriding thought that consumed his life, but he brushed it aside. And yet it wouldn't go away.

The money was Martha's. All the money was hers.

He punched the radio off the music station and onto one that gave continuous news. Perhaps they would have one of their helicopters overhead to explain the traffic snarl. He let his right foot do the driving, alternating it between gas and brake pedals, and tried to concentrate on the radio. The announcer droned on about a garbage fire in the Northside ghetto that had turned into a near-riot. The Young Simbas had held a street-corner rally, with Colley Watson burning a massive pile of garbage to protest the lack of attention paid to the ghetto by the city's Sanitation Department. But by now Ernest Flood was back to thought number one again.

You loved Martha even before you knew about her father and the mill. It was so hard to think back to those early days, and to keep that thought in mind. You loved her before you knew about the money. You were going to go back to college, after the service, but then there was all that money. It was easier, wasn't it, to begin learning how to run a carpet mill than to go back to school and become a teacher? Sure it was. And why shouldn't you and Martha have had a European grand tour as a honeymoon? And why shouldn't a man start at the top if he can? What was wrong with that?

But something began to happen. First to you, and then to her. The whole relationship began to change. The house in the County, the clubs you joined, waiting so many years to have children because you—no, she—was having so much fun. It's a hard thing to plan on a life of hard work . . . and then to be plunged, suddenly, into success without having to fight for it. There were three masters in the house from the beginning. The old man and his money. It was, in a way, like marrying him. She was his second in command. *Daddy says . . . Daddy wants . . . Daddy thought.* Daddy and the money and Martha. They reduced you to a stud, a paper pusher, not Ernest Flood any longer, but the man who married Martha Hanover.

There was a policeman ahead, waving at the crawling line of cars.

Flood looked off to his right, up on the shoulder of

the road. There was an overturned wreck and an ambulance beside it. Three police cruisers were on the scene. It looked like an awful smash. Broken glass and debris littered the road and a long gouge had been ripped in the grassy bank.

As he drew abreast of the wreck he could see a body being lifted onto a stretcher. The man was small and black. Two white-coated attendants placed the stretcher in the back of the ambulance.

The line of cars was halted again by a burly policeman standing in the road. Flood rolled the window down and called to him. "Is he dead?"

The big cop grinned. "Nah. The son of a bitch just busted himself up good. Serves him right. He tried to kill one of us, you know."

Before Flood could reply, the ambulance rolled across the grassy verge and swung onto the parkway. It rode away quickly, siren wailing, followed by two of the police cruisers and a policeman on a motorcycle.

After a few moments, the traffic began to move again.

9:40 A.M.

Greer checked his wristwatch as the city line flashed by. Right on schedule, he thought, exactly where they were supposed to be and in the clear. It was all coming off, all of it, just as he had planned.

He checked the rear-view mirror and looked at the girl in her back seat. She was still holding the fat little girl in her arms, but she was crying, her lips moving, tears running down her pale cheeks. Relieved, he waited a moment and looked again. Yes, those were tears all right. Now there would be no more scenes, no more threats. With the girl down, he realized, it would be easy to keep them all under control.

Everything was fine. He felt only a flicker of concern that Sparrow hadn't caught up with him. But he wasn't worried. The plan was finally in motion.

He was entering the city. Two more exits and they would be getting off. They were almost home.

9:48 A.M.

The Volkswagen was at a steady fifty miles an hour on the parkway leading to the city, but Joyboy's mind was still in Paris, a city he had never seen except in movies. It was, therefore, perfect. A place of style and sunshine, of groovy chicks and good times. He would be something of a king in that place. With money to burn and all the time in the world to enjoy the warmth.

The tune the radio was playing registered in his mind and after a while he began to sing along in a reedy baritone voice.

> "He's got the whole world—in His hands,
> We got the whole wide world—in our hands,
> We got all that money—in our hands,
> We got the whole thing in our hands . . ."

Enjoying it, he kept his eyes on the road ahead and shifted to the second chorus.

As the twisted wreckage of the Chevrolet came into view and then flashed by on the grassy bank to his right, he was too involved to notice.

9:50 A.M.

Philip Stuart stubbed out yet another cigarette butt in the alabaster ashtray. "I understand our tradition," he said as the headmaster paused for breath, "but I think it may be a trap, too. We're living in a time of change, of ferment—"

"All the more reason to hew to the past," Carew countered. "It is precisely at times like these that the old values become more important."

"I don't agree," Stuart began, but broke off as he saw Carew smile.

"Of course you don't, Phil," the headmaster said. "That's one of the reasons you are Dean of Boys." He swiveled his chair to face Stuart and put his hands on the desk. "You're not a 'yes' man. You think differently. I like that."

"Thank you, sir." Stuart felt a flush begin.

"Someday, I suppose, we will bring students in here from the city. From Northside. When the time is right."

"And when will that be?" Stuart said. He pointed out the window. "Every time I look at that construction site, and think of the money the new Science Wing is costing— Well, I get angry. Give me half of that, a quarter of that, and we could bring twenty or thirty new children up here."

"The board approved the expenditure six months ago. The money is committed. It's too late to change that now."

"So on the one hand you're telling me I'm too late. And on the other hand I'm too early, because the time isn't right."

"If you care to put it that way, yes."

"You won't put this proposal before the board?"

"No, Phil, I won't. I'm sorry."

"Well, so am I. I think we're missing a wonderful opportunity. We should be acting now, not in five years. Think of what a Sloane education would do for a black child from Northside. It could be the making of him."

Carew gazed briefly at the earnest young Dean and sighed. "There isn't a school in the country in our class who is doing what you propose."

"All the more reason for Sloane to be first."

Carew shook his head. "That's not our way. Sloane never seeks the spotlight. First let me see a black scholarship program succeed somewhere else. Give it a few years to prove that it doesn't disrupt the school. And then, perhaps, we can discuss it." Carew took Stuart's typed proposal from the desk and placed it in the top drawer of his desk.

There goes the ball game, Stuart thought. At least I tried.

"Now then," the headmaster said, "some further business. I have been noticing a decided lengthening of sideburns among some of the senior boys. How do you propose to handle that situation, Phil?"

9:58 A.M.

The littered streets of the Northside were dappled with light and shadow as the sun appeared from behind scattered clouds. The Cadillac was coming down Lenard Avenue, moving swiftly through the thin morning traffic. Kathy watched the streets flit by, looking but not seeing. Beside her, Junior Taylor watched with growing amazement. He knew exactly where they were, knew each cross street before they came to it. His father had driven this way many times when he had taken Junior with him to the clinic. In another minute they would pass by its front door.

10:00 A.M.

Sirens wailing, the ambulance flashed past the gates of County Hospital and rolled up the circular driveway. With a practiced economy, the driver shunted the vehicle forward and then back, aligning the rear of the ambulance perfectly with the edge of the ramp. When the rear doors were opened by a uniformed orderly, Patrolman Bradie was the first man out of the ambulance. Stepping aside, he watched the emergency staff bring a wheeled stretcher into place and lift the black man gently onto it. When they rolled the victim inside, into one of the three emergency receiving rooms, Bradie followed.

While a young resident examined the man, Bradie took a seat in a corner and began making notes for his report. "Negro/Male" he wrote in his pad. That's all the guy was at the moment. There had been no identification in his pockets. No wallet, for that matter. In his pants pockets there had been only a key and less than ten dollars in bills and loose change. Nothing more.

He noted the time and place of the accident. Subject evading police officer, he put down, and then made a notation of the specific violations that had caused him to give chase. Speed in excess of seventy. Weaving in and out of lane. Failure to stop when ordered. No driver's license, no automobile ownership, he put down. A stolen car, most likely, driven by the thief. Well, the license-plate number and serial number of the car were already being checked. If it was stolen then all these other charges would be thrown away. Possession of a stolen car, a felony rap, would be enough to put the man away for at least three years.

Bradie looked up as a nurse placed a bottle of whole blood onto an overhead support and plugged a tube into the man's arm. At least three years, he thought, that is, if the poor bugger lives.

10:02 A.M.

Greer brought the big limousine carefully down the street, sweeping the sidewalks and alleyways with his eyes. He saw no one. Ten yards from the garage he slowed and rapped the horn twice, then, as the garage door began retracting, he swung sharply left, bouncing the front wheels over the cut in the curb edge and shooting forward out of the sunlit street. The door closed rapidly behind him and for a moment there was only the blinding dark. He flicked the lights on and pulled the Cadillac forward to the back wall, leaving room for the others to enter when they appeared. Satisfied with the alignment of the limousine, he clicked the headlights off and turned off the engine. He was home.

He sat motionless for a moment and let the tension drain out of him. They had pulled it off. All the planning and scheming, the redirection of five lives, the long months spent with only one object in mind. And now they had the kids. And the car. And no one had stopped them.

He stepped out of the limousine just as Loretta Jo came running up.

"Oh, you're safe, you're safe, you're safe, honey," she was repeating as he stooped to take her in his arms. He kissed her neck and nuzzled his chin into the curve of her shoulder, feeling the bony curve of shoulder blades and the hard softness of ribs just under her dress as his hands moved her body closer to his. He tilted her chin and kissed her gently on the mouth and in that instant a tear wet his cheek. "It's all right," he said gently, "everything's going to be all right."

10:02 A.M.

Was he going crazy or was he only drunk?

Hamp Norris rubbed his eyes and looked again at the place where the big black limousine had been. There was no automobile to be seen. He brought the paper bag to his lips once again and, tilting his head back, let the sweet wine pass his lips. Rubbing a sleeve across his mouth, he regarded the deserted street. There was no car. He could see clear down this street and all the way down the hill to Lenard Avenue, six blocks away, and in all that space there was no car.

But he had seen it, just a minute ago. And he had heard it. The big engine approaching and the quick toot-toot of its horn. And then, when he had looked away to take a drink of wine, it had disappeared.

Was he going crazy or was he only drunk?

Hamp stood up from his seat on the front steps of the empty building and walked across the sidewalk into the sun. He ran his fingers through the few gray hairs that lined his scalp. What was happening to him lately? he wondered. First the headaches, then the pains through his chest and arms. And now this. . . . He brought a hand to his eyes to shield the sun and looked again. There was no car. Had there really been one? Or had he imagined the whole thing?

Wondering about it, Hamp Norris pushed his cart past the Elmer Garage and walked the middle of the street toward Lenard Avenue.

10:04 A.M.

The man's voice was so loud that Brenda held the telephone away from her ear. Across the desk from her, Carmine looked up. "Yes, sir," he heard her say, "I'm sure he'll be there in just a minute. In fact, he should have been there already."

What's up? Carmine asked with his eyebrows. Brenda made a face and put the phone back on its cradle.

"It's the airport call from North Rochdale. Carter's not there yet."

"Where the hell is he then?" Carmine asked of no one in particular. He should have been there half an hour ago.

"I only work here, Mr. Mancuso," Brenda said, shrugging.

Carmine looked at the chart behind his desk. Carter must have had a flat. Most likely he was stuck somewhere far from a phone, or else he would have called in.

"Get Charlie Noonan up there right away," Carmine told Brenda. He reached up and took Carter's nameplate off the ready chart and switched Noonan's from reserve to airport. While he waited for Brenda to come back from the parking yard, the thought of installing two-way radios in his limousines crossed his mind again. It was too expensive, the way he figured it. Of course, you paid for not having radios, with problems like this one.

When Brenda reached the customer again, Carmine talked to the man himself. But even as he soothed and assured the customer he'd make his plane, he was wondering what had happened to Carter.

10:05 A.M.

Greer got back in the front seat and lowered the glass. He let them look at him for a moment, then spoke to the blonde. He asked her name, and when she hesitated he asked again.

"Barnett," she said. "What's yours?" Her eyes looked as if they could burn.

"Never mind that. I'm talking to you because you're the oldest. And I'm warning you that if anything happens I don't like, you're gonna be the one that gets it. You understand me?"

"You'll never get away with it," she said, her voice breaking.

"We gonna live together for a while," he said. "Until certain arrangements are made. Then . . . if everything's peaceful like, and you all behave yourselves, why you probably get to go back home again. If not . . ." He shrugged and let the statement hang in the air.

He looked at the black boy sitting in the middle of the back seat. "What's your name?"

"Henry Taylor Jr.," the boy said.

"What you doing in this car? I never seen you before."

"I slept at my friend's house last night. And we were going to school together when you . . . when you—"

"How come I never seen you in this car before? You telling me you go to the Sloane School?"

The boy nodded.

"How many black kids they got? I didn't know they had any."

"There's some," the chunky white boy beside him said.

"I didn't ask you, *Chuck,*" Greer said. "You talk when I tell you to." He looked hard into the boy's brown eyes and purposefully flared his nostrils.

"I wanna go home," the chubby girl on the blonde's lap began to wail. "I wanna go home."

Greer looked at Kathy. "You better shut her up. I'm warning you. I don't want trouble in here. So you shut her up or else I'm gonna crack her one."

He raised the glass again and got out of the car. He had them buffaloed now, just the way he wanted them to be. In a little while, when Sparrow got here, they'd move all of them upstairs and settle them down on the mattresses. They'd be safe up there, with Sparrow and Joyboy to keep watch on them. In the meantime, he'd just let them sweat a little in the back seat, wondering what he was going to do.

He looked at his watch. What was keeping Sparrow?

10:20 A.M.

Joyboy brought the Volkswagen to a stop around the corner from the Elmer Garage, pulling up in front of the cluster of three tenements near the end of the street that were still occupied. He locked the door of the car and came around onto the sidewalk. You had to be damn careful where you left a car in this neighborhood. Turn around one minute and some fool kid will be making off with it.

He stepped cautiously down an alley, and boosting himself over a five-foot wooden wall he dropped lightly into what had once been the rear yard of the garage.

The earth here had turned black, covered over with droppings of oil and grease. Joyboy stepped around the hulks and remnants of old, forgotten automobiles and entered the rear door.

Greer and Loretta Jo were standing alongside the limousine. "Fantastic!" Joyboy said, as Greer shook his hand.

He told them how easy his part of the job had been, turning more than once to look through the glass windows of the car at the children inside. They were all there, under control. It was almost unbelievable.

"Did you see Sparrow on your way back?" Loretta Jo wanted to know.

"No. Last time I seen him he was coming around the corner where you stopped the limo, fixing to follow you. Why? Ain't he here?"

Greer slowly shook his head. "He should have been here by now."

"Something happened to him," Loretta Jo said, "I just know something happened."

"Won't do us any good to worry about him now," Greer said. "We just go on like we planned, without him. If he got caught by the pigs . . . let's hope he keeps his mouth shut."

"Maybe he got scared and took off," Joyboy said.

"Then we're better off without him." Greer crushed his cigarette under his foot and turned to the car. "Let's get moving, Joyboy. There's a lot of things need doing, and standing around wondering about Sparrow ain't gonna help." He walked to the front of the car and opened the door on the passenger's side. Behind him, Joyboy was looking over his shoulder at the crumpled body of the driver. "Wow," he said, "you sure must have whomped him."

"He'll keep," Greer said, reaching inside to release the rear-door switch. When the rear door opened, six faces looked anxiously at him. "Barnett," he snapped, pointing a finger at her, "outside!"

He slammed the door on the other children and walked the blond girl away from the car, holding her arm. In what had once been a small office, he turned her around to face him. Her eyes looked coolly into his. "Okay," he said, "here you are and here you stay. Until I finish making the arrangements for them to buy you back. You understand that?"

"I think you're a piece of shit," she said.

Without a blink, he brought his hand up and cracked her hard across the face. Tears started in her eyes, but her expression never changed.

"Watch your mouth," he said, "or I'll lay you out."

"You don't scare me."

He looked hard at her for a moment, surprised at her strength. This one was going to be trouble, he thought, but she was the key to keeping the younger children under control.

"Let us go now and we'll forget about everything," the girl suddenly said.

He cocked an eyebrow at her. "Jesus," he said, "you're really something, you know that? You're really a hard piece."

"We'll make up some story . . . something. And let you get away. How about it?"

"Forget it," he said, smiling. "You don't think we went through all this just for the exercise, do you? You stay . . . you all stay, until we're good and ready to let you go."

"*If* you let us go," she interrupted.

She's way ahead of me, Greer thought. "Look," he sighed, "we can do this friendly or we can do it mean. I really don't care. You want me to beat up on you some? Stomp on one of them kids out there? Is that what I got to do to make you behave?"

She thought about it for a long moment. "All right," she said.

He took her handbag, opened it and dumped the contents on a shelf. Then he opened her change purse and removed the two crumpled dollar bills that were there, and put them in his pocket along with her loose change.

"Now you're a thief, too," she said.

"Uh-huh," he said, taking her nail file. He fingered the litter of objects on the shelf and found a small plastic bag with two twisted cigarettes inside. "Jesus," he said, "grass?"

She nodded.

"Where'd you get joints?" he said. "What kind of school they running at Sloane, anyhow?" He slipped the plastic bag into his pocket, then took out his cigarettes and offered her one. She hesitated for a moment before accepting. For a few seconds they stood silently smoking, their bodies close together in the tiny office.

"You're going to kill us, aren't you?" she said quietly.

Greer took a deep drag on his cigarette. "I don't want to kill you," he said. "If they come up with the bread . . . and if they keep the pigs out of it . . . then we'll let you go."

"And if they don't?"

He shrugged. "We'll see how it goes."

"I don't believe you," Kathy said. "I think you mean to kill us either way."

"I don't care what you think," Greer said, an edge of impatience in his voice.

Kathy looked long into his eyes, trying to gauge his intentions. She decided that in the end he would do whatever he wished to do, and no amount of pleading would have any effect. A hard piece, he had called her. He might have been talking about himself.

"Look, Barnett," he said, stubbing out his cigarette against the wall. "I don't want to hurt you. If you behave, and help keep the little kids in line, it's going to be a lot better all around." He shoveled the objects on the shelf back into her handbag and held it out to her. "What do you say?"

She nodded slowly.

"Help me get them upstairs," he said, and he led her out of the office and back to the car.

They quietly trooped up the two flights of stairs and into the large room on the top floor. Greer posted Jimmy in the hallway to stand guard. With Joyboy behind him, he went back down the stairs and to the car. "Give me a hand," he said as he opened the front door. Together they managed to pull Carter out of the car, stretching him out on the floor of the garage. Greer knelt beside the body, his ear to the man's chest. He heard nothing.

"He dead?" Joyboy asked.

Greer searched the man's wrist with his fingers. There was a faint pulse. He looked at the side of the driver's head, just above the ear. A thin trickle of blood still oozed from the wound, but there was a jellylike clot forming. Even as he watched, the man's eyelids seemed to flutter.

"Let's get him upstairs," he said to Joyboy. "Then I have to call the school."

10:35 A.M.

Carmine drove past the Barnett house, his eyes working the road ahead. There had been no sign of the limousine along the pickup route and he was beginning to think he would find none. It was out of character for Carter not to have called. Something was wrong, he was sure of it now, something beyond a breakdown.

As he neared the Sloane School he found himself slowing down. He had better find out now if Carter and the kids had ever arrived. Don't get scared, he told himself, while he parked the car. It's probably nothing. Just poke around a little and make sure they all arrived here before you hit the panic button. It wouldn't be smart to upset anyone, especially if it turned out that Carter just had a flat on the way to North Rochdale.

Before he walked into the administration offices, Carmine had put a smile on his face.

10:40 A.M.

Pauline DeBusschere heard the headmaster's voice through the closed doors. Poor Phil, she thought with amusement, he's getting another lesson in the "Sloane tradition"—Lord help him.

She turned back to her work again and typed the last name on the list. She had just finished collating all of the absentee reports left on her desk by a succession of grade monitors. She had alphabetized the names and typed the official absentee report on a green form. In a few minutes, or whenever the conference in Dr. Carew's office was over, she would put one on his desk.

The telephone rang.

Pauline picked up the receiver and cradled it on her neck, her hands still busy extracting the green form from her typewriter. "Dr. Carew's office," she said.

"This is important," a man's voice said. "I want to talk to Dr. Carew."

"I'm sorry," Pauline said automatically, "Dr. Carew is in conference at the moment. May I help you, sir?"

There was a pause at the other end. Pauline thought she heard the sound of an automobile horn honking.

"I must talk to Dr. Carew . . . now."

Pauline wavered. "May I say who's calling, sir?"

Greer's hands were shaking. Maybe the girl was stalling, playing for time. They knew the children had been kidnaped and had already called the police.

"Hello . . ." the voice in his ear said, "hello?"

A feeling of panic welled up in him.

"Are you still there? . . . Hello?"

Forcing his eyes to the index card where he'd written the message, he said, "We have the kids. Do exactly what we say. The note is under the bush ten yards to the left of the front gate. Get it. I will call back later." He put his fingers on the hook and broke the connection.

Pauline put down the phone. She reached for a pencil to make a note of the call, then paused. "We have the kids." That's what the man had said, wasn't it?" At that moment, Carmine Mancuso walked through the doorway.

"Good morning," Carmine said. "How's everything going at Sloane today?"

Pauline hesitated, the confused phone call still on her

mind. A note at the front gate? "Fine, Mr. Mancuso, can I do anything for you?"

Carmine shrugged. "Not really. Just thought I'd come up and see if our service is still completely satisfactory." His eyes spotted the green sheet on Pauline's desk with its capitalized heading. Without asking permission he picked it up. "Is this today's?" he asked. He skipped down the list. Barnett, Katherine. Flood, Peter . . . Flood, Ralph . . . Porter, Heidi . . . Schwartz, Michael . . . Taylor, Henry Jr. My God, he thought, my God! They never got here.

Pauline saw Carmine's face go dead white as he scanned the absentee report. He swayed, and put a hand on her desk to steady himself. "What's wrong?" she said.

"I think . . . I think there's been . . ." What? ". . . there's been an accident."

Pauline stared, suddenly afraid.

"Or maybe worse," Carmine croaked. "A kidnaping."

Pauline heard the man's voice again. "We have the kids. Do exactly what we say."

Leaping up, she screamed and began running out of the room, Carmine pursuing right on her heels.

"A note . . . under a bush . . . to the left of the front gate."

PART III

Fathers and Mothers

THURSDAY

11:00 A.M.

Dr. Carew, his heart turned to stone, stared at the glass-enclosed clock. The pendulum rose and fell, steady as a heartbeat, as it had done ever since that day in 1879 when Dr. Josiah H. Werner, the first headmaster at Sloane, had placed it on the mantel.

The note lay not six inches from his hand, its sloppily printed block capital letters an obscenity against the polished surface of his desk. He looked at the note and read it through once more.

WE HAVE THE KIDS AND WE WILL KILL THEM IF YOU DON'T DO EXACTLY WHAT WE SAY. FOUR HUNDRED YEARS OF OPPRESSION ARE OVER. NOW IT IS TIME TO PAY THE PRICE. WE DEMAND AS RANSOM $100,000 FOR EACH KID. WE DEMAND THE MONEY IN SMALL BILLS—OLD BILLS. THIS BLOOD

PAYMENT WILL BEGIN THE REVOLUTION THAT WILL MAKE FASCIST AMERIKA CRUMBLE TO DUST. WE WILL CONTACT YOU BY TELEPHONE. DO NOT CALL IN THE RACIST PIGS—REPEAT—NO PIGS OR YOU WILL NEVER SEE THE CHILDREN ALIVE.

BLACK REVOLUTIONARY FRONT

Madmen. Fanatics. Holding the lives of six children—from the Sloane School!

They have taken my children, Carew thought. They were given to me to oversee their well-being and direct their education. And part of that trust was to protect them from harm. But who could have foreseen such an event?

It was my responsibility to protect them and it will be my responsibility to get them back. But how? Where does the act of dealing with a group of fanatics begin? The police? Should he call them at once? No, he must not. It would place the children in greater danger. And Sloane? Yes, it would tarnish the unsullied reputation of Sloane. Protect the name of the school, he told himself, for that, also, is part of your duty as headmaster. It must be kept *in camera*, for the school's sake as well as the safety of the children.

The children—were they already dead?

Was the remainder of this awful crime mere shadow play, an acting out of roles with all hope of success already snuffed out? No, no, no—they could not be dead, he would not again let himself think that they were dead, and he must act only on facts and not supposition. The parents would have to be notified at once. He would tell them here, not over the telephone, in this office where he would be witness to the terrible consequences of what he must say.

Carew raised his eyes and looked into the faces of the others.

Surprising even himself with his calm authority, he said, "All right. I think we had better get started. Pauline, the first thing to do is close the door."

11:05 A.M.

The Colley Watson who walked through the door of the staff room at the Garvey Clinic was not at all like the Colley Watson Henry Taylor knew from television. That Colley Watson was all fire and ice, created out of pure steel. The Colley Watson he saw now, the bearded, mustachioed one shaking his hand, was much smaller than his public image, mortal, surely, and very young. Not more than twenty-two or so, Henry judged.

"Sorry I'm late, Doctor," Watson said. "I didn't get myself sprung until about six this morning, and when Roy called I was just dropping off to dreamland. But when Roy said it was you, and that you wanted to get together, well, I rolled out of the sack."

"That's all right," Henry muttered, as Watson seated himself in the chair next to his desk. So Dr. Hart was "Roy" to Colley Watson. How involved was Hart with the Simbas, anyway? "Sprung?" Roy was saying. "From what?"

"The usual shit, you know," Watson drawled with easy humor. "Some cats over on 110th Street burned some more garbage last night, and the first thing you know the pigs are over at my place draggin' me in. Like, everything that happens in Northside they blame it on the Simbas, you know?" He winked. "Sometimes they're even right."

Why, he's a boy, Henry Taylor thought as he looked at Watson. Underneath his Che goatee and mustache he was just a cocky kid. And his speech, a slow, studied drawl, was like the image he had created for himself on television. An image, not reality. Colley Watson, Defense Minister and chief spokesman for the Young Simbas, the scourge of the Northside, was an actor playing a role.

"We don't usually have much to do with the police," Henry said softly. "We have enough problems as it is." He met Colley Watson's eyes and watched his grin fade.

"All right, pops, let's get down to it, huh?" Watson had his guard up now. His voice was crisp and flat. "You want something from the Simbas, right? That's what Roy's been talking about for quite a while. So let's hear it."

I ought to throw him out of this clinic, Henry Taylor thought, but something in Watson's look made him pause. He would make a bad enemy. "All right, let's discuss it." Henry reached automatically for his pipe and brought it to his lips. "Dr. Hart is convinced that we can work together. He says we're after the same thing, that with your help, with your manpower, we could begin to provide better medical services for the Northside. I must say, truthfully, that speaking for myself I'm not at all sure that we could work together—"

"Uh-huh."

"I want to spell it out now, so we don't get involved in something that's not going to do either of us any good, much less the people in Northside—"

"I dig."

"We will not become involved in any violent demonstrations." Watson seemed to be thinking of a private joke. "What we have in mind is a general health program for Northside. There are people out there who know nothing about sanitation or nutrition. We would start small. The Simbas could distribute a small pamphlet we would write—you could take all the credit you want for it—but you'd see that it gets distributed. Once we did that, and got used to working together, well, then maybe we could go further."

Watson turned to Roy. "I thought he was supposed to be a brother," he said, nodding at Dr. Taylor. "You didn't tell me he was an Oreo."

Henry felt a flush creep down from his scalp, but he held his tongue. Roy Hart shifted from one foot to the other.

"Easy, Colley," he said. "This conversation is just beginning."

"Oh shit, man, don't give me that crap. I could see the minute I walked in here that this guy's afraid of his own shadow. All these brothers who look at you and say 'Right on!'—and all the time they're saying, go raise hell, boy, but do it someplace cross town. Well, the Simbas don't play like that. If you're in with the Simbas, baby, you're in bed with 'em."

"Now wait a minute, Colley," Roy Hart said quickly, "You're wrong about Henry Taylor. I know him, I've worked with him."

"You don't have to defend me, Roy," Henry said. Sighing, he struck a match and lit his cold pipe. "I think we ought to begin all over again. Somehow, we got off on the wrong foot." He tried out a smile.

"No," Watson said, freezing a smile of his own. "Nobody uses the Simbas."

For an instant, Henry felt a chill of fear. "What happens is," he said slowly, "you use us, right?"

Colley Watson nodded and dropped a hand in his pocket. He brought out a piece of paper and unfolded it slowly. "Here's how it works. You ready?" He dropped his eyes from Henry's and read, "One, from now on every treatment in this clinic, even to those who can afford to pay, is free . . ."

"But it is free!" Roy Hart protested. Henry held up a hand: "Let him finish, Roy."

"Two, you will open at least two other storefront clinics away from fat-cat Lenard Avenue, both of them, so people don't have to come crawling here by bus. And you'll staff them with people the Simbas will provide.

"Three . . . the name of this clinic will be changed to 'The Young Simbas Medical Center' . . . and we will hold a joint press conference to make the announcement public."

Roy crossed the room in three strides and stood towering above the seated Colley. "You shit! Get out of here before I throw you out!"

Watson shrugged, not bothering to look up at the towering figure above him. He reached out and placed the paper on Taylor's desk. "These demands are non-negotiable, of course," he said coolly. "I'll give you some time to think about them. Say, a week, and then I'll have my pickets outside, marching up and down Lenard Avenue so no one will get in."

The veins stood out in Roy Hart's neck. "Why you bastard!"

Watson looked up at last. "Say *motherfucker*, Roy, it won't hurt you."

"You sucked me in, now you spit me out. You don't give a damn what happens up here in Northside, do you? As long as the Simbas come out on top!"

"I think, Mr. Watson, you had better leave," Henry Taylor said mildly.

Watson stood, ignoring the hovering Roy Hart, and walked to the door. He turned, the smile gone from his face. "Some free advice, Doc. Us . . . the Simbas . . . we're the only thing holding this goddamn place together. If you think *we're* wild, well, right behind us are the real revolutionaries. The kids . . . with a joint in one hand and a bomb in the other. You won't even be able to talk to them mothers. So as long as the Simbas stay on top, the Northside won't blow. You think on that, Doc, before you decide." With a casual wave, he was gone.

Roy Hart sank into a chair. "Oh, God, Henry," he groaned, "I really opened a can of worms, didn't I?"

"*Après mois le déluge*, eh?" said Henry. "Wasn't that his curtain line? The pity of it," he said, pointing his pipe at Hart, "the damn pity of it all is that he is probably right."

11:05 A.M.

"You go downstairs and help Loretta," Joyboy said to Jimmy. "I'll take over up here." He watched Jimmy get up from the chair and start down the stairs before he called: "Hey! You forgot something." Joyboy held out his hand. "The gun, Jimmy, the gun." Sheepishly, Jimmy came back and handed over the revolver.

One gun, Joyboy thought as he moved the chair into the room and tilted it back against the wall. Just one gun for all of us. It was ridiculous, but it was the way Greer wanted it. He looked around at the children. The younger ones were huddled together in front of the TV set, their backs turned to him, watching Andy Griffith.

The blonde—Barnett—was sitting on the floor next to the driver. She was attractive, pretty almost, if you cared for grays. Nice legs underneath that short skirt. Not much underneath the sweater, but they looked well-formed. More like an appetizer than the main course. Not a bad lay, probably, and innocent—that always made it interesting. He felt a quickening in his groin and was amused. He closed his eyes and began to fantasize a scene. He was helping her undress and she kept looking at him, asking questions. He helped her take the sweater off over her head. He cupped a breast. "Oh, that feels nice. Is that what we're supposed to do?" Her voice soft and feminine, her arms reaching back to unhook the bra . . .

"Ben, Ben, can you hear me?" Kathy was saying. Carter was beginning to groan. She balled her handkerchief and wiped the thin film of sweat from his forehead. The ugly wound in his temple had stopped oozing blood. As she spoke his name again she saw his eyes open and close. "Ben? Ben?"

"What?" he croaked, blinking, trying to keep her face from swimming away, "what?"

"He hit you and they took us. We're in Northside. They're holding us for ransom."

The kid on the road, the one with the map. A wave of pain rolled behind Carter's eyes and he bit his lip until it passed. The kid on the road . . . my God!

She held his hand and smiled. "I thought you were dead. I thought he had killed you."

"Never kill me," he whispered, his throat tight and raw. "Head's too hard." He saw her grin and felt better. It was like the first day of basic training in the army: everything hurt. "How many of them?"

She looked away for a moment, brushing back her hair. "Two guys, a boy, and a girl." He tried to rise but couldn't even lift his head. Silently, holding his hand, Kathy began to cry.

11:15 A.M.

Maxwell Barnett was beginning to panic. Sally had been calling Menakis nonstop all morning, and always with the same result. It was clear by now that Chris did not want to talk to him.

There were other negative signs, too. No one had come by to shoot the breeze, to have a cup of coffee. Even the mail-room boy, a kid out of Columbia University bucking for an assistant account man spot, had dropped the mail on Sally's desk and run. This morning, Maxwell Barnett was apparently a pariah.

Restless, he found himself walking the stairs to the floor below, to Eli Bernstein's office. To his surprise, Bernstein was there, small as life, bending over a large artist's portfolio and placing the contents of his drawing board into it.

"Eli," he said when Bernstein did not look up, "when did you get back from Chris's place? Why haven't you called me?"

The dapper little art director pretended he had not heard. Bernstein took a dozen type books off a window shelf and began putting them into a carton. Barnett walked over and touched his arm. "Eli," he said, "what are you doing?"

Bernstein straightened, looking at Max for the first time. "*Shmuck*, what does it look like I'm doing?"

"You're packing—but why? Are you moving upstairs? Have you quit?"

Bernstein opened the filing cabinet against the wall and took out the contents of a large manila folder. They were pink slips—telephone messages, Max realized with a start—and he watched Bernstein dump them into the carton on top of the type books. Who keeps telephone messages? he thought dumbly.

"What did Chris say?" Max demanded.

Bernstein opened the top drawer of his taboret and slid it out. He dumped this into the large carton, too, and Max saw a blizzard of paper clips, business cards, rubber bands, pencils, marker pens—most without caps—fall into the box. "Sit down, Max," Bernstein said at last.

Barnett sat.

"There's going to be a new agency in town," Bernstein began, "and their first account is already signed up: Tickee Toys. I promised Chris a whole new TV campaign—very visual."

Barnett stared. The account was moving, that's what Bernstein was saying. He was stealing it. Taking Maxwell Barnett's eight-million-dollar account and running off to start a new ad agency.

"This new agency," Barnett managed to say through dry lips, "who—who's behind it?"

Bernstein seemed to grow two inches as he smiled. "Me. Eli Bernstein Advertising, Incorporated. Sounds nice, huh?"

For a moment, Max thought he was going to fall off the chair. He made a face and closed his eyes. When he opened them Bernstein had a hand extended. "Max, baby, aren't you going to shake my hand and wish me luck?"

Barnett looked down at the soft, finely manicured hand, and spit squarely into its palm.

11:20 A.M.

When the telephone rang, Norman Schwartz was half asleep. He opened an eye, saw that Irene was, in fact, asleep, stretched out naked on the bed next to him, and reached for the phone. There was a woman on the line announcing Dr. Carew, and then the headmaster himself. Norman swung his legs off the bed and sat up. "Yes," he said with a faint stirring of alarm, "this is Mr. Schwartz."

"Your son, Michael," the Headmaster said, "he attends the Sloane School, I believe."

"Yes, that's right," Norman said. "Is anything wrong?"

There was a brief pause, just enough to convince Norman that he was about to hear something unpleasant. "A situation has arisen, Mr. Schwartz, that requires your presence at the school—in my office—at once. I'd like you to get here as quickly as you possibly can."

"Is he hurt? Did Mike have an accident?"

Again, that terrible pause. "I would rather not tell you over the telephone, Mr. Schwartz." Carew's voice held no emotion.

"Please, what happened? Is he all right?"

"Try and get here right away," Carew said. "And tell no one that you are coming, it's quite important."

"All right," Norman Schwartz said, but Carew had already hung up. He felt a pressure beginning to build in his chest and was frightened. He reached into his night-table drawer and took out a tiny tin. He put one nitroglycerine pill under his tongue, then another.

Something had happened to Mike. "Irene, honey?"

She stretched, her still-perfect model's body warm from the act of love. "Baby," he said, placing a hand on her flank and shaking her gently, "baby, wake up. We've got to get down to the school."

Norman swallowed hard, the pills suddenly tasting bitter in his mouth.

11:23 A.M.

Mildred Taylor, a polishing cloth still in her hand, sat dazedly at the gleaming teak table in the dining room. Junior was sick, or hurt. No, a small voice whispered, Junior is dead. He is dead, that's why Carew wouldn't say anything over the telephone. Her heart began to pound in her ears, but she wouldn't let go. She fought to gain command of herself. "He is not dead," she said aloud, for herself as well as the God who might be listening, "Junior is not dead."

She picked up the telephone at her elbow and dialed the clinic. Something has happened to Junior, she told Henry quickly, the school wants us up there right away. No, she said, answering his question, they wouldn't say what it was. "I'll meet you there, and Henry, please hurry."

She ran upstairs, throwing off the soiled housecoat she was wearing. She struggled into a black jersey dress and headed back down to the garage.

11:25 A.M.

Martha Flood could not decide what to wear.

She stood before her closet in the small dressing alcove, clad only in a half-slip and bra, and pulled out dress after dress. Damn that cold fish Carew, she was thinking, and damn the school, and especially—oh God!—damn those two boys and their terrible behavior. She started to put on a lively Pucci jersey, then changed her mind. Too bright for the headmaster's somber office. The twins must have really done it this time, she thought. At least three times a year she had her little talk with Carew. The boys were hard to control—no, *impossible* to control—and they continued on at Sloane only through the headmaster's sufferance and her father's generous yearly gift. But Carew had never summoned her to Sloane on such short notice before.

She pulled a Galanos suit from the rack and held it against herself, turning to see the effect in the mirror. Yes, the tweed was right, chic and yet not flashy. She reached into a plastic box on the shelf in front of her and took out a Hermes print scarf in pink silk. It looked fine, she thought, holding it against her throat.

She would be late getting to Pedro's studio, but she would phone him. She thought about the young Spaniard as she pulled on her panty hose. Her portrait was almost finished now, and, she supposed, so was their affair. The boy had very little talent with canvas. The only time he showed any passion was in bed. His skills there were very good indeed.

Fully dressed, she made up her face, being extremely careful with the blusher on her cheeks. Ready to go, she stood and gave herself a last inspection. Her wig was fine, the Galanos cut several pounds from her figure, as always. But the lines around her eyes . . . damn. She needed another week at Main Chance. When Pedro was finished with her, she decided she would go down to Main Chance and be remade, again, hopefully for the Mr. X who would follow Pedro into her bed.

The thought of telephoning her husband, or of telling Mary Gowers where she was headed, was not on her mind as she backed the white Mercedes roadster out of the garage and shot off down the driveway in a squeal of burning rubber.

11:30 A.M.

"That's it," Phil Stuart said, as he watched Dr. Carew put down the telephone, "that's all of them."

Carew nodded briefly and put a hand to his face, rubbing the bridge of his nose. "With the exception of the Cable boy, who we now know was not in the car."

"Right. I spoke to his mother. He's at home with a temperature."

"How very fortunate," Carew said. By and large the parents had accepted his summons calmly. The hysterics, he reflected, would come when he told them what had happened. "Take everyone directly to your office. When they have all arrived you can bring them in here. I want to tell them as a group."

"Yes, sir," Stuart said. "Should I have coffee and sandwiches prepared?"

"All right," Carew said. "But don't say for whom. Make up something. A sudden board meeting perhaps."

Stuart nodded his assent and was turning to leave when Carmine Mancuso spoke up. "Just a minute. There's a couple of things you seem to have overlooked." The burly man walked from the window to stand in front of Stuart, blocking his path to the door. "You can't handle this situation. My God, you know what you're up against? A gang of maniacs who lifted a load of kids right under our noses. So slick you didn't even miss them until they telephoned to tell you."

Carew's shaggy eyebrows rose and fell, but his voice remained calm. "Please lower your voice, Mr. Mancuso," he began. "It hardly seems necessary—"

"Of course it's necessary," Carmine interrupted. "Those kids' lives are at stake. You've got to call the cops. And probably the FBI. Every minute we wait around is going to make it that much harder to find the bastards."

"You needn't remind me that lives are at stake," Carew said, an edge creeping into his voice. "I am well aware of my responsibility."

"Yes, Mr. Mancuso," said Stuart, "too bad you weren't more aware of yours."

"What's that supposed to mean?"

"Only that it was your car, and your driver."

"You son of a bitch."

"None of that," said Carew, "not now. When this is all over there will be plenty of time to study our mistakes, and point a finger, if necessary."

"But what about the police?" Carmine's face was serious. "You're crazy if you don't call the cops."

"That is not my decision to make. At least not alone. We must tell the parents first, and then let them decide. By a majority vote, if necessary."

"Christ Almighty, that's crazy!" said Carmine. "You know what's going to happen when you tell them, don't you? There'll be weeping and wailing all over this room. And that bunch, half crazy and hysterical, you're going to let them decide?"

"Would you suggest I decide for them? And perhaps put the children's lives in further danger? No, that decision must be left for their mothers and fathers."

Carmine hesitated. He was sure he was right, but the headmaster had a point.

11:40 A.M.

Motorcycle Patrolman Michael Bradie cursed under his breath and threw the arrest report into the wastebasket. A typewriter, he was thinking, is a most undependable machine, not at all like a motorcycle. He placed a fresh form into the machine and very carefully typed the date in the appropriate box, using only two fingers this time instead of his customary five. In the box marked NAME, he typed "unknown," and in the square marked R he typed a lower-case "n." Before filling in the physical description he paused. How big was the black boy anyway? Deciding to make an educated guess, he wrote 5′2″, 110 lbs., hair black, eyes brown. He reported the age as under 21.

Sweating in the humid squadroom, Bradie looked at the clock. Just as he had thought; he wouldn't be back on post until after twelve. He settled down and described the action that had taken place on the parkway, giving himself full credit for having acted within the law. The little bugger was not his responsibility any longer. He had been delivered into the hands of County Hospital, and when he recovered—if he recovered—someone from Detective Division would pursue the investigation of the accident and its causes. Still, a cop had to protect himself from future squawks, especially the way things were going today. The Chevvy was on the current list of stolen vehicles. So there would be at least one charge against the guy that would certainly stick. The speeding and reckless driving with which he was concerned would probably be waived.

Bradie looked at the little pile of personal articles he had brought back from the hospital. Typing as he worked, he put them into a large brown paper bag. There wasn't a helluva lot. Eleven dollars and thirty-seven cents. No wallet or other identification. Two keys (one Yale, one Segal), a small penknife, one dirty handkerchief, one half-empty package of Salem cigarettes and matches, and a silver JFK half dollar mounted in a metal ring. Then he touched the binoculars. Zeiss Ikon, six x magnification, in a brown leather case. Very good field glasses for a kid. Like the Chevvy, they were probably stolen. He typed the serial number on the form. Some eager beaver could spend three weeks tracking that one down, if he wanted to.

The only other item was a road map of the County, found in the suspect's raincoat. As he was about to place it in the bag, Bradie saw that the map had been heavily marked. He opened it up on the desk in front of him. Perhaps the guy had written down an address or a telephone number that would help to identify him. Most of the markings were in the Rochdale and South Rochdale areas, and to Bradie's eye they were curious. Not exactly suspicious, just curious. The Sloane School, for instance, was ringed three times, and a notation: "Pig 8:30–9:00" was printed just outside the ring. What the hell was that about?

There were six other rings on the map, scattered throughout the South Rochdale area, and just outside each ring was a number. Across the map, connecting these rings, was a dotted line. The route started at Edgemont Road. Wait a minute, he knew that corner. It was where the Rochdale Diner was. Okay, so the guy probably had a cup of coffee there before starting out. So what?

Bradie looked at the numbers next to the rings and

realized they were times. The first one was 7:45 and the last, the one nearest the Sloane School, was marked 8:20. And, if you followed the dotted line it would probably be a pretty accurate schedule for reaching each of the ringed locations. But what did it mean, if anything?

There was one other interesting notation on the map. An X, at the corner of School Avenue and the bypass. Was he meeting someone there, a confederate perhaps? It could be, but then again it could mean exactly nothing.

Even so, when Bradie sealed the paper bag with a marked sticker, he did not put the road map into it. Instead, he clipped the map to the back of the arrest report and made a simple notation: "Map found on suspect, possibly suspicious in nature." Let the detective who followed up the case figure it out. Hell, that's what they were paying the guy for. And if it did turn out to be a clue, why then the credit for calling attention to the map would go to Patrolman Michael Bradie.

11:45 A.M.

Greer stood silently for a few moments, looking into the room, before speaking to Joyboy. With surprise, he saw that the driver, the man he had written off as dying, was sitting up and talking with the Barnett girl. He felt relief, and when he realized it, wondered why.

"No Sparrow yet, huh?" Joyboy asked, interrupting his thoughts.

Greer shook his head.

"Sonofabitch took off. Probably never see his ass again."

Let's hope so, Greer thought. "They behaving themselves?" he asked.

"Yeah," Joyboy drawled. "I think we put the fear of God into 'em."

"I'm going to talk to the driver for a minute." Greer walked into the room, squatting down in front of Ben Carter and Kathy. "How you feelin'?" he asked. "How's your head?"

So this is the kid who hit me, Ben Carter was thinking. He didn't look like much. Just a boy, really. Like one of the kids in the playground where he sometimes played softball. "I've felt better."

For a few seconds they stared at each other, neither knowing quite what to say. "Yeah, well . . ." Greer said, and let it go. He looked down at the mattress and scratched at a stain with his fingernail. "What's your name?"

"Carter."

"Uh-huh." Greer looked into the driver's eyes and felt a vague unease. Carter was not afraid. In fact, if there was anything in his stare it was anger. Greer felt a sudden urge to explain things. He wanted to apologize to Carter, to tell him he was sorry to have hurt a brother. He wanted to explain to Carter about the revolution, about rising up and extracting a price from the white racists who ran the country. He wanted to tell Carter that what he had done was for him, too. He thought of these things, but he said none of them. Later, perhaps, he would talk to Carter, without the white girl sitting beside him, or Joyboy staring into the back of his head—and they would talk for a long time and in the end he would make Carter understand. But he said nothing now. Turning, he walked from the room, his cheeks burning with a warmth he found surprising and somehow strange.

Carter watched him go, surprised by his own feelings, and in his ear he heard Kathy asking: "Ben, is he afraid of you?"

11:45 A.M.

Shirl Barnett drove the white Mustang over the bridge and put her foot down to the floor as the hill came up in front of her. Trees flashed by in a green blur as she hurried through the bypass that would let her out at School Avenue, just down the road from the Sloane.

The ice-cold voice of the headmaster had terrified her. She had put down the phone in the study and sat shaking with fear. But as she sat she had been able to see herself at that moment, a spectator at her own death. The mirror over the desk reflected the coffee stain on the hem of her housecoat, the torn and ragged edges of her white slippers, her drab uncombed hair. Suddenly she ran up the stairs to the bathroom and popped a green tranquilizer into her mouth, swallowing it dry while watching her own grimace in the mirror over the sink. Salvation was at the other end of the telephone. For ten awful minutes they had tried to find him, switching her call from floor to floor throughout the agency while she waited through an eon of self-revilement. But Maxwell Barnett was nowhere in the building and his secretary was away from her desk. "Is there a message, Mrs. Barnett? Is there a message?"

"Max, Max, oh help me, Max!" she had cried out, falling to the floor and weeping.

But there was no one to help her now, no Max to shield her from events. The house was empty. No one would help her.

Strangely, as she began to comprehend this, sitting up and wiping at her eyes, she began to feel stronger.

No longer a spectator, she stood and went to wash her face. The eyes that stared back at her from the mirror were her eyes, bloodshot and puffy, needing mascara and eyeshadow and something, God knows, to hide those black rings and ugly pouches, but those eyes were her own. She dropped her housecoat and slippers and stepped into the shower, remembering only at the last minute to slip on a shower cap. Turning the tap on fully, as hot as she could stand it, she turned her face up to the spray, letting it sting and burn. Alone, she was thinking, you are alone and you have been alone for a very long time.

Drying herself roughly, she inspected the body she had begun to hate so much. That was wrong, too, she knew. She had become a person she despised—because of Max or to spite Max—to hold his attention or to punish herself? No matter now, this gross and ugly body was the only body she would ever have, and hating it led only to the same endless circle of guilt and pain. No more, she told herself, she would have no more of it.

She dressed slowly, thinking of the walls she and Max had carefully built to keep themselves apart. A long time ago she had lived through him and loved it, exulting in his rise up the ladder in the agency, accepting the house as her reward. But now, when he would not share, when they could not talk, this house was her cell, because she had built nothing of her own. She would write him off, then, wasn't that the business expression for a loss you had to leave behind? Maxwell Barnett was a write-off. To replace him she must now begin to create a life of her own.

She put on her best black wool dress and searched

through her jewel box for the single strand of real pearls she had once liked to wear. Sitting at the dressing table, she spent long minutes combing her hair, savagely breaking through the knots and tangles and thinking of how far she had let herself descend. What trouble was Kathy in up at school? What had she done? Whatever it was, she would find a way to cope. Her own way, without Max. Marching to the bathroom before going downstairs, she reached in to turn off the lights. All alone, the small vial of green pills on the sinktop stared at her. She hesitated, started to reach for them, and then directed her hand to the light switch. Even with the light off she could still see them. With a bitter cry she grabbed the small vial and thrust it roughly into her handbag, then ran down the stairs and out of the house.

11:55 A.M.

"There's scotch in the cabinet over the sink," Sally called to him from the bedroom.

Maxwell Barnett already had the bottle of J&B in his hand, but what did you do for a glass in this place? She had worked for him for three and a half years and he had never been to her apartment. Why had he come here today? He peeked into a small, half-rusted metal box on top of the refrigerator and found a glass. In the sink he could see the remains of this morning's breakfast cereal, and a litter of plates and pots underneath testified to the greasiness of last night's dinner.

Max took his drink and went out to the living room. A bed that might also function as a couch took up the space between the two narrow windows. It was awash in a rumple of blankets, sheets, and pillows. "Be Prepared!" said the poster on the chocolate wall above it, and a very pregnant Girl Scout looked down at him. Very funny, he thought sourly, and taking a drink cursed Eli Bernstein yet again.

"There! I told you I'd only be a minute." Sally had replaced her sweater and skirt with a see-through lace lounging robe held at the waist with a single tie and cut dangerously low on top.

"Nice place you have here," he said, and she laughed. She sat down on the floor at his feet and grinned at him.

"Now, isn't this a better place to drink than some silly bar?"

"Yes, much better. When I get looped I won't start fighting."

"Can I freshen your drink?"

"Yes," he said, draining his glass in a long swallow. She disappeared into the kitchen for a moment and came back with another drink, munching a pickle. She handed him the drink and put the pickle to his lips, offering him a bite. "It's very good for you," she said as he shook his head.

"I don't want things that are very good for me," he said. "Just scotch."

Shrugging, she crunched at the pickle. "I can't believe Eli's going to take the account, Max."

"Believe it, sweetie, it all adds up. The little bastard has probably been setting me up for it for a year. And I've been so busy holding Chris's hand, I never noticed the snot creeping up on me."

"And what happens now? I mean, to you."

Max laughed, short and bitter. "What happens when

you get shot down in flames, love? You die, right? So I'm dead."

"Poor Max," she said, "poor baby." She put her head on his knee and stroked his calf.

He looked across the room. "They'll probably put me on some other account for a while, to make things look good. And then they'll let me go."

Sally rested her chin on his knee and looked up at him. "I'm sorry, Max, really I am. You're a very lovely man, and bad things should not happen to a lovely man."

"Don't worry about me," he said, looking into the top of her robe, seeing the line where her faint tan ended and her very white breasts began. "I've been on the beach before."

"Poor baby," she said, and rising, sat on his lap and put her head on his shoulder.

He felt a wet, slow kiss on his neck, and he smelled her breath, warm and somehow sweet. He let her take his hand in hers and lead it into the parted folds of her robe. "No," he said, very low, "Sally, please no."

"Come, Max," she whispered, "come with me, sweet Max." Her tongue licked at his ear.

He turned his head away from her as his eyes began to mist. He felt a heavy tenderness, and he was grateful, but it all suddenly made him want to cry. An image of Shirl, very young, came into his mind.

"Come, Max, let me make you feel happy." She stood before him, her robe fully open.

He leaned his head back in the chair and shut his eyes, crying softly now, overwhelmed at the sweetness of her gift, but knowing it was one he would not, he could not accept. "No," he said, his throat thick, "no!

Oh, God . . . it's the only thing left I've never done to her. . . ."

12:00 P.M.

"Do you mean to say you've made me come all the way up to school and now you won't tell me what it's about?" Martha Flood said angrily.

"You'll be told, Mrs. Flood," said Stuart, "you'll all be told by Dr. Carew." He turned toward the other parents waiting in his office: "It will only be another few minutes, please be patient." Nervously, he ran a finger inside his shirt collar.

"I demand to know what's happened!" Martha Flood said. "What have my boys done?"

Phil Stuart looked into Martha Flood's angry face. At another time he would have met her petulance with anger of his own. But not today. "I'm sorry," he said, as quietly as he could, "please try to be calm. What has happened is . . . is very serious. I think, if you haven't done so, you might want to call Mr. Flood. He should be here with you."

For a long moment Martha Flood said nothing. The anger drained from her face to be replaced by a look of stunned anxiety. She sat down in the chair near his desk and opened her handbag, searching through it until she came up with a pack of cigarettes. She lit one and said, "Are they hurt?"

"I can't tell you."

"Are they in the hospital?"

"Please, please, Mrs. Flood. You'll know very soon."

Stuart looked at the other parents sitting quietly in his office. The black woman, Mrs. Taylor, and Mrs. Schwartz were huddled together on his couch. Mr.

Schwartz sat nearby, staring into space. Emma Porter was dabbing gently at her eyes and trying not to sob. Where was the Barnett woman? If she would only get here, Carew could take over.

"May I use your telephone?"

He nodded and backed away from his desk to allow her some measure of privacy. The hard look about Mrs. Flood's eyes, the determinedly angry set of her face, had changed very little. As she spoke to her husband she looked and sounded like a woman talking to a naughty child. Just as she hung up, Shirl Barnett appeared at the door.

"Is this . . . is this Dr. Carew's office?"

Thank God, thought Stuart. He turned to the others: "Dr. Carew will see you now."

12:00 P.M.

Greer came downstairs and stopped in the doorway of the second-floor office. Jimmy was sitting on the floor, listening to the portable radio. "Turn that fucking music off!" he shouted. When the boy stared at him, surprised at his sudden anger, Greer marched across the room and snatched the small transistor from his hand. "Goddammit! Can't no one here do what they're supposed to! Get on your feet and help Loretta." He extended a hand and jerked the boy to his feet.

Loretta stared from the sink. "Honey?" she began.

"Feed them," shouted Greer. "You help her, Jimmy."

Loretta began to say something and thought better of it. She turned to the refrigerator and began to assemble bread, mustard, and bologna on the sinktop. Something must have happened upstairs. She told Jimmy to fetch some plates, then let him help her put the sandwiches together. Greer was sitting at the table, his face sullen, and she could hear him muttering under his breath. "It's a fucked-up world," he said, "you know that? Fucked-up."

She nodded. "You want a sandwich?"

"Did I ask you for one?"

She shrugged and turned back to the sink, piling sandwiches on a plate. Jimmy picked up an armful of Pepsis and had begun to follow her to the door when Greer stopped them. "Did I say take it upstairs?"

"No, honey, but I thought you meant me to."

"You thought, you thought," he mimicked, leading them up the stairs. An anger he could not identify filled him as he glared at the kids from the doorway. They were so neat, so shining, so well dressed. Even here, even now. They looked at him with a confidence that inspired rage. They had never scrabbled for a nickel, or gone hungry at any time in their lives.

"Hey, hey! We eat!" one of the twins shouted when Loretta walked through the door. Laughing, the boy turned from the television set and raced his brother to the plate. In no more than a moment, both boys were gobbling at sandwiches and reaching for Pepsi-Colas. Greer looked away, remembering a cold room where a boy sat at a table wearing a dirty coat and a large tired woman crying as she watched the boy eat. "Don't cry, Mama," the boy was saying, "I like it, it's great," chewing into the sandwich that held mustard and no meat, the bread dry in his mouth, the hot taste of mustard seed filling his throat, going down hard. "Don't cry, Mama, it's really good." And eating it, smiling, trying to cheer her by making her think he enjoyed it. And his baby sister, her arms thin as wire, crying out from under his mother's coat on the big bed near the window, crying to breasts that held no milk, to a room that held no warmth, and outside the big wet flakes of snow coming down on the streets of this city that held no friends.

"I don't like bologna," a small voice said.

Blinking, Greer looked down at the chubby little girl.

"I don't want bologna," she said, her chin defiantly upturned. "I want pizza!"

With a hoarse cry his hand flew in a wide arc and slapped her face. Thrown sideways by the force of the blow, she fell against the wall. He knelt quickly, grabbing her by the arms and shaking her. "Eat it! Eat it! God damn you, eat it!"

Tears welled in his eyes. He let her go so roughly she fell again. Kathy Barnett picked her up. Greer felt a hand on his arm, Loretta's. Her eyes were very frightened.

12:15 P.M.

Dr. Carew watched the parents file through his door. He let them be seated and paused. How does one inflict pain easily? What is the antidote to hysteria? "I have terrible news," he said finally, "and there is no way to conceal it. But please, please, remain calm. Your children have been kidnaped and are being held for ransom—"

A collective gasp rose from his audience. Carew raised both hands. "Please," he said, "please let me continue." Mrs. Barnett began to wail. Next to her, Martha Flood's ashen face was riveted onto his own.

"They are being held for ransom by a group calling

itself the Black Revolutionary Front. A note was discovered shortly before eleven o'clock this morning. I called you immediately upon determining that what the note said was, indeed, so. As far as we know, the children were taken sometime this morning on their way to school. The driver of the limousine is missing as well as the vehicle. Shortly before eleven my secretary received a telephone call telling us where to find the note, and saying the children were being held captive. . . ."

Two of the women were crying now, but quietly, trying not to miss a word. Carew felt a curious detachment. This moment was the worst. He glanced at Carmine Mancuso, who was standing at the window. Arms folded, face impassive, he too was hanging on Carew's every word.

"Mr. Mancuso, who operates our limousine service, as you know, became aware that the car used to transport the children to Sloane was missing. He retraced the limousine's path to the school and was here when the telephone call was received. . . ."

I must lie to them now, Carew thought, it is necessary. A small lie, in the service of mercy.

"The caller told Mrs. DeBusschere that the children were safe and that they would not be harmed so long as we followed their instructions and did not inform the police. . . ."

He's pulling it off, Carmine Mancuso was thinking, the old prune was making them believe. That hard face, those icy blue eyes . . . Carew was like the teacher you daren't argue with, the schoolmaster in whose class you never raised your voice. He was commanding them to listen and by God they were!

"Their note, by the way, emphasizes that same point. Do exactly as they say and the children will be returned safely. Here, let me read it." The parents listened spellbound. They seemed to have shrunk from one another, with the exception of the Schwartz couple, who clung, heads drooping, in a close embrace.

The headmaster finished reading the note and silently let his hand fall. "You see now why I acted as I did. It is absolutely essential that we remain calm and act rationally . . . difficult as that may be under the circumstances."

He would never see Mike again, Norman Schwartz was thinking, feeling the heavy dread in his throat and in the irregular beating of his straining heart. He stroked Irene's hair, wanting to break down and cry and knowing that he must not. Mike, Mike . . . a day in the park, dappled sun under a cover of rustling maples. Mike was three, a sturdy, running, darting three, but this day he was down on his knees, silent and unmoving as he studied the earth. How long did you watch him there, a spot of sunlight illuminating his hair, his face grave as he concentrated on the ant hole in front of him? Many minutes later, satisfied that he had seen something terribly important, Mike running over to shout the news: "Daddy, Daddy! Ants have brown eyes!"

This wasn't the way to think now. He had to concentrate on getting Mike back.

"I realize how difficult it is," the headmaster was saying, "the shock and pain you feel, but we must not let ourselves be carried away by our emotions."

"Dr. Carew," Norman asked, "you are sure they have been kidnaped?"

"Quite sure, Mr. Schwartz, yes."

"And no one saw it happen? Or missed them until later?"

"As far as we can tell," Carmine Mancuso said from the back of the room, "it happened sometime between picking up Miss Barnett and arriving at school."

"And they weren't missed? Their teachers . . . their classmates, no one missed them?"

Carew's white eyebrows drew together. "We knew they were absent, yes. But as for the rest of it—"

"Why not, goddamn it! Why the hell not?" Martha Flood demanded. "How could they be missing for hours . . . hours!"

"I'm sorry, Mrs. Flood, there was no way on earth we could have known in time to have done anything."

"Why! Why!" Her shout was a cry for help.

Carew's voice was gentle. "Who knows, Mrs. Flood, who can prevent madness? A student climbs a library tower in Texas and begins shooting people. A group of dissidents burn a bank in California. Madness, Mrs. Flood. A peculiar disease of our time."

"Headmaster," Norman Schwartz said, "we can spend hours talking about who's to blame. Now we have to act."

"Exactly," Carew said.

"I want to know about that driver," Martha Flood interrupted, "I want to know about that black bastard who took my children!"

"Hey, hey! Easy, lady!" Carmine Mancuso walked to the front of the room to stand beside Dr. Carew. "He's not a black bastard, he's Ben Carter. And I don't want you—or any of you people—to go shooting your mouth off about him. We don't know he's involved, and dammit, I'm not going to let you assume it."

Martha Flood jumped up. "Of all the nerve! For all I

know you're in it with him. You and the other niggers who grabbed my boys." She turned on Mildred Taylor and pointed a finger. "And what is this one doing here? Is she the driver's wife? What right does she have to be in this room at a time like this?"

Mildred Taylor's head came up slowly. Her voice was barely audible. "My son was in that car."

Martha Flood seemed to shrink back, but only for a moment. "But he didn't belong there. There weren't any nig—black kids—in my boys' car. What was he doing there?"

Norman Schwartz tasted bile. "It's a long story," he said, going over to Mildred, "not that you deserve to hear it—"

"Ladies and gentlemen, please!" Carew protested.

He's losing them, thought Phil Stuart, they're beginning to fall apart and he won't be able to get them back under control.

"Would you please be seated, Mrs. Flood?" said Carew. "And you too, Mr. Schwartz."

"Yes, behave yourselves, dammit!" Carmine Mancuso growled. He looked at the headmaster. "Isn't that what you're trying to say?"

Carew coughed. "Yes, Mr. Mancuso, exactly. And I think that you ought to take a seat, too."

"Okay." Carmine gave the headmaster a strange look and walked to a chair in front of the fireplace. He felt a growing impatience with Carew. My God, what a windbag the old man was.

Suddenly the door opened. Everyone turned to look.

Henry Taylor stopped, obviously surprised at the number of people in the room, his eyes searching for his wife. Ignoring Carew's greeting, he strode over to her and said, "Is he dead?"

When Mildred shook her head, no, he felt his heartbeat slow. It was not what he had feared then, riding up the parkway like a madman, his mind coming to one inescapable conclusion. Junior was dead, there had been an accident at school, and now they wanted to have them up at Sloane, Mildred and him, so they could tell them the dreadful news together. Thank God, he said to himself, thank God.

"He's been kidnaped, Henry, they've all been kidnaped. They took the limousine on the way to school." Henry Taylor looked up into Norman Schwartz's white face.

"But they're alive?"

"Yes, Dr. Taylor, we presume they are," the headmaster said. "We received this note, and there was a phone call about two hours ago."

Henry took the note from Carew and read the printed message. A sense of horror filled him. Black people had done this—his people—and now they held his son. If only Junior had not slept away from home last night, he found himself thinking, if he had not been with Mike Schwartz— Immediately he was filled with an overpowering sense of shame.

Norman Schwartz saw his anguished face and put a hand on Henry's arm. "Are you all right?"

"Yes, I think so." The heart patient, worrying about the doctor. Norman Schwartz, who looked as if he might collapse at any moment. Incredibly, Henry wanted to laugh. "Norm, you'd better sit down." He glanced at the others. Emma Porter, he knew the young widow, had met her at various school functions in the past. Mrs. Flood, yes, the woman who had twins at school (boys, weren't they?). She had raised such a fuss the last time tuition was raised. Mancuso, of course, from the limousine service. And the pale woman in the raincoat, he didn't know her.

Henry turned to the headmaster. "The police," he said, "have you called in the police?"

Carew drew a slow breath before answering. "No. I was waiting until we were all together. I felt we ought to discuss it first."

"Yes, of course," Henry interrupted. "You couldn't call them on your own, could you?"

"No. I felt it had to be a mutual decision."

Henry nodded, turning to the others. "The headmaster hasn't called the police," he said, "because he can't speak for us. So it seems we have a fast decision to make. Do we call them, or try to handle this ourselves? Norman, have you any thoughts?"

"None. Only that I want Mike back, that I'll pay anything to get him and no questions asked."

"Yes . . . yes, we have to do what they say," cried Emma Porter, still crying.

"I think we should call the police," Henry said. "Raise the money, hand it over, but notify the police too."

"Wait a minute," Martha Flood said, "who put you in charge?"

Henry looked into eyes that were charged with hostility. He knew that superior look, he had met it many times before. "You're in charge, if you like," he said coldly. "What do you think we ought to do?"

He watched her face lose some of its high color. She looked away, biting her lip, and when she spoke her voice was not much more than a whisper: "I . . . don't know."

"Thank you," he said, turning to the pale woman in

the raincoat just as the headmaster spoke her name: "Mrs. Barnett?"

Cope, Shirl, the voice in her head whispered, say something. What? What should they do? If only Max was here, she thought, if I could just speak to Max for a minute. "Whatever . . ." she said, "whatever you decide."

Carew paused before speaking. "Everyone except Dr. Taylor has agreed not to call in the police. We'll do what they say, handle it ourselves."

"Just a minute," said Carmine from the back of the room. "I don't think you know what you're doing."

"Mr. Mancuso," Carew said angrily, "I think you should let the parents decide this."

"Let him speak," Henry said. He knew the man and he had always struck Henry as being level-headed and sensible.

"You're crazy to try and handle this yourselves," said Carmine. "Look: this bunch is professional. They grabbed the kids and the car and we didn't know a thing about it until they called to tell us. Which means they've probably been planning this for months. And that they're hiding someplace where only the cops can find them. Now how can you people hope to deal with a professional outfit like that?"

"We have no choice, I'm afraid," Schwartz said. "They have my son. I want him back. So we have to deal with them, on their terms."

"But the cops would help," Carmine insisted. "I know, you're afraid the gang will guess we called them and maybe hurt the kids. But the police have dealt with kidnapings before. I'm sure they'll be able to protect the kids."

"Just a moment," said Carew. "I must point out the additional danger to which we will be subjecting the children if we notify the police. At this moment, only those of us in this room are aware of the situation. But think what will happen if the police come to the school. The students and faculty will see them and start asking questions. Some word may leak. The newspapers could get the story. How can we take such a chance?"

"A crime is a crime," Carmine said flatly. "You've got to call the police."

"No," Henry said, "we don't have to, Carmine. The choice is ours. I think we should call the police, but the other parents don't. It has to be a majority decision. No one of us," Henry said slowly, "can take the responsibility of forcing a decision on the others. And we can't sit here debating it. So now we raise the money and hand it over in good faith."

"Oh, Jesus!" Carmine exploded, "in good faith? With these crazy maniacs? Black Revolutionary Front, or whatever they call themselves? That's a helluva chance to take, Doc."

"We're just wasting time arguing," Norman Schwartz said. "I think we should be talking about how we're going to raise that much cash on such short notice."

Emma Porter had been listening with quiet anxiety, but she could control herself no longer. An image of a dark pit came into her mind, a small grave dug in the floor of a cellar, a band of grinning black monkeys holding her little girl . . . She began to weep. "The money . . ." she cried, "the money, it's all tied up . . . in a trust fund. I can't touch it. I won't be able to get Heidi back . . ."

Henry looked at the small round woman and swallowed hard. The money, somehow the parents would have to raise it. And collectively, for the lives of all the children hinged on a collective payment. Six hundred thousand dollars, in cash. How long would it take to collect such an enormous sum?

As if he could read Henry's thoughts, Norman Schwartz spoke: "We're in a bind on the money, Henry. I've been sitting here trying to figure it out and I think we're in trouble. I don't see how we can get our hands on that much cash until sometime next week. Tomorrow's Friday. We have only today. . . ." He looked at his watch. "An hour and a half until the banks close. Three more hours to reach my broker . . . The thought of them holding Mike over the weekend . . . till we can come up with the money . . ."

Henry nodded. They would have to help each other out, there was no question of that. Somehow they would have to get six hundred thousand dollars, extending loans to each other, like to the Porter woman, in order to meet the payment. How much could he contribute, he thought, knowing that it would mean everything if it had to. Cash first, of course; they had twenty thousand dollars in the bank. His mutual funds, they were worth fifty-five to sixty thousand dollars. His other stocks—God! The market was down. How much could they be worth at this moment? Eighty, ninety thousand dollars? And how much time would it take to convert all of this to cash? And how many of the others would come up short, besides Mrs. Porter?

He looked into Shirl Barnett's rabbit face. "We don't have a penny saved," she said. "Not a penny." She cast her eyes down and looked at the floor. "Living up here, sending Kathy to Sloane, vacations . . . we've never been able to manage to save anything—"

"We'll have to stall for time," Norman said. "I'll call

downtown and get whatever cash my company has, but it won't be enough, eighty or ninety thousand dollars at most. But maybe—wait a minute, I just had an idea." Excited now, Norman reached down for his wife's handbag and extracted a pack of cigarettes. He lit up and began pacing the floor in front of the fireplace. "What if we all managed to get our securities together . . . all of us who own stocks and bonds . . . and made a pool. Then we add our life insurance policies and property. Hell, we could put our homes in the pool. They ought to be worth a helluva lot collectively. And then, with the pool as security, we go to my bank—or someone's bank—and get a fast cash loan."

"A loan?" Henry asked.

"Sure, a loan. To start to convert everything to cash, why we'd be running around like chickens. And there's no time."

Phil Stuart followed the conversation from his place near the door, thinking how fortunate the headmaster was to have parents like these in the room. Dr. Taylor had walked in at the opportune moment, just when they were about to break down into name-calling and chaos. He'd saved them from that and forced them to think, to react. And now Schwartz was holding the floor. Money must be his thing. But even though they were trying to deal with the realities, it was still amateur night. The police should have been called at once. It was Carew, really, who had prevented it, and Stuart thought he knew why. The school, damn him. Not the children, not that, but the school. Scandal was what the headmaster feared, and he'd stage-managed the entire scene to make sure the police were kept away.

Dr. Carew was sitting in his swivel chair listening to

the conversation. Martha Flood was interrupting now to say that she would contribute what was necessary . . . in her case, two hundred thousand dollars, Carew realized, the twins . . . So she would raise her portion of the money needed, and Schwartz, from the way he was speaking, would put in more than his share to help the Barnetts and Mrs. Porter. Suddenly Carew realized what he must do. There was no real choice. And the responsibility, that would be his also, as it had always been.

"Mr. Schwartz," he found himself saying, "none of this will be necessary." How curiously calm he was, Carew thought, how controlled his voice, when inside he knew the decision he had reached could mean the end of his career. "None of you will have to raise any money. The school will pay the ransom money. Sloane will. It is the only thing to do." He stared at the surprised faces and smiled. "We are famous, you know, for taking care of our own."

PART IV

Northside

THURSDAY

1:45 P.M.

Ben Carter walked cautiously toward the door, his hands upraised, watching the black hole at the end of the gun come up to meet him. Ten feet away from the guard at the door he stopped, his hands still up, signaling his peaceful intentions. "Can we rap some?"

Joyboy shrugged. "It's your mouth."

Carter sat down, crossing his legs under him, feeling lightheaded at the sudden exertion. "How long are you planning to hold us here?" he asked.

"Till we finished with you."

"I mean, when do you think that will be?"

"Sometime."

"How long is sometime?"

"Sometime."

Talk to the wall, Carter thought, this bastard isn't

saying anything. Still, it didn't hurt to try. And maybe he could learn something. "You holding us for ransom?"

No answer.

"Are you doing this for money?"

"No. Love."

Carter grinned. "All right. I mean, how much?"

"Enough."

What did you expect, birdbrain, the truth? "Uh-huh. And when do you expect to get it?"

"Sometime."

Right back to the starting point again. "All right, man, I'm just trying to find out what's happening. There's no harm in trying, is there?"

Joyboy didn't answer.

"You guys ever pulled anything like this before?" asked Ben.

"Yeah. We had Nixon here last week, didn't you hear?"

"Uh-uh."

"And next week, we gonna grab the Pope."

"Okay, I dig you're an experienced bunch. How many are you?"

"Couple a thousand."

"That many?"

"Listen. Why don't you give it up? You ain't gettin' nothin' outta me."

"Maybe I like the conversation."

"Uh-huh."

"That other guy who was up here? Is he the boss?"

"Could be."

"He's kind of young, ain't he?"

"Uh-huh."

"I mean, you look old enough to be his father. You ain't, are you, by any chance?"

"Ain't what?"

"His father."

"Fuck off, sonny. This game is over."

"Aw, come on now, it was just getting interesting. Is that his girl? The kids tell me they saw him kissing her."

"That ain't his girl, that's your mother."

Carter shook his head. "Nasty. That is not nice. And just when we were getting acquainted, too. She givin' you any?"

"Your mother givin' you any?"

"We playing the dozens, or are we talking?"

"You're talking. I'm just listening."

"Look, are you going to be a brother, or are you going to be a shit?"

"Both."

His face never changes, Carter was thinking, no matter what he's saying. There was absolutely no way to read his thoughts, the guy didn't give you a clue. "When you get the money, what are you going to do?"

"Take it."

"I mean with us."

"That's for you to figure out."

Slowly, Carter rose to his feet, watching how carefully the guy held the gun on him all the way. It would be hard to catch him by surprise, perhaps impossible. He seemed to know what he was doing all the time. And that, Carter realized sourly, was about all the conversation had revealed.

1:55 P.M.

"Mr. Norris," Kaplan called from behind the grille, "are you coming in or not?" Peering out of the top of his bifocals, the old pawnbroker watched the junkman standing in the doorway.

Hamp Norris decided, closing the door behind him in a tinkling of bells and walking into the gloom. "Kaplan?"

"Over here behind the grille."

You couldn't see a thing in this place, it was so dark, thought Hamp. The old man, Kaplan, he liked it that way. He kept the pawnshop dark and himself locked away behind a heavy metal screen that ran from floor to ceiling. Because of the stickups, Hamp supposed. He knew that Kaplan had been robbed many times.

"So, Norris? What you got for me today?"

"Few things," Hamp mumbled, opening the drawstring sack and pulling out the first one. He placed the silver coffee server on the counter and waited while Kaplan opened and closed the wicket, taking the server over to a gooseneck lamp for a closer inspection.

The server was silver, all right, the pawnbroker saw, not that that made it worth much. He ran a gnarled finger over the inscription engraved on the base, reading: "Edna and Charles, 25 Years of Love, from your Children on your Silver Anniversary." A beautiful sentiment, Kaplan thought, but it made the server unsalable.

"How much?" asked Hamp.

A good question. Melted down, the server was worth perhaps ten dollars. "Nothing, really," he said. "But for you, two dollars."

"Three?"

"What else you got today? Let me see, maybe we'll make a deal."

Hamp pulled the remaining items from the bag and placed them on the counter: an enamel shaving mug, three spoons, a calico doll with one missing leg, a dirty work shirt, a small Swingline stapler, and a double-sided picture frame.

Sighing at the impossibility of such a collection, Kaplan reluctantly snapped on the light over the counter to get a better look. But the first thing he looked at was the junkman. Norris looked awful, much worse than usual. He's been drinking this morning, Kaplan thought. "Mr. Norris, you're not taking care of yourself. You look terrible."

Hamp studied the pawnbroker, weighing his answer. Should he talk about the vanishing limousine or would Kaplan just laugh? "I guess I'm just not feelin' so good."

"So who is?"

"Drinkin' too much."

"Yah."

"Tell me, Kaplan, can a man begin seein' crazy things without him bein' crazy?"

"Depends. Why? You seen something crazy, Norris?"

"Mebbe. Mebbe I did. I don't rightly know."

"What?"

"A car, Kaplan. A big black Cadillac. First it was there, clear as day, just a-comin' down this old street. And then, the next minute, gone! Just jumped clear off the face of the earth."

"Hmm. That's crazy, all right."

"That's what I said."

"If you don't mind my saying, Mr. Norris, maybe you're drinking a little too much?"

"Mebbe." Hamp ran a hand through his gray stubble. "Anyways, Kaplan, how much?"

Kaplan looked at the junkman, and at the bedraggled collection spread before him. Anything I give him, he thought, he's going to go out and drink up. "It's worth nothing, you understand. But for you, Norris, three-fifty."

"Four dollars."

"Done." The pawnbroker opened the wicket and counted out four singles.

2:00 P.M.

"All right," Carew said. "I think we'd better get organized. I'll have to get in touch with the bank right away. I don't imagine it will be simple. Mr. Schwartz, would you come with me? Will your wife be all right if you leave her?"

"Yes, yes, I think so," Norman Schwartz said. He looked at Irene, who was talking with Mildred Taylor.

"Good."

"I'd better stay here," Henry Taylor said, glancing at Shirl Barnett. "I have some sedatives in my bag. There's no telling . . . we may have a couple of hysterical women to deal with."

Carew nodded. The black doctor was proving to be a godsend.

"It would help if they ate something," Taylor said. "And it might take their minds off things."

"There should be coffee and sandwiches outside," Carew said. "I'm just going down the hall to the bursar's office. If there's a call, I'll take it there. Phil, I'm making you responsible for security. You'd better sit outside with Mrs. DeBusschere. Make sure no one comes in. We don't want anyone suspecting what's going on."

Phil Stuart hesitated. "I'd like to speak to you for a moment . . . alone."

Carew paused a moment and then said, "Very well, if you insist," and led Stuart to his private washroom.

Closing the door behind him, Stuart began. "You're making a mistake, sir. The police . . . I think they have to be notified. No matter what the parents may think."

Carew shook his head. "That has already been decided."

"I know, but it wasn't the parents who decided, it was you."

"What?"

"I know what you're trying to do," said Stuart, "and I think it's madness. You decided not to call the police when we first learned what happened. You told the parents not to speak to anyone because you had already decided that the police weren't going to be called under any circumstances."

"Wait a minute, Phil, you don't know what you're saying."

"Like hell I don't! It's Sloane, isn't it? The school comes first. And so your only hope is to bribe these parents by putting the money up—"

Carew interrupted, his eyes blazing. "You'd better not say any more, Phil."

"You managed this whole thing, didn't you? You're willing to gamble the lives of six kids to save the reputation of your school."

"How dare you!"

"Call the police," Stuart said. "Call them now. They're going to be told eventually. And when they are you'll have a lot to answer for!"

"That's enough!" The headmaster's face was flushed, and as he moved toward the door Stuart thought the older man was about to strike him. But the arm that came up only reached for the door handle. "Second guesser!" hissed Carew. "You're a professional second guesser, Stuart. Why didn't you speak up when we were discussing the question? Why did you wait until the decision had been made?"

Stuart blinked. He started to speak, but found he had no words.

"When this is over," Carew said, "we can have things out. But until then, I demand your loyalty!"

Stuart stepped aside as the headmaster opened the door. Before he had a chance to answer, Carew had brushed past him.

"Mrs. Barnett?" Dr. Taylor looked down into a face that seemed to have lost touch with reality. When she did not acknowledge his presence, he put a hand on her arm. "Mrs. Barnett?"

As through a dream, Shirl heard someone speak her name.

"There's coffee outside," Henry said, "and sandwiches. I wonder if you wouldn't mind serving everyone. I think Mrs. DeBusschere might need some help."

"Yes . . . of course." She sat unmoving in the chair.

"Mrs. Barnett?"

"I'm very . . . warm. Is it warm in here?" Why was everything happening so slowly?

"Yes, it's warm. Perhaps you ought to take off your raincoat."

That's a good idea, she thought, but why was this man speaking to her from so far away? Why didn't he come nearer? "My raincoat," she said.

"Let me help you," Henry said. He placed a hand under her arm and another behind her shoulders and Shirl felt herself being lifted. She was floating now, her feet barely off the floor, and someone undoing the belt of her coat and slipping it off her shoulders.

She's going to faint, thought Emma Porter, stepping to her side. "It's all right, dear," she said, taking her arm, "it's going to be all right."

Shirl blinked, then fell, weeping, into Emma Porter's arms, hugging her close and sobbing. To her surprise, Emma burst into tears too, and the two of them stood hugging each other, rocking back and forth, crying for the loss that would be too much to bear.

"Would you mind repeating that again, Doctor," said Alfred Rossman, bursar of the Sloane School.

"I'm saying that I must have six hundred thousand dollars in cash this afternoon, in small bills."

Rossman looked at Carew. The headmaster's face was as grave as he had ever seen it. "What's the money for?"

"I can't tell you that, Al."

"But you can't expect me to just hand it over."

"Look, Al," Carew sighed, "there isn't any time for explanations. But for God's sake, think! I need six hundred thousand dollars in small bills, and I need it right away. Now why on earth would I be making such a request if it wasn't a matter of life and death?"

"Jesus Christ, a ransom? My God, is that it?" The look on Carew's face told the bursar that he was right.

"Six hundred thousand dollars, Al," Carew said. "As quickly as we can raise it."

"I don't think we can get that much together. It's impossible!"

Norman Schwartz cleared his throat. "I don't suppose you have that much cash—" he began.

"Hell, no," the bursar said sharply. "I'd hate to tell you how much cash we've got in the safe. No more than five hundred dollars, probably. I don't like to have more than that because, why make it tempting? And we don't have anywhere near that kind of money in our checking account, either. Just enough to meet our next two payrolls, about sixty thousand dollars."

"Is that all?" Schwartz said. "But I always thought Sloane . . . Well, you know, it's supposed to be a rather rich school."

"It is, Mr. Schwartz," Rossman said impatiently, "we're very well endowed." He cast a guarded glance at the headmaster, not wanting to reveal more of the school's financial position than he must.

"You can speak freely, Al," Carew said.

"All right then," Rossman continued, "maybe if I spell it out we can come up with an idea." He drew a deep breath and began: "Sloane is worth, conservatively speaking, between twelve and fourteen million dollars. Very little, of course, is in cash. The only cash we see here is tuition money, and believe me, it doesn't begin to cover our expenses. We get most of it in the fall and we invest it right away in Treasury bills and commercial paper, items that are very liquid and yet provide some sort of return. What I do is work out a schedule with the bank, figuring our cash needs as far in advance as I can see, and we buy and retire these short-term items on a rotating basis. The payroll is covered that way, and part of our kitchen expenditures.

"At any rate, tuition payments are really a drop in the bucket. Our major financial resource is our endowment. Commodore Sloane started us off with the land the school is on, plus this main building we're sitting in, and a million dollars of his railway stock. Through the years, alumnae and parents of students have made various contributions, in cash, securities, real estate, and what-have-you. You'd be surprised at some of the things Sloane has owned, at one time or another, especially in recent years when the tax laws have rewarded charitable contributions. Most of it we converted to cash and invested. Some of it, because it was so specified in the terms of the contribution, has been held in its original form. The Delany Fund is the biggest item in that latter group."

"And what is the Delany Fund?" Norman Schwartz asked.

"Robert C. Delany, the oilman, if you remember him. He gave the school a large piece of property about twenty-five years ago." The bursar smiled. "How does that old joke go? 'It's called downtown Dallas?' Well, Delany gave us a good hunk of what is now downtown Rochdale."

"You mean the Miracle Mile?"

"A part of it, yes. And most of what has since become the Negro section of town, behind the shopping district. We own it, through a separate corporation set up and run by our bank. According to the terms of the

Delany Fund we can't dispose of the property even if we wanted to. So we skim the profits and invest those."

"And who handles your portfolio?" Schwartz asked.

"County Bank and Trust, right here in Rochdale. It just so happens we're their landlord."

"Perhaps I should explain," Carew put in, "Jim Abernathy of County Bank is an old friend. We went to school together. About fifteen years ago, when Jim became president of the bank, he approached us. Al and I agreed to let Jim handle everything. Since then, I think he's done a remarkable job."

Rossman shook his head in agreement. "The man's top-notch. Of course, we also happen to be County Bank's largest depositor, so perhaps we do get special treatment."

"So Abernathy is your portfolio manager, investment counselor and banker all in one," Schwartz said. "That's fine. He's our man, then."

"He is also one of our trustees," Carew added.

"No question," Rossman agreed. "The trouble is, as I was trying to explain, we're not that liquid at the moment. "I don't think we have more than two or three hundred thousand easily available."

"A loan, then?"

"Yes, that's what I was thinking." Rossman looked at Carew and picked up the telephone. "Maggie, get me James Abernathy at County Bank. And when you get him, Maggie, make sure you don't stay on the line." He sat back in his chair while he waited for the connection to be made and looked at Norman Schwartz. "She's a good girl, but sometimes she likes to hear things she shouldn't."

2:20 P.M.

Maxwell Barnett walked about the city hardly aware of where he was going. He thought of Sally and the sad smile on her lips as she saw him to the door. There was half a lifetime between them, he thought now, the bitter half; she had not yet endured the rejections, the compromises, the putting down of roots. She was free. She could offer him coffee in the morning and her body in the afternoon. Tomorrow, laughing, she would be free to do neither, seeking new friends, new jobs, new pleasures wherever she wished.

Thinking of Sally, he realized that he, too, had thrown off a weight. No longer would he have to sit at Chris Menakis' feet, a lapdog to catch and fetch at his master's bidding. That part of it, at least, was finished. Max wondered how Eli Bernstein would take to finding girls, arranging parties, being awakened at any hour of night to hear a mocking voice ask: "Hey, what adjacencies did you say are available in Cincinnati?" Are you ready for that, Eli? God, he was through with it! Free. I have some good news and some bad news, he thought to himself. First the good news: you have been lifted out of the shit, the account is gone. Now the bad news: you're probably out of a job, which means you'll be falling back into the shit very soon again.

Advertising, what had ever made him go into it? (I never killed anyone before, your honor, it just sort of happened.) Where else could a man who is bright and glib work so hard, accomplish so little, and be so wildly overpaid? Mountains of bright, articulate, gifted people laboring a lifetime to increase the net of some corporation by a few percentiles, maybe.

Surprised by his own vehemence, he walked to a bench and sat down.

All right then, no job. Followed very quickly by no money. They hadn't been able to put away more than a few thousand dollars. How long would that last?

We could sell the house, and one of the cars.

You've muffed it, Max, he told himself, you've fucked it up. You've worked very hard, and what have you achieved? A house in the County, two cars, a miserable marriage, and a daughter who doesn't know you. God, life is funny. You bust your back to make your wife happy and end up busting her instead.

Max looked at his watch. He wouldn't be going back to the office today. What was the point? Screw them, screw them all. He'd go home to Shirl, and say what he had to. And maybe, maybe for once they could sit and talk like human beings.

It's almost two-thirty, he thought; if I get to the station quickly I can probably catch the two forty-five train.

2:22 P.M.

Greer came up behind Loretta and squeezed her in his arms, feeling her stiffen, then relax as she recognized his touch. He kissed her wetly on the neck, smelling her warm skin.

"You goin' out now?" she asked. He nodded, resting his cheek against hers. "Maybe you ought to eat somethin'."

"Hey, girl," he said, breaking the embrace and standing away from her, "why you want to keep mothering me, huh? Do I look like I'm in need of that?"

"Yes," she said, mocking him.

"Well!" he sniffed. "Now I heard everything. Don't you know they call me Killer Greer?"

"Tough, huh?"

"The toughest. I run with the snakes and lay down with the tigers. Catch bullets in my teeth and spit out coffin nails. Hard? Why I got a piece of half-inch steel 'stead of a backbone, child."

"That make it hard to tie your shoelaces, don't it?" Loretta asked as Jimmy burst out in giggles.

Greer pointed at the boy. "And that one there, the fool laughin' his head off—they call him Jimbo the Assassin. Anyone I'm too tired to take care of, why he just naturally knocks him off."

Loretta nodded. "Mighty glad you told me. I was worried you was goin' soft."

Loretta tried to keep a straight face, but broke down into giggles. She was his strength, Greer thought, he could talk and touch her and she would make him laugh and give him hope. If someone like Loretta believed in you, why there wasn't a thing in the world that could stop you.

She turned to him and stroked his cheek. When she started to speak he put a finger on her lips. "Yes, Mama," he said, "I will be careful."

2:25 P.M.

"Hello, Al," the deep voice at the other end of the phone said, "how the hell are you?"

"Fine, Jim, just fine," the bursar said. He looked at

Norman Schwartz's tense, controlled face. "Listen, Jim, something's come up. We have an emergency on our hands and you'll have to help us out."

"I'm listening," Jim Abernathy said.

"We need cash, a lot of it, and we need it fast. And Jim, I can't answer any questions." Rossman paused and drew a breath.

"How much cash?" Jim Abernathy asked.

"Six hundred thousand dollars. As fast as you can get it together."

Jim Abernathy sat up straight in his padded leather swivel chair and put his cigar into the mottled marble ashtray on his desk. He held the receiver away from his ear for a second and cocked his head. "Listen, Al," he said, still trying to keep his tone light, "are you kidding me?"

"Six hundred thousand dollars in cash. I wouldn't make a joke like that," the bursar said.

"No, no . . . of course you wouldn't." The heavy-set banker looked at the Buffet print framed on the wall. Alfred B. Rossman, bursar of the Sloane School, did not make jokes. Rossman dotted every *i* and crossed every *t*, and probably, under his conservative suit coat, the man wore suspenders as well as a belt. So if he said he needed six hundred thousand dollars in cash, he undoubtedly did.

"Are you there, Jim?"

"Yes, I'm here. Look—you've thrown me for a loop. Six hundred thousand dollars in cash. Why, Al? What's it all about?"

Rossman sighed. "I wish I could tell you, but I can't. I need—that is, we, Sloane, need six hundred thousand in cash right away. In small bills. I realize it will be difficult."

"Let me think for a minute," Abernathy said. "I don't want to have to say no. Right off the bat I'll tell you we don't have anywhere near that kind of cash on hand."

"You don't?"

"Hell no," Abernathy growled. "There isn't a bank in the County or in the city that keeps cash on hand in such large amounts. There's just no need for it."

"So what you're saying then . . . You can't do this for us?"

Abernathy swore under his breath. "No, I didn't say that. Yet."

Carew grabbed the phone. "Look, Jim, we must have the money. It's an emergency."

"I appreciate that," said Abernathy, "but we don't have six hundred thousand dollars in cash on hand. When we need cash in large amounts we order it from the Federal Reserve in the city."

"Then you're telling me it can't be done."

"I'm afraid so."

"But couldn't you go to another bank? Couldn't you borrow it from them?"

Abernathy found himself smiling. "I wish it worked that way, Charlie, but it doesn't. They're strapped just the way we are. Not a nickel goes out without being accounted for. Now, let me get to problem number two. Sloane doesn't have six hundred thousand dollars in cash on deposit right now. So there's no way I could hand over the money even if I had it—which I don't."

Carew looked past Rossman, out the window, seeing the sweep of green lawn that stretched away in the distance, and beyond that the brown scar of newly dug earth that marked the spot where the new science wing would someday stand.

"Jim, listen," he said into the phone, "I'm on a spot and you've got to help me. I think you know I'm not an emotional man. But there are lives at stake here. I must have that money fast."

There was a long silence and very slowly Jim Abernathy said, "I'll do what I can. Six hundred thousand in small bills. What's a small bill, Charlie?"

"Tens. Twenties. Nothing larger than a hundred, I suppose. And not new."

"All right. I've got that. What I'm going to do is put in an immediate request to the Federal Reserve for the cash, and pull every string I can downtown to try and get it here tomorrow. But Charlie, I can't guarantee it, I want you to know that."

"I do. And thank you."

"Hey, not so fast," Abernathy said. "I'm going to make you a loan against the securities I'm holding. You've got to give me a good reason for making this loan. Do you understand?"

"Yes," Carew said. "You'll have to tell the Federal Reserve people something that makes sense."

"Exactly."

"I need it to . . . My God, Jim, I don't know what to tell you."

"I'll make believe I didn't hear that. Come on, Charlie."

Carew looked at the bursar and Schwartz, then out the window again. The hole in the distance caught his eye. "The new science wing," he said deliberately. "We need the money to build the new science wing."

"All right," Abernathy said, "but why do you need the money in cash?"

"Because the builder, Slattery, offered us a reduced contract if we'd pay cash."

"I've got that word for word," said Jim, "and that's the way I'll send it through. I'll try to get back to you in a few hours. One more thing . . . you'd better call Slattery, just in case some eager beaver downtown decides to look into the matter. How well do you know him?"

"Slattery?" the headmaster said. "Joe Slattery's son is in the upper form. He's a disciplinary problem, I do believe."

2:30 P.M.

They sat alone, away from the others, in the far corner of the headmaster's office; Ernest Flood, his face buried in his hands, sobbed uncontrollably, while beside him, her face turned to the window, Martha Flood smoked yet another cigarette. On hearing the news he had broken down completely. "My boys, my boys," he sobbed.

"Ernest," Martha whispered, her voice low and controlled, "get hold of yourself. Stop carrying on this way."

He peered at her through wet fingers. "I . . . I didn't know. Went out to lunch . . . all that time. I . . . could have been here."

"There was nothing you could have done. It didn't matter. Now, Ernie, please, stop making such a scene." She took a deep drag on her cigarette, the pale blue smoke drifting up in the shaft of sunlight that streamed through the window.

"God, Martha, what are we going to do? If anything happens to those boys I'll . . . I'll . . ." Groaning, he felt a surge of tears.

"Nothing is going to happen to our boys," she said, her voice flat and toneless. "Now stop making a fool of yourself." She looked at her husband with distaste. It was just like him to fall apart. There was no strength in him, no backbone. Now, when she could use his strength and support, he was doing what he always did, collapsing and letting others decide. He wasn't like Father, she thought, not at all. And yet, wasn't his softness, his easygoing affability what had attracted her to him in the beginning? A man different from Daddy, a man you didn't have to fear. And how could it be that what she admired so long ago and wanted for her own, was what she hated now? How many years ago had she taken over the role of father in their home?

"Mrs. Flood?"

The doctor—Taylor wasn't it?—stood behind her chair.

"He's taking it pretty hard. Perhaps he ought to lie down."

Who was he to interfere? Who wanted his help? "That's all right," she said, not bothering to look up, "he'll be all right."

"I have some tranquilizers with me," Henry offered. "They might make it easier for him."

"That won't be necessary." Her voice was cold.

Henry shifted. Bitch, he thought. She cuts the balls right off a man. "Well," he said, "you let me know. I'll be here." He waited for a moment, and when she did not reply, turned away.

2:45 P.M.

Greer took the paper plate of hamburgers in one hand, the cup of orange drink in the other, and walked to the standup counter that looked out on the parking lot. He put the food down on the counter, stooping to retrieve a dime that jingled to the floor. He was not hungry but he would eat, if only to get it out of the way. Mechanically, he swept the pickle off a burger, poured ketchup from a dispenser on the counter, closed the bun, and took a bite.

The White Hut was almost empty. Two old men sat behind him at the counter, sipping coffee; a scattering of cars dotted the wide expanse of blacktop outside the window. The phone booths were right outside, and empty. It was a good choice. He would make the call here instead of riding all the way downtown.

He swallowed the remains of the first burger and fixed the second. Twelve-cent hamburgers don't take very long to eat, he thought. The Hut hadn't changed very much since the riot. He had been fifteen years old when it happened. Out there, on the parking lot, he had come riding by in Buddy's beat-up Buick and had thrown a brick right through this window, and then they had roared off into the night, down Van Sicklen Street, to bust into the pawnshops and the big appliance store at the corner of Lenard Avenue.

What a waste that had been. What had they accomplished with all the burning and looting? Who had they hurt? Our own, that's all. Sure, Whitey began to get scared, and the President went on television, and a lot of shit was promised by a lot of shitty politicians, but it hadn't gotten them anywhere, had it?

Wrong, all wrong. Now what should have happened —and damn it, it was going to happen—was for the brothers to hit them downtown. Twenty, thirty cars zooming out of the night loaded with molotovs, just blowing a hole ten or twenty blocks wide smack down the middle of the Gold Coast.

The last time, they had got it all wrong. Buddy dead, and a lot of people losing everything they had in the fires, and a bunch of kids who had nothing to do with it in jail or shot up.

That ain't going to happen again, he thought. You got to grab Whitey's balls, not your own, and squeeze till they're hurting. Even the fucking bombs didn't do it. Three times we hit them and left our notes behind, even sent it into the papers and got it printed on the front page, but it didn't mean shit. It was a waste of time with Chuck. The machine was too big to bring down with a few bombs. Whitey has all the money in the world, and he just throws a little bit back into it and makes that machine good as new.

But they had graduated from those days. The white machine was made of money and the only way you were going to stop it was with money. Money and terror.

Six hundred thousand dollars, say, for starters. Jesus, you could round up a potload of guns, and guys to use them, for that. All of them getting ready, training and planning, until the night they went into business. Blasting out of Northside and burning and shooting up in the County, and downtown. And Marin County from Oakland the same night, and Philadelphia, out in Main Line country. In Detroit, busting up Dearborn, Oak Park in Illinois from Chicago, Shaker Heights in Cleveland, smacking Westchester from out of Harlem, the suburbs around Boston, Chevy Chase and Georgetown from out of the capital, Dallas, Omaha, New Orleans, Pittsburgh, Cincinnati, Denver . . . All over the fucking country they got us penned into ghettoes while outside they go on living high. But a year from now, two years maybe, and the big bustout will change all that.

It was time. Man, it was overtime. And the Black Revolutionary Front was going to do it. Not the Panthers, not the Muslims, not fucking Nay Nay Cee Pee, not CORE or Slick or Wilkins or any of those other old-timey burrheads who only knew how to use their mouths and not their guns. The Man ain't listening, he never did and he never would. You had to bust him up so bad he was lying on the ground in front of you and then, while you kicked him in the head to make sure he was listening, you told him what you wanted and then you took it out of his pocket. That was the way, baby, that was the only way.

Martin Luther started it, he woke us up, but they took care of him. And Malcolm—God, he would have been the one to do it—so smart and fine and perfect you wanted to cry just thinking about him—but they got him in the end, too.

A sour feeling rose up in his chest as he swallowed the last bite of the second burger. He looked at his watch and checked it with the clock over the serving counter. He felt strong now, and sure of himself. You couldn't let feelings get in your way when you were working on something so big. The driver, Carter. Just a little while ago he had felt bad about hitting him, because he was a brother. And the kid, the black one. That had been a surprise, too. But sometimes you've got to sacrifice your own to get what you're after. They'd all have to go when the time came. They knew too much. They'd make it too easy for the pigs to pick us up. But first the money.

Taking a dime out of his pocket, Greer walked out the door and around the corner of the White Hut. The three telephone booths outside were all empty and there was no one around. He stepped into the first booth.

3:00 P.M.

When she heard the voice on the telephone, Pauline DeBusschere stiffened in her chair.

"I want to talk to Carew, Dr. Charles Carew."

"Yes, yes," Pauline stammered, her fingers fluttering over the buttons on the bottom of the telephone, "just a minute." She punched the call onto hold and hit the intercom buzzer. "He's on the line," she said breathlessly when Carew picked up the receiver.

"Put him on," Carew said, "and stay on the line. He looked across the room at the others. "Be quiet now."

He heard a click in the phone and then Greer's voice.

"Is this Carew?"

"Speaking."

"Well," the voice said, "you know who I am. The price is six hundred thousand dollars. You know that, don't you?"

"Yes," Carew said. "We are trying to get it together."

"Good. And what about the cops?"

"We have no plans to call them," Carew said quickly.

He heard a short laugh. "You're not shitting me, are you?"

"No, I assure you. We realize the position we are in and we plan to act accordingly."

"Well, that's smart," Greer said. "Now about the money."

"As I said, we've begun the arrangement to—"

"What arrangements?" the voice rasped, rising in pitch.

"Take it easy," Carew said. "Don't get excited." He felt himself growing flushed. "We've requested the money from our bank, in small bills. There's no problem except that it may take some time to send it over."

"Why?"

Carew began to speak more quickly. "They don't have all that cash on hand. It's quite complicated, you see—and what we are—"

"You're fucking with me," the voice said. "What do you mean the bank don't have the cash?"

"No, no, I'm telling you the truth. We expect to have the money tomorrow—or Monday at the very latest. Please believe me, we're all doing our best to hurry."

"Listen, honky—you fuck with me and you won't see those kids again."

"Please," Carew said, "try to understand. We're trying to cooperate. Give us time to get the money together and I assure you we'll make no trouble. All we want to do is to get the children released as fast as possible."

Carew took a breath and waited for a reply, but there was none.

"Hello? Are you still there?"

"A bank don't have six hundred Gs—that's shit, man. How come, in the movies, they always get the money?"

The voice was softer now, Carew thought, almost a

whine. It was asking, not demanding. Shall I dare it, he wondered, can I take the chance? "That's the movies," he said. "This is life. We're raising the money. But what about the children? How do we know they are still safe?"

"They're safe. Don't worry, we're taking good care of them."

"How do I know I won't be paying you for nothing? How do I know that you haven't killed them all? *I insist on speaking with one of them.*"

"The money, when you going to be ready to hand it over?"

"Never mind the money. I won't pay you until I'm sure those children are alive. So if you do something foolish, you will have done it for nothing. Listen to me—I mean what I say. We'll have the money tomorrow, or Monday. And we'll say nothing to the police, believe me. But I want some assurance from you that the children have not been mistreated—"

"I can't wait till next week. You get me the money tomorrow or that's gonna be the end of it."

The man was faltering, Carew thought. "No," he said firmly, "you don't get the money until I speak to one of the children. I want to know they are alive and well, then I'll hand over the money, not before. Do you understand me?"

In the long silence Carew could hear his own heartbeat.

"I'll think about it."

"Call me back," Carew said as he heard a click at the other end of the line. "Call me back," he said again, although he knew that this time he was speaking only to himself.

3:20 P.M.

While he waited for the doctor to appear, Detective (2nd Grade) Charles P. Tuttle stood looking out the window at the end of the long corridor on the sixth floor of County Hospital. The day had turned out fine, Tuttle was thinking, a real April beauty with a strong sun to dry things off after the rain. You could see half the County from up here. God's country it was, so lush and beautiful, especially now that the winter was over at last.

"Mr. Tuttle?"

The detective turned to meet the gaze of a young resident.

"They told me you wanted to talk to the patient we operated on this morning . . . the one from the car wreck."

"That's right, Doctor. There are just a few questions I'd like to ask him."

The resident paused, his brown eyes blinking behind his rimless eyeglasses.

"What kind of shape is he in?" asked Tuttle.

"It's touch and go right now." The doctor turned to walk down the corridor and Tuttle fell into step beside him. "Severe internal injuries—he must have hit the steering wheel or the dash with terrific impact. Ruptured spleen, some liver damage. We did what we could, but it doesn't look good."

"That serious, huh?" Tuttle said, surprised. They turned a corner and started down another hallway. At the end of the hall Tuttle could see a uniformed patrolman standing guard outside an open door.

Before they entered the ward the resident stopped.

"Try not to excite him. He's really not in very good shape."

Tuttle nodded and followed the doctor to the curtained bed. The prisoner was young and he seemed lost in the welter of tubes and bottles. A pint of whole blood hung off to one side. But the boy was awake, and staring hard at the policeman. Tuttle leaned down and spoke slowly. "I'm a detective, son. I want to ask you a few questions about this morning . . . about the accident."

The patient's eyes fluttered, but he said nothing.

"We need your name, son," Tuttle said. "We don't know who you are."

Very slowly, his lips held tight, the boy shook his head.

"Your name. We'd like to tell your people you've been hurt."

The patient's eyes shifted to the resident, as if seeking help, but his lips did not move.

"You must have somebody you'd like us to notify," said Tuttle. "Your mother, maybe, or your girlfriend."

The boy's face relaxed, and for a moment Tuttle thought he saw a smile. There was something wrong. The kid looked as if he were playing a part, a deathbed scene in a cheap gangster film. Maybe he simply couldn't speak.

"Anything wrong with his throat, Doc?" Tuttle asked.

The young resident shook his head. "He should be able to speak . . . if he wants to."

Tuttle turned back to the patient. "Come on, son," he said, "I'm not here to hurt you. I'd like to help, if I can. Just tell me your name, okay?"

The boy's lips moved and Tuttle leaned closer. "Fuck you, pig," Sparrow said.

"Glad to see you found your voice," said Tuttle, "even if you just want to cuss me out. We got a make on the Chevvy you smacked up. Stolen last week down in the city. That's one to five years, in case you didn't know." He paused, looking hard at the man in bed and giving him time to respond. No answer. "But what I'd really like to know about is this." Tuttle took the folded map from his coat pocket and held it. "Is this a list of burglaries? Were you staking out the spots for some friends? Because if they go ahead and pull these jobs, you become an accessory. So if you want to tell me about it, maybe we can reduce the stolen-car rap. How about it?"

Even as he spoke, Tuttle knew it wouldn't work. But there was time. The boy would be around for quite a while. He signaled to the doctor and they left the ward.

3:30 P.M.

Carmine was driving. Phil Stuart sat beside him enjoying the reprieve from the highly charged atmosphere at the school. They looped through Edgemont Road, taking the short way back to South Rochdale, avoiding the winding streets of the Evergreen Housing Development and the heavy traffic that would be on the road near the IBM plant. There wasn't anything either man could do at Sloane. But Ben Carter's family had to be told. Carmine insisted on it and Carew had agreed, deputizing Stuart to represent the school.

"What do you know about the Carters?" Stuart asked as they swung off the Miracle Mile.

"Now much," Carmine said. "I know Ben pretty well, he's been working for me for more than a year. I know he lives in town here with his mother and sister. She's younger than he is, the sister, goes to Rochdale High. I don't know what his mother does, but I know she works."

"You've never met them?"

"I said hello to his sister once. Other than that, I couldn't tell you."

Watching the street numbers carefully, they drove slowly down Altadena Avenue. In the middle of the block, next to a dry-cleaning store, Carmine spied a parking space and pulled to the curb. Number 81 Altadena Avenue was a low three-story building with a television repair shop on the ground floor and two floors of apartments above it. In the little vestibule Carmine searched for Carter's name and, finding it, he pushed the button underneath for a long moment. "Maybe she's not home from school yet," he said as they waited for the answering ring that would open the inner hall door. As Stuart was about to reply the harsh buzzer sounded. They walked up a steep narrow stairway carpeted in linoleum. As they turned the landing, a door opened a crack at the end of the short hall.

"Miss Carter?" said Carmine.

The door opened a bit more.

"My name is Carmine Mancuso . . . Ace Limousine Service. Your brother works for me."

The door opened wider and Stuart saw a slender, very pretty young girl, her high-cropped Afro hair style framing a face that might have passed for oriental. "Oh, yes, Mr. Mancuso, we've met," the girl said in a light voice. "Won't you come in?"

She led them through a neat kitchen to a sitting room that looked out through gauze curtains to the street. A plaster crucifix hung over the small couch, and two deep armchairs flanked a round mahogany table near the window. Stuart looked about curiously. It was the first time he had ever been in a Negro's home. He introduced himself, learning in the process that the girl's name was Jackie. The men sat down in the armchairs while the girl seated herself at the edge of the couch. "Has anything happened? Is my brother all right?"

"Yes, he's all right," Carmine said. "But I'd rather wait until your mother gets here before telling you what it's all about. When will she be home?"

"Not long. About half an hour or so," Jackie said. She looks like a bird, poised at the edge of that couch, Stuart thought, some kind of rare jungle bird. She wore a flaming-red ribbed sweater above a plaid miniskirt, and a silver peace medallion on a thin chain hung between her breasts. "Has he done anything wrong?" she said. "Is he in some kind of trouble?"

"He hasn't done anything wrong," Carmine said. At least I hope not, he thought. "Maybe we'd better wait . . . till your mother gets here, I mean."

They stared at each other for a moment that stretched into several minutes. Outside, Stuart heard the sounds of the street. In the apartment above, a toilet flushed noisily.

"What does she do? Your mother," Stuart said at last.

"She's a dietitian."

"Oh," he said, feeling uncomfortable, "that's nice."

"Uh-huh," Jackie said, smiling.

"I teach at the Sloane School," Stuart said. "I'm Dean of Boys."

"Oh, wow," the girl said, "that's a good school, isn't it?"

"Yes. Yes it is."

"Terrific," she said.

Stuart squirmed in his chair. He smiled at her, then looked away.

"Nice place you got here," Carmine said.

"Thank you."

"Yes," Stuart added, "it is nice."

Several more moments passed before the girl offered to make coffee or tea. Both men declined, and they settled back to survey the room and each other in silence.

Stuart thought of asking her what she thought about civil rights, the Black Panthers, and how it was to live up here in the County. But all he said was, "Nice weather today, isn't it?"

"Yes. It cleared up fine," she said.

"Do you have any other brothers or sisters?" he said.

"Yes," Jackie said, "a married sister—Deborah—she doesn't live with us."

"I see." Stuart looked at his watch. It was going to be a long half hour.

3:45 P.M.

"Well, I don't like it," Joyboy said, his nostrils flaring. "I think they just playin' cat and mouse."

Greer lit a cigarette and listened. Joyboy's thoughts echoed his own. It could be a trick, a delaying tactic to give the cops time to track them down. "I'm telling you what Carew told me," he said, "and I don't like it any more than you do. But what can we do about it?"

"Christ," Joyboy broke in. "What kind of bank don't have six hundred Gs on hand? Man, you got to be some kind of fool to swallow that."

"Yeah, well, I told him we were going to dump the bunch of 'em unless he come across, but the sonova-bitch stood his ground. And then I figured—Jesus—if he's fuckin' with me, he's either got an iron pair of balls, or just maybe he's tellin' the truth."

"Truth, my ass," Joyboy said. "I'm telling you it's a trick, Greer. While he's stalling us they got the pigs out lookin' . . . maybe the FBI by this time, too."

"Well, we can't worry about that," said Greer. "If they don't play it straight, we're dead. So don't bother your burrhead about it."

"I won't," Joyboy said, returning Greer's grin with a frozen stare. Just as long as you get back here with the money, he thought, that's the only thing I'm worrying about. Just get it over with and get back here with the money and then we'll see about what happens after that.

"There's something else," Greer said. "They want to talk to one of the kids. Make sure they're still okay or they won't go through with the deal."

"Carew said that?"

"Uh-huh."

"Man, he's a hard-ass, ain't he?" Joyboy said, whistling through his teeth.

"I said I'd think about it, and I have. I figure we ought to do it, maybe tonight sometime."

"What if it's a trap?"

Greer shrugged. "I think the old bastard wants to

make sure he's payin' for the real merchandise. That we ain't killed them yet. And I want him to think the kids are okay, because that way he's sure to kick in."

"Goddamn," Joyboy said sourly, "first Sparrow disappears, then we can't get the money till tomorrow—or maybe next week—and now this. It ain't going right, Greer."

"I never said it was gonna be easy," Greer said. "And goddamn if I ain't right again."

"Yahba-daba-DOO!" Fred Flintstone yelled.

"What a stupid program," Ralph Flood said, turning away from the TV set. "Isn't there something else on?"

"I like *The Flintstones*," Heidi Porter said, her eyes fixed on the cartoon figures jumping about in half-animation.

"Well, let's see what else is on," Ralph said. He moved forward onto his knees and reached for the dial.

"Let her watch it, twinny!" Kathy called from across the room. "They're getting bored and jumpy," she said to Ben Carter. "Perhaps I ought to organize something to keep them occupied."

Ben, lost in his own thoughts, did not reply.

"Come on, Pete," Ralph said to his brother. "I can't sit here and watch this *baby program* any more." He stood up and, extending a hand, pulled his brother to his feet. "Let's take a walk."

The boys turned and moved away from the door, passing back into the grid of empty, dusty shelves in the rear of the large room. "I've had about enough of this," Ralph said when they were partially hidden from the others by the network of shelving. "I think it's time to go home."

"Swell," his brother said sarcastically, "all we've got to do is learn how to fly."

Ralph grinned. "Oh, no . . . there's a way to get out of here, all right." He looked at his brother in a superior way. "Of course," he added slowly, "if you're too chicken to try it . . ."

"Tell me what it is first."

Ralph sighed. "Just what I thought. Chicken." He made his special fist, with the middle knuckle extended, and punched his brother on the bicep of his arm.

"Ow!" Peter said, keeping his voice down. "That hurts!"

Peter rubbed at his arm. Ralph had that crazy look again, the one that always got them into trouble. Like the time they had broken the windows in the Flaherty house on Willow Lane when they were throwing rocks. Ralph and his ideas, they never worked. But sometimes, saying no to Ralph was worse than doing what he wanted. "All right," he said, "tell me about it."

Ralph chuckled and put an arm around Peter's shoulder. "It's a cinch to get out of here. Now here's what we do. There's only that kid watching us now, right? . . ."

Jimmy sat on his chair outside the door, the gun tucked into the top of his pants. The TV set was turned at an angle from him, but he was watching *The Flintstones*. Every once in a while he flicked his eyes about the room. Kathy Barnett and the driver were talking, sitting in the corner to his right. The older boys were playing with some cards. And the twins were taking a walk through the shelves.

He wondered when Joyboy was going to come back upstairs to relieve him. He was getting hungry. Loretta must have something besides bologna. Or maybe, Greer would let him take a walk over to Lenard Avenue and he could get himself a hamburger at Porky's.

Inside the room, Ralph edged along the front wall. He had to be careful. If Ben Carter knew what he was trying, he'd stop him for sure. He looked over at Pete, who was standing near the TV set. He inched a few more feet toward the doorway, walking sideways, his belt scraping plaster. He felt bubbly inside and very excited. The poor sap at the door wouldn't know what hit him.

He looked at Pete again and nodded. His brother moved squarely in front of the TV, blocking the screen from the kid on guard. Ralph leaned forward slightly, on the balls of his feet, waiting to spring.

"Hey!" Jimmy called from just outside the door. "Your father a glazier? Get outta the way!"

Pete pretended not to notice, standing perfectly still.

Hearing Jimmy's shout, Ben Carter looked up. His eyes widened as he saw Ralph launch himself into the doorway, hooking an arm on the doorjamb as he swung around the corner. "No!" Ben shouted, "No!"

Ralph swung his right arm like a club as he made the turn, knocking boy and chair and gun backward to the floor. In two steps he was down the hall and on the stairs, taking them two at a time.

Jimmy slid across the floor to the wall, stunned for

the moment. "Greer!" he screamed, "Greer!" The little kid had gone down the stairs already. He pulled the gun from his waist and scrambled on all fours. "Greer, look out!"

He heard yelling behind him and he turned back to the doorway. If he chased the kid the others could escape. "Get back!" he yelled, brandishing the gun, but it was not necessary. They were just standing in the room, frozen, looking at the doorway.

Greer and Joyboy heard the commotion at the same time, and for an instant they did not react. Then they were on their feet, knocking the card table over in the process, and scrambling for the hallway. As Greer stopped through the door a small figure shot by, just escaping his reaching hand. He pivoted and leaped for the corner but the boy was already halfway down the stairs that led to the ground floor. "Stop!" he screamed, stumbling on the half-landing. The boy was flying ahead, leaping down the last five steps.

Ralph landed running on the main floor of the garage and headed for the front door. He heard them coming behind him, yelling, and now he was scared. Ten running bounds carried him past the limousine. Now he was at the door. He pushed at it but it did not move. He looked down and saw a handle and he reached for it, grabbing hard and pulling up with all his strength. It did not move and he felt his heart drop. They were almost on him. He turned as the tall man lunged for him and ducked away. Joyboy had reached the garage too. Ralph ran along the wall and got behind the limousine but they were already closing in, one at the front of the car and one at the back. As they edged toward him he put his foot on the door handle of the car and shot up onto the roof, sliding across it on his belly, turning in one motion and dropping off onto the floor on the other side. The men leaped for him, cursing. Ralph saw Greer lunge for him and stepped backward. Then he was falling, falling.

Greer stood at the edge of the grease pit and watched the boy get to his knees. His legs felt watery and he was breathing hard. Sonovabitch, if the kid had turned to the back door he'd be all to hell and gone. He was slippery as a cockroach. "You all finished?" Greer said.

Ralph looked up at him, his eyes blazing. There was a smudge of grease on his cheek and his shirt was covered with it. "You're lucky I slipped," Ralph said, "or else you'd never catch me."

Greer moved to the steps that led down to the pit. "Come on up here," he said.

"Come and get me!"

Joyboy put a hand on the floor and jumped down. He grabbed the boy by his hair and pulled him to his feet. Twisting Ralph's arm behind his back, he marched him out of the pit.

Greer looked at the boy briefly before they went upstairs. There were tears in the kid's eyes, but his mouth was set in a firm line. He was a tough mother, this little one. He had to be taught a lesson.

On the second floor, he motioned to Joyboy and they brought the boy to the table, under the light. "Hold him," Greer said to Joyboy and he reached into his pocket and took out his knife, flicking the button in the same motion so the four-inch blade clicked into place.

He heard Loretta gasp when she saw what he was doing. "No," she said, "Greer, don't."

"Shut up!" He rested the point of the blade against the boy's throat. "You're a dumb kid," he said to the boy, holding the child's eyes with his own. "Which twin are you?"

"None of your business," the boy spat.

Greer reached down and grabbed the boy's wrist, turning it over to read the name on his silver bracelet. "Ralph," he said, "you have fucked with me for the last time." He twisted the boy's arm and brought the knife down against the inside of his forearm. Then he changed his mind, laughing. "I know a way to tell you apart," he said, dropping the boy's arm. Carefully, Greer brought the knife up. He circled the boy's head for a moment. Then in one fast slash he cut the boy's cheek open from the tip of his ear to the edge of his mouth.

"You're Ralph now," he said, releasing the child and watching the blood well in a red line across his face. "Now you're always gonna be Ralph."

4:00 P.M.

Maxwell Barnett parked the blue Chrysler Newport halfway down the driveway and stepped out of the car, automatically reaching behind the front seat for the attaché case that was not there. He smiled at himself as he looked at the floor mat. The smart olive leather case was another touchstone that was missing today. He had left it in the office. Twelve years ago, that neat, hand-tooled piece of leather had cost forty-seven dollars. A present he had given himself when he made the big leagues. On planes and trains and buses and cars, it had traveled thousands of miles with him, filled with plans and presentations. It held shirts, too, and underwear on his short overnight trips. On his lap, it was a writing platform to scribble the notes that would later be transcribed into call reports and schedules. And today he had left it behind. Well, there wasn't any paperwork to catch up on any more.

He walked slowly up the gravel driveway toward the house, noticing the purple bloom of wild irises that had sprouted along the hedge. A picture of old Sam Bloom popped into his head—God, that was years ago. Sam Bloom, former jeweler, now retired, had picked up rent money by working as a part-time messenger boy at the agency, when he, Max, had been a mailroom boy fresh out of college and on the way up. Sam Bloom—sixty-seven years old and still working, because he had to. Going out to bring back coffee for the secretaries he would always take his briefcase with him, piling buttered rolls, doughnuts, and danish into the bag and stuffing cardboard containers of coffee on top, and always managing to maintain a kind of odd dignity when the coffee spilled and made the doughnuts and danish soggy. People complained, but Sam Bloom would never carry coffee in a paper bag like the other messengers did. "I might meet someone I know," he told Max one day, his breath smelling faintly of tobacco, the white line of his mustache solemn, "somone from the old days, in the jewelry business. How would it look if they saw me delivering containers of coffee?"

So sad. What made Sam Bloom come to him now? Is that the road for me, a castoff hanging on, dying but dignified, grubbing for a buck in a well-tailored suit?

As he walked up the front steps, Max automatically straightened his tie and put on a smile. Get ready, Shirl, the former breadwinner is home. But the front door was locked. And when he entered, the house was dark. Could she be sleeping? At this hour?

He looked through the bedrooms, then looked again at his watch. All right, he thought, I give up, where is she? And where was Kathy? The girl should have been home from school by now. Darker suspicions loomed but he cast them away. What an anticlimax, taking the confessional away from the penitent.

He hung his suit coat away in the closet, stripped off his tie, and shucked his shoes. In stockinged feet he padded down to the bar. He was about to pour a hefty drink when the phone rang. It was Sally, back in the office, her voice tight and controlled. "Where the hell have you been?"

"Never mind. What's up?"

"Your wife phoned after we left and twice more since then. She wants you to meet her at school, it's something to do with your daughter."

"Oh?" What the hell was that all about? Had Kathy done something? "How about the office? Anyone looking for me?"

"No, Max, there hasn't been a soul."

"Thanks," he said, wanting to say more and not finding words. He let Sally hang up and put the phone down, looking at the Van Gogh print over the fireplace. *The Bedroom at Arles,* the world on a slant. He'd always liked that picture. Old Vince, living like a peasant while painting masterpieces that would make others rich. The world on a slant, like always.

Moving very slowly, he walked upstairs to find his shoes.

4:20 P.M.

"Now you just listen to me," Floogie Williams said from behind the long bar. With the bar rag trailing down from his fist, he pointed a finger at the old junkman. "Talk like that is just gonna get you in a mess of trouble, hear? Specially with me."

"I seen what I seen, Floogie," Hamp Norris insisted, his voice rising and trailing off into a whine. He took another sip of the muscatel. The world was crazy, sure enough, and was filled with crazy things. But if one of those crazy things happened to you, did that make you crazy too?

The heavy-set bartender filled a beer glass and walked it down to the end of the bar, placing it in front of the woman sitting there and removing the empty glass with a polished gesture. She smiled through layers of powder and rouge. "He sure is carryin' on, ain't he?"

"Crazy wino," Floogie said. "I've almost thrown him outta here three times this afternoon." He turned away from the whore. "Maybe I shoulda," he added, thoughtfully, "but what the hell. It don't harm nothing." He took the empty glass to the middle of the bar and jerked it up and down in the soapy water.

"What's ailing the old man?" asked a man in a gray fedora.

Floogie shrugged. "Ghosts."

A flicker of reflected light danced on Gray Fedora's teeth as he smiled. "Is that all?"

Floogie laughed his respectful bartender's laugh. "Son of a bitch says he seen a fat Cadillac flyin' through the air this morning. Just a takin' off into the sky like a big-ass bird." He stood watching the man in the gray fedora. He was well dressed, and in no hurry.

"All kinds of nuts in this world, hey?" the man said.

"Yeah," Floogie said, "there sure are." He walked away down the bar to find his cigarettes.

4:35 P.M.

Mrs. Regina Carter sat rigid on the couch next to her daughter, staring hard at the two white men in her parlor who had brought her such terrible news. Tears filled her eyes, running slowly down her dark cheeks. She dabbed at them with her handkerchief, fighting to hold herself under control. For Benjamin Lee was not dead—the men had said that right away—and there was no reason for mourning.

Jackie's arms were about her mother, a hand stroked the back of her white uniform.

"And so, you see," Stuart continued, "our hands are tied. We've given our word not to call the police. Tomorrow, or Monday, we hope to deliver the money—and have the children and your son returned to us safe and sound. So hang on and pray—that's all I can say—and tell no one what has happened."

"My brother had nothing to do with this," Jackie said, looking at Stuart.

He gazed back into her wide-set eyes. "No, no," he said. "We're not saying he did."

"Hell, no," Carmine added in a rough voice. "He's a good kid, Ben."

"Why?" Mrs. Carter said. "Why do people want to do evil? What makes them hurt their own?" She looked out the window, her eyes very far away.

Stuart looked at the large black woman, at her daughter sitting next to her, one as heavy as the earth, the other light as air. "I don't know," he said pensively, his voice trailing off. "Every day we seem to find new crimes . . . new ways to hurt each other." On the wall behind the two women the plaster Jesus twisted on the cross. Stuart rose to his feet. Behind him, Carmine walked to the doorway leading out into the kitchen. "It's time we were going," he said softly. "Not that there is much we can do back at the school. . . ."

"I'm going to pray for them," Mrs. Carter said.

"Yes," Stuart said. "I'm sure you will."

"For all of them, Mr. Stuart. The children and Benjamin Lee . . . and the men who have taken them away."

Stuart turned and followed Carmine from the room. Pray well, Mrs. Carter, he thought. It's about the only thing we can do now.

4:50 P.M.

The slanting sun threw sharp shadows on the wall as Jim Abernathy dialed Carew's office. While he waited for the call to go through, he poked a hand inside his jacket. His armpits were soaked from undershirt to suit coat, and he felt cold. In the ashtray, three dead cigars lay half buried under piles of gray ashes. It was quiet in the bank at this hour, the clerks and secretaries had gone, no typewriters chattered. Abernathy's tongue felt heavy, there was a foul taste in his mouth, and the banker suddenly felt very old. "Charlie? It's Jim. You must have been born under a lucky star."

"You have it?"

"Yes. Tomorrow, late in the afternoon, it'll be here. All of it."

He heard Carew cough sharply into the phone. "That's fine, Jim, fine. I knew you could do it."

"That made one of us, then, Charlie. You have no idea what I went through to get the money. I don't mind telling you my neck is stretched from here to Timbuktu, and if one of the federal boys cares to look into it, I'm in serious trouble."

"Was it that difficult?"

"No, Charlie, not at all." Abernathy paused for a moment to light yet another cigar. "All I had to do was break about ten banking laws, commit a minor fraud, and blackmail some poor slob who used to like me very much." He blew a cloud of blue smoke at the ceiling. "I can't recall a Federal Reserve shipment ever having been detoured before. I'm a little surprised myself that it could be done."

"I appreciate it, Jim," Carew said. "I hope to be able to tell you what it's all about very soon."

"Never mind," the banker said, "I've got a pretty good idea." He looked down at the notes scrawled on the yellow pad on his desk. "A hundred and fifty thousand in tens, fifty thousand in fives. I've got it all. Nothing larger than a fifty. Most of the bills are old."

"Fine, Jim, fine," the headmaster said. "I'll speak to you further in the morning."

"Hey, wait a minute," Abernathy said, "don't run away."

"I have some people here, Jim," Carew said, "and they're very anxious to hear what you've told me."

"Just a few more things, Charlie. I've got three pieces

of paper for you to sign, and I'll want Rossman's signature, too. I'll have Alice type them up at home tonight, I wouldn't want my secretary to see them. So you'd better figure on dropping by here in the morning."

"All right. We'll be there."

"You're sure you don't want an armed guard?" Abernathy asked. "It could be arranged, you know. That's a lot of money to be carrying all alone."

"No, Jim, no guards. This is something I'll have to do myself."

"I thought as much. All right then, I'll see you tomorrow." There was something else the banker wanted to add, but he had difficulty putting it into words. "Good luck, Charlie," he said slowly, "I hope this thing turns out the way you want it to."

5:00 P.M.

Maxwell Barnett held his wife in his arms and buried his face in her hair, while the others looked away and tried not to hear their words. "Shirl, Shirl," he said, holding her against him. The note had paralyzed him and Shirl's ravaged face told him the rest of the story. She had been through all this alone while he had wandered through the city feeling sorry for himself. He felt a flood of shame. "I couldn't find you, Max," he heard Shirl saying, her voice a monotone, empty, "I needed you and I couldn't find you." He squeezed her harder, his guilt overcoming the other feelings. "I know how you are about business," she said, looking at him now, her pale eyes vacant and dreamlike. "I thought you'd think I was making it up—"

"Shirl, please—"

"I didn't think you'd come . . . I . . . wasn't sure you'd come."

Max bit his lip. He wanted to hide himself, to shrink into nothingness and run away, fleeing from the shell of a woman who stood before him. She was like a child now, there was no anger or accusation in her, nor was there any passion at all. Limp and pale, a blond blob . . . *"I didn't think you'd come . . ."* Wasn't that what she had just said so simply, without rancor, as if it would be perfectly natural for him to choose business over her or Kathy at any time, that they could lie bleeding or dying and he would not come at once, placing business before them, again, always and forever, as he had been doing for so many years? He looked at her incredulously, realizing in that long moment how sick she was, how twisted her view of him had become. I've failed, he thought, failed you by so much that if I live a thousand years I will never be able to make it up. He put his arms on the mantelpiece and cried unashamedly, his racking sobs loud in the quiet room, where all but his wife stood looking the other way.

5:30 P.M.

"It feels fine, Kathy, really it does," Ralph Flood said. He held Ben Carter's handkerchief hard against his cheek. "It doesn't even hurt any more."

"Let me take a look," Ben said. He pulled the handkerchief gently away from the wound and saw that most of the bleeding had stopped. "I think you're going to live," he said, "but you better keep holding the handkerchief that way."

"That was a dumb thing to do, Ralph," Kathy said. "They might have killed you."

"Yeah," the boy nodded, grinning, "but I almost made it. A few more feet and I would have got clean away. And then I would have run and called the police and they would have come and caught these guys and we all could have gone home."

"Sure we could have," Carter said, "or maybe, by the time the cops got here, we would have all been dead." He leaned forward and put a hand on Ralph's knee. "Listen to me now, no more tricks, no more escapes—not unless I give the word. You understand?"

"Ah, gee, Ben," the boy said, "you act like you're afraid of them."

Ben sighed. "I am afraid of them, Ralph. These guys play rough. And while they've got us locked up here I don't want to give them any excuse to hurt us"—he looked closely at the boy—"or maybe kill us. So no more stunts, understand? Not until I say so."

"All right, Ben."

"Good," Carter said, as Kathy leaned forward to whisper something. "Don't look now," she said, "but we've got company."

"You and you," Greer said as he came through the door, pointing to Kathy and Ben, "come with me." He walked to the rear of the room, away from the children. Ben and Kathy followed slowly.

"I've got some news," he said. "I talked to Carew. He says he's getting the money, but it may take a couple of days."

"And what happens when they get the money?" Carter asked.

Greer looked the driver straight in the eyes. "Why, they turn it over to us and we let you go."

"Just like that, huh?" Carter said.

"No. Not just like that. We lock you up in this place first. Then, when we have the money and we get where we're going, we telephone the school and let them know where to find you. At least, that's the way I got it figured now."

You're lying, you bastard, Carter thought. It's just rolling right off your tongue and all of it is crap. "I see," he said. "And why are you telling us all this?"

"Because I need your help," Greer said. "No more stunts like the twin pulled before. First thing you know, we'd have to kill somebody, and that's something I don't want to do . . . unless I have to."

Carter felt a chill, as if someone were walking on his grave. Now he was certain that they were doomed, that before this crime was complete they would be dead, shot down or stabbed, one by one. "I get the message," Carter said. "You want us to cool the kids."

"Right. No tricks, no surprises. I'm putting a lock on the door so you can't pull that shit again. But I don't want no trouble when we come up here. Fuck around and you'll all be dead. Play it cool and easy and you'll all be home in a few days."

"Okay," Carter said evenly. "I'll try to keep the kids under control."

"One more thing. They want to talk to one of the kids before they hand over the money." He pointed a finger. "What's his name?"

"Taylor. Henry Taylor."

"Right. I'm gonna take him with me a little later. I want you to talk to him before we go. Because if he tries anything while he's with me, he gets it, and then you all get it. Understand?"

"I'll do what I can."

"Do better than that," Greer said. "There's a lot of money riding on this and I don't want any mistakes. A killing don't do neither of us any good. So make sure he don't try anything."

"I'll take care of the boy," Ben said. "You take care of your part of the bargain."

"Done," Greer said, turning away. "I'll be back in a while," he said, as he began walking toward the door.

Ben Carter held fast to Kathy's arm as Greer walked through the doorway. He saw the door close slowly. From outside, in the silence, he heard the sound of a padlock snapping into place.

6:30 P.M.

"Come on, Norman," Henry Taylor said, "let's take a walk."

From his seat near the door Norman Schwartz smiled at the doctor. Then he rose and followed Henry from the room.

"I have to keep moving, Norm," Henry said. "This sitting around and waiting . . ." He shook his head.

The school was quiet, the children and staff having departed some hours before. The silence drew the two men together as they paced the length of the long corridor and turned back again. In front of the large oil of Commodore Sloane, Henry paused and looked up, studying the face of the old man and the figures in the background behind him.

"What's bothering you, Henry?" Norman asked, breaking the silence.

Henry looked away and ran a hand across his cheek. "I just have this feeling, Norman . . . it's hard to describe. As if we were trapped . . . pinned down."

"Yes," Norman nodded, "I know. All the decisions being made on the other side. But what can we do?"

Henry's square face was clouded. "Norman, I wouldn't say it in there, but I don't trust those bastards worth a damn. We should have called the police at the outset. It's like medicine, Norm, the faster you diagnose an ailment and attack it, the better off you are. Always."

"No," Norman said, "no police. You can't take a chance when they're holding a gun to your child's head."

"I don't agree." Henry's voice was grating. "Carew convinced you and the others that no one should be told, and all I can do is go along. He was right about one thing, no one of us could have made the decision alone."

"We pay up and hope for the best," Norman said. "We're trapped."

Henry shook his head. "There must be some way to get those kids back before it's too late. They're down in Northside, I know it, I can feel it in my bones. It's the one place, the only logical place they could take the kids and feel safe."

"What do you mean . . . 'before it's too late'?"

"Look, Norm," Henry said, "the way I spoke in front of Mil and Irene and the rest of them in that office, that's one thing. To you I'll speak my mind. When we hand over the money, I don't think they'll let the kids go." Henry's voice trailed off and he turned, looking away.

"You think they'll kill them." It was a statement, not a question, and it hung in the air between the two men.

Henry nodded. "Yes. I think they will. I think they've meant to all along."

"Do you think they've already done it?"

"No," said Henry. "I think the kids are safe until the gang gets its hands on the money."

"And after that?"

Henry grimaced. "We've got to find them before that, Norman. Before tomorrow afternoon."

"But how? Henry, how do you go into a rabbit warren like the Northside and find someone in twenty-four hours?"

"Somehow," Henry said doggedly. "Somehow there has got to be a way."

7:30 P.M.

Greer finished the coffee and sat back in his chair, enjoying a cigarette as he surveyed the Taylor boy. Carter had obviously convinced him to behave. The boy sat quietly in his chair, not saying a word. He was a good-looking kid, with a strong nose and finely etched cheekbones under his light, coffee-and-cream skin. And just scared enough, Greer thought.

"You all set, kid?"

The boy nodded.

"Stand up a minute. Let me get a look at you." The kid was almost as tall as Jimmy, but if anything he was built a little broader. "What do you think, Loretta?" Greer said. "Does he look like he belongs in Northside?"

"Now that you mention it, he looks a little too good. That raincoat is kind of fancy. And that shirt and tie . . . I don't know."

Greer chuckled. "He makes me look like a poor relation." He made the boy take off his raincoat and tie, exchanging them for Jimmy's soiled jacket. With a few last instructions to Loretta out of the way, Greer led Junior downstairs.

"Before we go outside," he said at the door, "I wanna make sure you know what you're supposed to do."

"Don't worry," Junior said, "Carter told me all about it."

"Just you remember, kid. You make any trouble and everybody gets zapped. Everybody. So just don't figure on bein' no hero."

"I won't."

Greer led him out the back door and across the pitch-black yard, helping him over the fence and through the alley to the next street. Once inside the Volkswagen, Greer drove slowly out of the neighborhood, turning north on Lenard Avenue, the boy silent beside him, watching the lighted streets and stores flash by outside the window. "You got a name," Greer asked, "besides Taylor?"

"My friends call me Junior," the boy said, not turning his head.

"How old are you, Junior?"

"Eleven. I'll be twelve in July."

"You live in a nice house, up there in the County. I been by there quite a few times. You like livin' up there?"

"It's all right, I guess. I don't know, I never lived anyplace else."

Greer turned off Lenard Avenue and headed for the parkway. "How would you like livin' down here, in Northside?"

"I probably wouldn't," Junior said. "It's all closed in, like. No grass, no trees."

"Yeah, you right about that. And kinda dirty, too. Or hadn't you noticed?"

"I noticed," Junior said. His voice was restrained, tense.

"And half a million of us livin' in that garbage. While Mr. Charlie, Mr. Whiteass, he lives up in the County or downtown where they clean the streets regular and the only shit you see is from their fancy pooches. We gets the shit and they gets the rest. How you like that, Junior? How you like that for a world, huh?"

The boy looked over at Greer for a few seconds, then looked straight ahead out of the window as the Volkswagen climbed the ramp to the parkway.

"You don't mind it, huh?" Greer taunted as the boy's silence lengthened. "Just as long as you get yours, why you don't rightly care about your brothers, eh, kid? That the way you figure it?"

"No, it's not," Junior said.

Greer didn't let him go on. "But that's the way your Daddy sees it, right? I got mine, the rest of you go kiss ass. Ain't that right?"

"No, that's not right," the boy said, his voice rising, then trailing off. "I don't know . . . we don't talk about it much."

Greer's tone was mocking. "Course not."

"Well, we just don't, that's all. But I know my Dad's not that way. He cares a lot, about black people. The Garvey Clinic on Lenard Avenue, he started that, you know. And I've heard him talking about patients who can't pay him, and how it doesn't make any difference . . . and I know he gives money to the NAACP all the time . . . there's a plaque on the wall in the den . . . and . . . and . . ."

Greer laughed. "Aw, gee, ain't that nice. Throw the poor darkies some crumbs, Mandy Lou, just as long as we got cake for supper. Come on, Junior, you're breaking my heart. Your Daddy's one of the richest bastards up in that County. Damn it, whatever he's doin' it ain't enough. Whatever he's got, he got off the backs of black people. It belongs to them, don't you see? He's got no right to get rich while one black man walks around in rags, while one black child goes hungry. Is that fair for you to be driving off in a limousine to some faggoty white school, while other black kids ain't got enough to eat?"

Junior looked confused. He'd never heard ideas like these before, and it was clear he didn't know how to handle them.

"In the revolution, baby, every black man that ain't with us is against us. There's no in-between. Just remember that, Junior, and start doin' some thinking on your own."

Greer slowed the Volkswagen as the County line loomed ahead. He pulled off into an empty rest area and parked next to the outdoor callbox. He looked at Junior and sighed. This kid wasn't about to join any revolution. He would have to be killed like the rest, shot down and left behind in the garage. And Carter would be dead, too. And the first casualties of their revolution would be black people as well as white.

Greer placed a hand on the boy's shoulder. "Never mind me, Junior," he said, smiling. "Sometimes my mouth has a way of running off ahead of the rest of me. Don't take it too personal, okay?"

The boy nodded slowly, now more confused than before.

"Okay, kid," Greer said, sighing. "Let's go make that phone call, huh?"

8:15 P.M.

A number of cots had been set up in the faculty dining room, and the women had been sent in to rest. Only Shirl Barnett slept, however, the result of a heavy sedative administered by Dr. Taylor.

Surprisingly, in the hours of waiting, Emma Porter and Martha Flood had become friendly. The small, dowdy widow listened wide-eyed as Martha talked tirelessly of places she had visited—yes, she had actually had dinner in a Greek *taverna* on a night when Jackie and Ari had danced and listened to the *bazouki* until the sun came up—and she told Emma about the retreats in Geneva and Lucerne where women she knew had wrinkles removed and years taken from their tanned faces. In turn, Martha smiled when Mrs. Porter talked of Heidi and Paulie, of diapers and dishpans, and the special problems of raising two children in a fatherless home.

Nearby, drinking coffee at the round Formica table near the window, Mildred Taylor and Irene Schwartz spoke very little. The tray of sandwiches that had been brought to the table from the headmaster's office was largely untouched. Earlier Carew had urged the women to go home. They had refused. As long as there was a chance that the kidnapers would call again, they insisted on waiting.

The men waited, too, in Carew's large office. Pauline had insisted on remaining at her desk and was trying to concentrate on some routine jobs. She stopped typing when the telephone rang.

Carew picked up the receiver and nodded when he heard the now-familiar voice, telling the fathers that this was the call they were expecting.

"I got a child here wants to talk to you," Greer said. "Now make it quick and no tricks, understand?"

He held his hand over the mouthpiece and leaned down to Junior. "You just tell him who you are and that you all right, boy. And nothin' about where we're keeping you, understand?"

The boy nodded his head and squeezed into the callbox in front of Greer.

In the headmaster's office, the men were crowded around the desk. "He's putting a child on the phone," Carew said.

Greer leaned down and put the mouthpiece of the instrument in front of the boy's face, holding the receiver away so that he could hear what was being said at the other end. His right arm hung free, about the boy's shoulder, ready to swoop a hand across Junior's mouth at the first sign of treachery.

"Hello," Junior said.

"Who is this, please?" Carew asked.

"Henry Taylor Jr.," the boy said.

"Your son, Dr. Taylor," the headmaster said, and Henry leaned forward snatching the phone from Carew's outstretched hand. Carew went to the outer office, where he took the receiver from Pauline.

"Junior? This is Dad. Are you all right, son?"

"Yes . . . yes, Dad."

God, God, Henry thought, I thank you for this. "They haven't hurt you?"

"No . . . I'm fine."

"The other children, too?" Carew asked. "Are they all right?"

"Yes."

"The driver, Carter—is he with you or them?" Carew asked quickly.

Hearing the question, Greer snatched the phone. "He ain't with us," he said. "Ain't that right, kid?" He held the phone down again until the boy said yes, and then put it to his mouth again. "All right," he said, "now what about the money?"

At the sound of this man's voice Henry Taylor felt the bile rise in his throat. He listened silently while Carew spoke.

"Tomorrow," said the headmaster. "We'll have it tomorrow."

"When?"

"In the afternoon. Before three o'clock."

"Good," said Greer. "I'll call you tomorrow and tell you where to take it."

"Can we speak to the child again tomorrow?"

"Forget it. We don't take no more chances. I'll call you tomorrow."

"But what about—"

"Tomorrow, honky," Greer said, and he put the receiver back on the hook.

Behind them traffic buzzed on the parkway as they walked the few steps across the pavement to the Volkswagen. Greer paused before turning the key to start the engine, looking at the child. Junior's balled fist worked at his eyes, wiping the tears that flowed and made him feel so ashamed. Greer's hand reached out and brushed the boy's hair. "Come on now," he said, his voice soothing. "Tomorrow night this time you'll likely be back home with your Mama and your Daddy—so hush up now, and think about that, hey?"

Junior looked miserably at Greer. "Tomorrow," he said.

Greer wiped a tear from the boy's cheek with a finger. "Tomorrow, guaranteed."

Then he started the engine and drove slowly out of the parking area and back onto the parkway.

PART V

Ransom

THURSDAY

8:30 P.M.

Carew was smiling as he addressed the parents. "I am enormously relieved," he said. "At least we know that the children are safe and well and that, God willing, they will be returned some time tomorrow.

Phil Stuart was startled by the headmaster's jubilance. Well, he'd handled things in his own way and it looked as if he would be successful. The parents, sitting in a loose circle about the room, seemed to reflect Carew's air of optimism. For the first time the oppressive tension seemed to have lifted. Emma Porter was smiling, actually smiling, and the others looked comparably relaxed. Except for Dr. Taylor, Stuart saw, who sat near the desk, nervously rubbing his forehead.

"Dr. Carew?" Henry finally interrupted. "I still think we must be very careful. Six children will be missing from their homes tonight. People are bound to ask questions. A lot depends on how you answer. Since we voted not to notify the police it would be extremely dangerous if anyone outside this room learned of the kidnaping." Henry's eyes sought out Carmine Mancuso. "You have a car and a driver missing. How are you going to handle that?"

"I already have," Carmine answered. "I told my secretary that I found Ben Carter at home sick this afternoon, and to scratch his name off the ready roster for a few days. No problem. I told her I put the car in a shop downtown to have some work done. So we're covered all around."

"And who's going to pick up his children tomorrow and take them to school?"

"Jesus," said Carmine, "I never thought of that. You're right. The boys will know something funny's going on if we don't cover that run." He thought for a moment. "Hell, I'll do it myself. I'll call in late tomorrow and say I'm out covering for Ben. It'll be okay."

"Fine," Henry said. "Now, everyone, be prepared to answer questions. What about your other children, friends, a maid?"

Martha Flood smiled to herself at this, looking at Henry Taylor in a strange way. Wasn't he the clever one, she thought. Some of them had to be bright, though, think of Ralph Bunche. "My *au pair* girl," she said. "All she knows is that I've gone off to school to see about the boys. I suppose I'll have to tell her something."

"And my housekeeper," Emma Porter said. She looked anxiously at her wristwatch. "My God! She must be wondering where I am."

Henry nodded. "Make sure you have a story set before you go home. And make it a good one.

"I also think we'd better start making plans for tomorrow. It will look strange, to have all of us up at school two days running."

"Quite right," Carew said, "an excellent point. He looked around. "Mr. Schwartz, I'd like you to come with me to the bank. And Mr. Mancuso, perhaps we can avail ourselves of your transportation."

"Anything you want," Carmine said, "you got it. Cars, drivers, you name it."

"Very good." Carew turned to Dr. Taylor. "And since you seem to understand these people, perhaps you ought to be here with me, also."

A spark of anger flared within Henry, but he held it in check. These people, he thought. As if my color makes me an instant expert. And do you speak for all whites, Carew? "I'll try to make it," he said dryly.

Emma Porter rose to her feet. She seemed hesitant. "I think, if we're not all going to be here tomorrow," she began slowly, "maybe we should be together, anyway somewhere. To be alone at a time like this . . ." Embarrassed now, she stared at the floor.

Martha Flood broke the silence, reaching out from her seat to touch Emma's hand. "That's a fine idea, Emma," she said quietly. "You come over tomorrow." She turned in her chair. "And if anyone else wants to come along," she offered, "you'd be welcome. It's a big house."

Irene Schwartz and Mildred Taylor exchanged glances, but neither woman spoke.

"That's settled then," said Carew. "In any case, call Mrs. DeBusschere tomorrow and let her know where you can be reached. We'll keep in touch throughout the day." He smiled in dismissal as the parents began filing from the room. The Floods, with Emma Porter in tow, were the first to leave. Behind them the Taylors and the Schwartzes walked together.

Down the hall, Maxwell Barnett stood looking down at his sleeping wife. He kneeled and ran a hand over her hair. "Babe," he said as he kissed her on the cheek, "wake up, babe, it's time to go."

Her eyelids fluttered open and she stretched, smiling. "Is Kathy home yet?" Her voice sounded very young.

"No," Max said very gently, "not yet, honey." He helped her sit up on the edge of the cot and began to put on her shoes. "I have to make chocolate pudding for dinner," she said. "Kathy likes chocolate pudding."

A copper penny soured on Max's tongue. He nodded at her empty smile. "Yes, yes, I know," he said. He helped her rise and took her raincoat over his arm.

"It has to cool before we can eat it," she said. "I'm making all her favorites tonight. Lamb chops . . . and asparagus . . . and we'll all eat together . . . and I'll put flowers on the table. We haven't had flowers on the table in a long time, Max, have we?"

He began walking her to the door, his arm around her waist. "I'll want the crystal bud vase. . . . I think it's on the top shelf in the hall cabinet . . .you'll have to get it down for me, Max."

"I'll get it, Shirl," he said in a choked voice, "I'll find it for you."

Smiling, she walked beside him down the long hallway.

9:25 P.M.

Irene and Norman Schwartz were sitting in the Taylors' living room while Henry used the telephone in his den. "The answering service must be going crazy," Mildred said as she poured out drinks. "I know Henry hasn't checked in for hours." She looked up as Henry appeared in the doorway.

"I'm off," he said. His raincoat was draped over his arm.

Norman Schwartz looked at his friend, his eyebrows framing the question: "Off where?"

"To Northside," said Henry. "I don't think we can count on things going as smoothly as Carew pretends. And I'm convinced the kidnapers are hiding out in the ghetto."

"But honey," Mildred protested, "what can you do?"

"Poke about. Keep my ears open. Perhaps I'll hear something. Down there it doesn't take much to start drums beating. Anyway, I just spoke to Roy Hart and I'm meeting him at the clinic in forty-five minutes."

Norman sighed. When Henry got an idea in his head he could hardly ever be budged. "I don't think it will do any good," he said, "but I'll put my coat on and come with you."

"No, thanks, Norm, you're not in shape for this. And besides, where I'm going that white face of yours would get in the way."

Norman smiled. "It still seems a losing proposition. How do you know they're even in Northside?"

"I don't. I've just got a feeling, that's all."

"All right, okay, you've got a feeling," Norman said, his hands gesturing. "Let's say, by some miracle, you find them. What then?"

"I'll worry about that when it happens."

Norman shook his head. "Off he goes, into the night. Super-Doc. Henry, I think you're being foolish."

"Look, it's something I have to do. If I don't pick up anything on the wire, I'll just turn around and come home. Okay?"

"Sure, sure," Norman said. "What the hell is '*the wire*'?"

"It's our own jungle telegraph," Henry said. "Let something happen in Northside and inside an hour every soul in the ghetto knows about it. If those kids are holed-up down there, someone must have seen them. I have to find out for myself."

Mildred didn't even try to make Henry change his mind. One look at the set of his jaw told her it was useless. "Be careful, darling," she said, "and good luck."

Henry nodded and then, as an afterthought, went back to the den on his way out. He opened the small wall safe behind the picture over his desk and reached in. It had been years since he had looked at the small .22-caliber automatic. He opened the magazine and checked to see that it was loaded. Then he put it into the pocket of his raincoat and headed for the door.

9:45 P.M.

Ben Carter paced amid the wooden shelving. There was no doubt in his mind of their ultimate fate. He had written in his mind's eye: a) They cannot release us when the ransom is paid because we are the only witnesses to the crime and we could identify them fully and completely to the police, even down to details like the sound of their voices and the nicknames they use for each other.

b) We know the exact location of this building, and the police would find here enough evidence, including their fingerprints, to convict them when they were apprehended, as they must finally be.

c) Kidnaping is a capital crime, the penalty is death. Add (a), (b), and (c) and the conclusion is inescapable. When the money is in their hands they will kill us all.

All right then, he told himself, face the facts. They will kill us all when they get the money. They won't act before the ransom is handed over in case someone insists on speaking to one of the kids again before paying.

Carter squatted down against the wall and lit a cigarette, forcing himself to think. All right, Sergeant Carter, what the hell do you know? How do you lead a gang of children and fight your way out of this trap? Estimate of enemy strength: one pistol, one knife, already in action. Hell, they could have an armory downstairs. And you wouldn't know that until they opened up.

All right then, in the army the book said: Keep the enemy occupied, concentrate your forces in one area, assault enemy positions until you have broken through a hole, hold open the breakthrough until all of your forces have withdrawn. So said the book.

He stubbed his cigarette out on the floor, grinding the remains under his shoe.

A frontal assault on the door, then. With what? Four boys, two girls, one man, not too healthy at the moment. Weapons? None. Unless . . . he took one of the shelves in his hands. A board would be better than nothing, wouldn't it? But how were the damned things connected to each other? He moved to the end of the rear line of shelves and looked at the beams that stood upright from floor to ceiling. *They weren't connected at all!* Quickly, he walked to the next vertical bracing a few feet away and checked further. It was true. There were only small six-inch cross boards attached to the vertical beams. The shelves merely rested on these, held in place by their own weight and the weight of the objects placed upon them.

Carter lifted one shelf and carefully swung it clear, placing it against the wall. The piece of wood was about six inches across and an inch thick. It stood slightly higher than the top of his head. He turned back and removed another shelf, placing it against the wall like the first one. Easy as pie. They could dismantle all these shelves whenever they wanted to. And even as he thought this, another cold knot of dread turned in his stomach. They could never just beat their way out.

Now think, damn you, he said to himself, and even as he said this an idea began to take shape in his mind. The shelves . . . and the mattresses. It was a long chance at best, but perhaps their only chance. The timing would have to be exact, and the children would have to move swiftly when he gave the order and do exactly as they were told.

He smiled then, as he took yet another shelf down and stacked it against the wall. Yes, it could work. And if it did, those mothers were in for a surprise. Not all the weapons were on the other side, and not all the power. And God—God!—wouldn't it be something to beat them.

10:30 P.M.

Roy Hart was waiting inside the front door of the clinic when Henry Taylor got out of his car. Hart led Henry to the lighted staff room and listened incredulously as Henry told him what had happened.

"They ought to be strung up by the short hairs!" he exploded when Henry finished. "Revolutionists, huh? And the first thing they do is kidnap a bunch of innocent kids. Man, if they hurt Junior, I swear I'll take them apart piece by piece!"

"We've got to find them first, Roy," Henry said quietly. "That's why I need your help." He spoke of the conclusions he had reached. "It's probably hopeless but I don't know what else to do."

"You're right, we have to try," said Hart. "So you call people . . . and I'll call people, and maybe we'll be lucky." He ran a finger inside the neck of his sweater. "But we've got to be damned careful because the wire works two ways. Ask around about something and the next thing you know *you* end up on the wire yourself. I don't think we can ask about the kids."

"The limousine," said Henry. "I thought we could use the car as a cover. Perhaps we can say that it's my limousine, and that I'd be willing to pay a reward to get it back, no questions asked."

"And emphasize no cops," Hart said. "I like that. People get uptight around here when you mention the police."

"Exactly." Henry glanced at his watch. "It's getting late, we'd better get started."

As he made his first call, Henry found himself thinking that maybe luck would be on his side. Thirty minutes later, however, despair returned. He had spoken to almost twenty people—his barber, two grocers, several lawyers, accountants, various businessmen he knew from long acquaintance to have their fingers on the pulse of Northside—and in every case there was no news. There were others to call, retailers, most of whom were always an instant source of information about the rich street life of the ghetto. These calls he would make in the morning. But from the reaction of the people he had already spoken to, there was nothing on the wire about a limousine, stolen or otherwise, or any news at all about a kidnaping.

When Roy Hart poked his head through the door, his face downcast, Henry was not surprised. "A blank," Hart said, "an absolute blank. If there was a limousine hidden away in Northside today, the wire doesn't have anything on it. At least," he added, trying to sound cheerful, "there's nothing on it *yet*."

Henry pulled out his pipe and began to fill it. "I think we ought to try the street next. We'll split up, that way we can cover twice as much ground. The bars and clubs are our best bet at this hour. It's almost twenty minutes past eleven. Let's try to meet back here in two hours." He stood and gathered up his raincoat, and the two men left the clinic together. Hart paused just outside the door as Henry put on his coat. "Two hours," he said, "let's hope we hear something." He stood watching Henry hurry down the street. To cling to even a small shred of hope must give the older man some comfort. At least it was better than just sitting and waiting.

He thought of the boy then. In the Easter vacation he had come to the clinic with his father and his presence seemed to fill the place. He had kept himself busy with chores the whole day, there wasn't a pencil in the clinic that hadn't been sharpened to within an inch of its life.

Please, God, Hart said to himself, don't let them harm the boy . . . not this boy. He turned and walked swiftly north in the harsh glowing neon of Lenard Avenue.

11:30 P.M.

. . . She must have thought about it all night because that morning she ran to the window as soon as she awoke. Three years old then, she spent the morning looking out into the yard, watching the heavy skies for the first sign of snowflakes. And then she saw them, the first thin scattered fall of white, early that year, a day in November. And running full tilt she came into the kitchen, those green eyes open wide, her cheeks thin then, and pulling my arm, looking up and shouting "Mommy, Mommy—blurries! I saw them! Snow blurries!" Laughing at the words, we hugged, and I kissed her, getting dressed then, the two of us, pregnant with Paulie then, and we walked down the path, bare hedges flecking with white, and Heidi running and laughing with me, as the white snowflakes flicked at her blinking eyelashes . . . and it was always blurries, after that, our own private word, and even later when snow came she made the joke, "Snow blurries today," and the memory never fades . . .

Tears stung her eyes and Emma Porter sat upright in the big bed, sleep gone now. Throwing on a robe, she walked down the hall to stand over Paulie's crib and look down at him sleeping, one hand rubbing the small of his back, saying soothing words and crooning gently. She stood there for a long time.

FRIDAY

12:00 Midnight

Hart heard them giggling and stopped, walking back into the side-street darkness. They were huddled against the door at the top of the stoop, three or four of them, he couldn't be sure. "Hey now," he called, his voice falling into a practiced slur. He put his hand on the brownstone railing.

"What you want?" A boy's voice, suspicious.

Hart grinned and hunched down to put a foot on the first step. "Little info, that's all. Friend of mine lost a car around here somewhere. Cadillac limousine . . ."

"You the law, baby?"

"Hell no!" Hart laughed. "Just a friend. He's lookin' to get it back and he'll pay for it, no questions asked. Big black Cadillac. License plates from up in the County. You seen it, or heard anythin' about it?"

A girl's voice floated down, high and rich. "If I seen it, would I be here, man?"

"Okay," Hart said as the others laughed. He turned to go.

One mocking voice. "Was your mother a giant?"

The tall man waved and continued down the street.

12:20 A.M.

Better-dressed than the other customers, Henry Taylor stood waiting at the counter of Adam's Ribs, watching the fluid motions of the fry cook as he turned the sizzling potatoes out of the drop basket and onto a paper plate. The odor of hot grease and frying chicken filled the air. Two women waited in front of Henry, their hands on the scarred linoleum countertop. A blue neon window sign flashed, CHICKEN/RIBS . . . CHICKEN/RIBS. In the rear of the tiny store a flashily dressed young man smiled into the telephone, writing a number in pencil on the wall.

Adam Harris finished wrapping the ribs and potatoes and made change out of his apron pocket for the two women.

"What's yours, chief?" he said to Henry.

Henry laid a dollar bill on the counter. "Looking for a car," he said. "Cadillac limousine. Black, with County plates." He saw the counterman's eyes blink, twice, and a curtain come down over his face. "No cops," Henry said, "just a friend wants it back before whoever snatched it beats it up."

The counterman grunted. "No cars here, mister."

"I figured maybe you might have heard something," he said as the man shook his head. Henry forced a smile. "If you do hear anything, call the Garvey Clinic tomorrow. Cadillac limousine, County plates. There'll be some money in it for you."

The counterman nodded and laid a hand on the dollar bill. When Henry nodded he stuffed the bill into his apron. He can't be law, the man thought at this. Law never pays for nothing.

1:25 A.M.

Waking, his mouth dry, Greer heard her breathing next to him in the dark. He put a hand on her back and rubbed slowly at the base of her spine, grinning when he heard her groan. Why not, he thought, why not?

He rolled away and pulled off his pants, then turned back and ran a shivery hand between her thighs, just brushing the hair on her cunt because he didn't want to wake her up yet. Very softly now, he found one nipple and rubbed it with the inside of his hand, coming back over the spot again and then just holding it, firm but not hard. Loretta moaned again and rolled toward him in her sleep. He kissed her neck where it met her warm shoulder, thinking that his hair was probably tickling at her ear and that she liked it. "Hey, now," she said suddenly, her voice thick with sleep, "what you doin'?"

He led her hand to his hardness in reply.

"Jimmy's here," she whispered, jerking her head toward the sleeping boy. "And Joyboy, too."

"Shit," he said softly, not really annoyed.

"No," she said, but he already had another idea. He got to his knees and helped her up. "Where we goin'?" she started to say but he shushed her. As she got up, he lifted her off the ground to his shoulder as if she weighed nothing.

He carried her through the doorway that way, his

free hand still rubbing at her back. He hurried down the stairs, not feeling the oil and grime under his bare feet, already laughing at what he was about to do. "In the car, chick," he said as he fumbled with the handle, gently dumping her onto the wide rear seat.

Then he closed the door and came to her, his mouth on hers, tongue reaching deep, and she fell back lifting her dress, already throbbing inside at the thought of what was to come. They began to pump on the soft seat and she said "FUCK FUCK" very loud as it started to build and he did and he did and it exploded.

"We never did it in no Caddy before," he whispered a long time later.

1:40 A.M.

Henry Taylor was seated behind the wheel of the Olds when Roy Hart came down the darkened street. One look at the older man's face told Hart that Henry's luck had been as bad as his.

"Maybe in the morning," Hart said after they had compared notes. "When the back-fence people and the stoop sitters come out, maybe then there'll be some word. It's been less than twenty-four hours."

"Maybe." Henry stared out into the street for a few moments, then started the engine.

"You don't have to drive me home," Hart said.

Henry grinned. "Don't worry, I'm not. Not yet, anyway. I thought we might drive around a bit. You never can tell, maybe we'll see something." He pulled away from the curb and drove slowly toward the corner.

Hart started to speak but stopped himself. Henry knew as well as he that the Cadillac wasn't parked on the street.

Henry turned the Olds toward the river and began to drive slowly through the quiet streets. They passed a brightly lit beauty parlor and two or three candy stores where men idled in the dim light cast out into the street. The liquor stores were open, too, and Hart soon lost count, there were so many of them.

Once, on a side street far from Lenard Avenue, they passed a Cadillac limousine parked at the curb and their hopes rose. But the plate was from the city and the color was a deep blue instead of black.

A half hour passed, and then an hour, and Hart began to have trouble keeping his eyes open. At last, the river lay before them, and Henry pulled the car over to the curb. "Damn it," he said quietly, "maybe I'm wrong. Maybe they're not here." He rolled down his window and let the river breeze sweep in. "But I can't get this feeling out of my head, Roy. Junior's here . . . someplace. I know it."

The look in Henry's eyes was too painful for Hart to meet and he turned away. "Go home, Henry," Hart said woodenly. "Get some rest, man, or you'll fall on your face. In the morning we'll try again."

Henry made a U turn and began driving back toward the center of Northside. "I'll drop you off," he said after they had been driving for a few minutes.

"What about you?"

Henry shrugged. "I'll keep on cruising for a while. Maybe the other side of Lenard Avenue. I don't know . . ."

Ten minutes later, Hart was standing beside the Olds in front of his home. He promised to meet Henry at the clinic shortly before nine o'clock, and the two men shook hands before the Oldsmobile pulled away. Hart stood watching as Henry turned the car left at the corner, heading east toward Lenard Avenue, driving in the same direction from which the sun would be rising in just a few short hours.

7:00 A.M.

A shaft of sunlight streaming through the naked window awakened him and he sat erect quickly, somehow frightened and unaware of his surroundings. The white walls of the clinic stared back at him and Henry realized dumbly that he had fallen asleep on this high leather examination table when he had only thought to take a few moments rest. His watch told him that he had slept for two hours. Dry-mouthed and blinking, he moved to the toilet and stripping his shirt, washed his face.

Awake now, he surveyed himself in the mirror. It was true, he did look as terrible as he felt. He opened the cabinet and using Roy Hart's razor and cream, shaved carefully, then combed his hair with Hart's comb.

A sense of urgency told him to get moving and he obeyed, collecting his raincoat and moving out to the reception room on his way to the door. But he paused, sat down at a desk, and began to pick up the telephone to call his wife, then stopped himself. No, it was too early. He had talked with her when he came back to the clinic, about two hours ago. She had not slept either, nor had Norman and Irene Schwartz who were spending the night, Mildred said, and what had he learned in Northside?

What? Nothing, he answered. Except that on certain streets no limousines were to be found, and in certain well-known places no information could be obtained. My son is lost and I cannot find him, he thought then, the words repeating themselves in his mind until he willed them to cease. Never look back, never feel sorry for yourself. His father had said that. Junior's grandfather had said that, except that he hadn't lived to see or know the boy who was his grandchild.

Henry opened and closed his hand swiftly. Stop it, cut it out. Think of now, concentrate on the next step. Crying only makes your eyes red, it doesn't get you anywhere. Hart would be here soon. Together, they would begin to look again.

What now? His stomach supplied the answer, growling. He thought then of when he had last eaten, and for a few moments it escaped him. Yesterday, but when? He couldn't remember eating anything after breakfast. No wonder his stomach was rumbling. Energy, he thought, I need food to keep going. He shrugged into his raincoat and walked out the front door, locking it carefully behind him.

Lenard Avenue shone bright in the spring sun. The air was cool and bracing, and Henry breathed deep. Nothing terrible happens in the morning. Why was that, Doctor? Why did fevers rise in the evening and lower themselves by day? What mysterious forces were at work there? How many times had he seen patients chipper and cheerful at morning rounds, only to find these same patients beginning to lose ground at night, failing and slipping back, sometimes dying during the deepening hours of night?

That's cheerful, he thought wryly, dropping it. Food. Where does one have breakfast on Lenard Avenue? There was a coffee shop someplace, they usually brought lunch from it for the clinic. But where?

He tried to decide which way to walk. Trucks rumbled past heading downtown, and the beginning of what would later be a stream of commuters, their cars slipping by, windows rolled up. I haven't been on the street here in the morning in a long, long time, he thought, I feel like a stranger. He began to walk north. On the corner, a line of women carrying shopping bags, waiting for a bus. The black brigade, heading downtown to wash and clean and cook and serve at the apartments of people on the Gold Coast. Have you seen my son, he thought of asking them? A quiet boy who looks like me, maybe a little tall for his age, good in school. Answers to the name of Junior or Henry or Hank. Eyes brown, hair black. Can catch a baseball, throws right, bats left. Have you see him?

Tears came and he stood blinking and wiping his eyes with the back of his hand. Fool, he cursed himself, stop it now. He will turn up today and it will be fine. They will get the money and they'll let him go. Behave yourself!

He felt a tug at his sleeve and looked down.

"Hey, mister," the boy said, "you got change for the bus?"

"What?" Henry stared at the hole in the child's sneaker, took in his tweed cap and soiled jacket.

"Be a pal, huh, mister? I ain't got no money to get to school."

A ragamuffin, Henry thought. How do you send a child off to school looking like this? "Where's your mother?" he asked, as the boy's face clouded.

"Shit, never mind." The boy turned away.

"Wait. Come back."

"Yeah?" Sullen, angry, he might spit at me. Henry

dug into his pocket and brought out a handful of change. The boy edged closer, staring at his palm. "How much do you need?"

"Thirty cents."

He landed the child two quarters and watched him put the coins into his pocket. Nodding, the boy turned away.

"Hey!" Henry called. "You're welcome." The child's tough manner made him smile.

At a safe distance now, the boy turned and stopped. Folding one hand onto the bicep of his opposite arm he twisted his wrist at Henry and made a sucking, derisive noise. "Fongoo," he called, then skipped lightly away down the street, sneakers flashing, cutting in and out of the groups of people walking on the avenue.

7:15 A.M.

Detective Tuttle parked his car in front of County Hospital and went in the side entrance, asking at the desk for the young resident he had met yesterday. He was told where to look and, going downstairs, he walked through a maze of corridors until he found the staff cafeteria. The resident was sitting at a table against the rear wall, alone, smoking a cigarette and drinking coffee. He looked up and nodded sourly at the detective as Tuttle sat down.

"You're late," he said, taking a sip of coffee. Tuttle looked at his watch.

"I didn't figure on coming here at all," Tuttle said. "But I thought, you know, maybe on the way in I'd stop by and see him."

The doctor nodded, looking at him levelly over the

rim of his cup. His brown eyes looked watery behind the thick glasses.

"How is he? Can I talk to him?"

"No," the young resident said shortly. He took a deep drag on his cigarette and flicked the ashes onto the floor. "He died about an hour and a half ago."

Tuttle felt the hairs on his neck begin to rise. "Jesus. Just like that?"

"Just like that."

"He didn't look that bad," Tuttle said.

The doctor sipped his coffee. "It happens."

Tuttle rose and picked up his hat. "Well, then, I guess we won't ever know about that map."

"I guess you won't. Was it important?"

"Probably not," Tuttle said, "but who knows?" He turned and walked away.

7:25 A.M.

Two little girls in pigtails came giggling up behind him as he walked. Turning, Henry Taylor looked into beauty, white ribbons holding their hair, faces washed and shining. Holding hands, the two of them, no higher than his waist. It made him smile they were so perfect, so black and beautiful to see. "Good morning, ladies," he said, and they giggled all the more, skipping past him down the block and turning into a store near the corner. He followed slowly, still looking for a place to have breakfast.

He smelled food at the same time he was stopped short by a hand-lettered sign proclaiming "THE YOUNG SIMBAS." Flanking the sign at either side was the symbol of the party, the head of a roaring lion executed in black on a green background, inside a large circle. The windows of the store were plastered over with a profusion of signs and posters, some obviously professionally done. Large photos of Mao and Che and Eldridge Cleaver stared out onto the pavement. "OFF THE PIG!" read one hand-letter square, and below another sign read "FREE CLOTHES FOR OUR PEOPLE!" Curious, Henry peered into the interior of the store.

The place was jammed with children eating. He'd heard of the Young Simbas' breakfast program; obviously this was it. He opened the door and walked cautiously inside.

Long trestle tables ran down either side of the narrow room. Children ranging from three to teenage sat eating breakfast. Cartons of milk and orange juice were set out on the table, along with plates piled high with bread, butter, and jelly. A serving table stood in the rear, presided over by a young girl in dungarees and a black turtleneck sweater. She was spooning out hot oatmeal for the children waiting in a short line to be served. Other girls, similarly dressed, sat at the tables with the children helping some of the little ones to eat.

Posters adorned this room as well as the windows, but they were of a different kind. A large photo of Colley Watson (it must have been four feet square) smiled down from the wall, his leather beret set at a jaunty angle. There were more slogans and more pictures, but none of the children seemed to be paying much mind to the propaganda. They were too busy eating.

Henry stood transfixed. He didn't hear Colley Watson come up behind him until the Simba leader said softly, "Hey now, look what the cat drug in."

Henry just turned back to the children.

"Makes your heart proud, don't it?" Watson said after a moment.

"Yes," Henry said, not looking at him, "it does."

"Maybe we ain't as bad as you figured."

Henry said nothing, thinking that yes, it was not what he had expected. There was more protein than propaganda being ladled out here.

"You in a hurry?" Watson asked. "Care to take a look around? I was just gonna get me some breakfast. Maybe you'd care to join me, Doc?"

Henry nodded and followed Watson toward the rear of the room. It was a slow walk, with Colley pausing to stoop and pat children as he went, saying "Hi there," and "Hey now!" and greeting some children by name. "He eatin' good?" he asked one of the girls seated next to a small boy who, Henry saw, was still wearing diapers under his overalls. She smiled up at Watson, and he walked down to where three teenage boys sat together. "Scoff it up, chillun," he said, "and you'll grow up big and strong." "Like you, Colley," the boy in the middle said, his eyes shining with admiration.

It was a performance, Henry thought, like his television appearances, but damn—it worked.

At the rear of the room, Watson scooped up two soup bowls and held them while the girl ladled out the hot oatmeal. He jerked his head for Henry to follow and led him through a door into a smaller room. A bridge table stood near the wall and beyond this was the kitchen. "Sit down, Doc," Watson said, "I'll hustle us up some coffee." Henry looked around. A large street map covered the wall, with red and green pin flags mounted in various places.

It covered the entire area of Northside, from the bend of the river in the north to Adolphus Park at the bottom. The scale was large, as if to emphasize the vast amount of real estate that Northside encompassed. And somewhere, in that grid laid out so clearly, was Junior with the other children.

Watson appeared with two steaming mugs of coffee. "Nothin' like oatmeal to get you started in the morning," he said.

Following Watson's lead, Henry spooned sugar on the cereal and ate slowly, the two men regarding each other in silence until their bowls were empty. Watson lit a cigarette and sat back, relaxed. "Well now," he grinned, "I figured you were gonna talk to me sometime, but I didn't think you'd walk right into the lion's den."

"Some den," Henry said wryly, "some lion."

Watson laughed, tipping his chair back, and Henry thought, here, at last, the man was being himself. Watson was deceptive. Filled with nervous energy, he seemed to overcompensate by his drawl and slow, studied movements. But his eyes gave him away; they never missed a thing.

"I didn't actually come here to talk to you," Henry said. "I was looking for a place to have breakfast and found you by accident."

"Did you enjoy your breakfast?" Watson countered.

"Fine. Haven't had oatmeal since I was a pup."

"Sticks to your ribs," Watson said, taking a sip of coffee. "And did you like what you saw too?"

"I think so," said Henry. "The kids are eating and I guess that's the main consideration."

"Uh-huh. That's what it's about," Watson agreed.

"How about the stuff on the walls, what'd you think of that?"

"Not much," Henry said, "not very much."

"Yeah, well . . . I didn't figure you'd be too hip on what we believe. But then, it just naturally takes some people longer to see the way, don't it?"

"Maybe so," Henry said. "How many kids are you feeding out there? It looks like a small army."

"I couldn't really tell you. Couple of hundred, probably. It's hard to keep track the way they keep coming and going. The girls open this place at six. We got mothers then, bringing in their kids on the way to work. Then they just keep fallin' in here until sometime after nine o'clock. Some of these younger kids, you know, why they just stay right here all day—until their mothers come back for them in the afternoon. It's a kind of a day-care center we run, not strictly speaking, but close enough. If we could get that mother church to give us room, like we been trying to do, why then we'd have something even better."

"Must cost you a bit, I imagine."

"No, not really. Most of the food is contributed. Supermarket around the corner supplies the milk and butter and oatmeal. And we got a bread company that delivers free."

"How about the kitchen? It must have cost something to set that up."

"A brother," Watson grinned. "In the restaurant supply business. We talked to him a while and damn if he didn't supply us with the whole shebang—on the arm."

"Very convenient," Henry said.

"Yeah, well. We get a lot of things that way, you

know. Just by talking to people and asking them for what we want."

"You never threaten them, I suppose?" Henry said.

Watson waved a hand. "Not any more," he said honestly, "we don't have to. We come around the corner on that a while back. Now we find people more willing to listen, and when they listen a while we end up converting them. Look, there's two kinds of people in Northside. Those that think we're right and want to be with us, and those who are just plain scared of bein' against us."

"And how do you figure me?"

"Just about in the middle, deciding which way to jump. Thinking about how I can be a bad ass if I go head to head with you, and sucking around me some to see if you can't work out a better deal. How's that, Doc, pretty close?"

Henry's smile was enigmatic. "You're working hard at converting me, aren't you? Hiding your claws, so to speak?"

"Yes, I am. I'd be a bad revolutionist if I didn't proselytize." Watson's gaze was open. He snuffed out his cigarette. "Hell, I don't want to fight any fights I don't have to. If there is some kind of accommodation we can come to, fine. I'd like to work it out."

"Those demands of yours . . . they were rather stiff, as I recall."

"Oh, that," Watson said airily. "Forget that. You've always got to ask for a helluva lot more than you want. That's salami tactics. Demand the whole salami, and then take a slice."

"All right," Henry said. He could see now why Roy Hart had been taken with Watson. The man could be very disarming. "Let's talk about what you really want from me then."

"Okay," Watson drawled. He leaned forward in his chair, elbows on the table. "I want you, Doc. And I want the clinic. I want that big public ceremony we talked about yesterday. I want a sign to go up over your door: "THE YOUNG SIMBAS MEDICAL CENTER." And I want it known that you support us and believe in what we're doing. If we had that, why there are four or five other situations that would come into line in twenty-four hours. We'd be on top then, and there wouldn't be a thing in the world could stop us."

"Very neat," Henry said. "You want to win without a fight."

"Damn right. You and I both know that if I put my people on the street I can close you up. Ain't nobody going to cross our picket line, you know that. And if the pigs come in and try to stop us, why most of your patients will be afraid to come in. But who wants all that? Not me. Or you, I think."

"No," said Henry. "I can't say I want that either." Slowly, he unbuttoned his raincoat and took it off. He could see why the supermarket and the bakery were helping the Simbas. The mere threat of violence was enough to make any rational man think twice about opposing Watson. A protracted street war outside the doors of the clinic would not serve the people of Northside. Watson was right about that. And if he did put up a fight against the Simbas, which side would win? Or did it matter? By negating the services of the clinic, Watson would hold all the cards. "I'll have to think about it," Henry said.

Watson was all smiles. "Sure, sure, take your time. There's no rush."

"You want a blank check, Watson, and I don't give that easily," Henry said. "I want to know more about you. What you're doing. You said before that if I endorsed you, you'd really be rolling. Where to?"

Watson's laugh sounded very real. "You want it bent, or straight?"

"Straight. No curve balls."

"Okay. I could give you the ten-dollar version. Our political philosophy and all that crap. But that's just scare tactics. If we ever really did make a revolution in this country we'd be the first ones up against the wall, and we know it. The fucking hard-hats and rednecks would like nothing better than getting out the gun to go shoot black ass. Man, they'd have a ball.

"No, we're too smart for that.

"Power is the answer. Moving up. Getting our hands on the machinery.

"We started with the pigs, started shooting back at them. Well, they made a lot of noise but they stopped beating up on us so much. When's the last time they shot a kid up here? You know, casual-like, just taking a life because they feel like it? Been a long time, ain't it?

"The Mayor downtown, he's shitting a brick trying to be nice to us up here. Forget that nice crap, he's just plain scared. And that's where it's at. Long as we can keep the whites thinking that we really are going to rise up one day and start shooting, then I think we can get somewhere. Nothing else works. But fear works. Terror works. Getting on television and strutting like a wild man, that works. . . ."

Watson broke off abruptly and took a long drink of coffee. He lit another cigarette, looking at Henry, coolly appraising. "The clinic will be put under some kind of community control. I'm on the board, with a couple of other cats. You handle the medicine, I'll handle the politics. We'll get these two other clinics I want too. Either by pressuring the city for more bread, or through contributions from the fat cats. Don't worry about it. When you throw your hand in with us, that'll be it."

Henry dropped his eyes to the table. He felt suddenly tired and old. He was out of touch with this place, with Northside. The suburb was his home now. But the real world no longer ended at the County line. That was the message Watson was delivering. This ghetto and all the other Northsides in the country was where the struggle was taking place. The infection was here, and it was spreading. There could be no bystanders any more, you could not cheer from the sidelines. Everyone was involved, like it or not. And the choices were not easy. Nevertheless, they could not simply be left to groups like the Simbas to decide.

He looked at Colley Watson, no longer listening to his words, but trying to judge the man himself. And the idea that had struck him as early as yesterday returned. If Junior was held in Northside, Watson would know about it. If there was any hope at all of finding his son, he had to have Watson's cooperation. But how far could he trust him?

"Tell me," Henry said, glancing casually at the street map on the wall and back to Watson again, "how many people do you have altogether?"

"That's a military secret," Watson said blandly. "A

hundred, more or less. That's hard-core. Then there's about fifteen hundred kids we can call on anytime. And in a pinch there are several thousand more who would line up when we gave the word. And if push came to shove, a showdown say, maybe forty or fifty percent of Northside would be on our side. And about a hundred percent of the kids under twenty."

"I see," Henry said. It looked as if he would have to take the chance. He needed Watson's help, and if getting it meant committing the clinic, well, he would face that later on. "There's something I'd like to ask you," he began, but Watson held up his hand.

"First let me ask you something, Doctor," Watson said, leaning forward. "What's so important about that limousine? Why have you been down here all night lookin' for it?"

PART VI

Death

FRIDAY

8:25 A.M.

Greer led the small procession up the stairs to the third floor. Behind him, Joyboy carried the plate of sandwiches and Jimmy toted two Pepsi bottles filled with water, the Pepsi having been exhausted by the evening meal. At the door, Greer stopped. "Let's just be careful now," he said. "That's one thing wrong with locking the door. You never know what could be waiting for you on the other side."

He told Joyboy to put the plate on the floor and stand ready with the revolver while he opened up. If he was expecting a surprise, Greer did not get it. His prisoners sat well away from the door, looking, if anything, even more docile than they had the day before. Their clothing was rumpled and their faces looked tired. "Good morning, folks, breakfast is served. Sorry we don't have no grits or bacon, but the kitchen has plumb run out."

Jimmy set the water and sandwiches on the floor inside the door while he watched. There was no rebellion in those faces, he thought. He could leave them here under lock and key with a clear mind. "Eat hearty," he said as he closed the door again. "Won't be much longer now."

Ben Carter heard the lock snap closed in the hasp and the sound of footsteps retreating down the stairs. The children sat in a tight little circle about him, no one making a move toward the food. They looked pathetic. Ralph Flood's cheek was angry and swollen, and above it his eye had closed to a thin slit. Crusted blood stained his neat sweater and half his shirt collar. Beside him his twin sat glum and disconsolate. No jokes passed between the brothers this morning, or daring plans for escape.

"We might as well eat," Mike Schwartz said. He and Junior brought the breakfast from the door and set it down inside the circle. Each child took a sandwich from the plate and passed the water bottles around. They began to eat without appetite, mechanically chewing and swallowing. Behind them, unwatched, the TV blared as *Marine Boy* moved through his underwater world.

"Anybody know any good jokes?" Carter asked, and when no one spoke he chided them. "Come on kids, cheer up. Things got to get better because they can't get much worse."

"Wanna bet?" Kathy said.

8:55 A.M.

Colley Watson's face was grim. When Henry had finished he banged a fist on the table. "Stupid!" he spat. "Maniacs!" His hands shook as he lighted another cigarette.

"So you see," said Henry, "when my search drew a blank I turned up here. I guess, subconsciously, I'd been thinking about it all along."

"You know who's gonna be blamed for this, don't you?" Watson said. He speared his own chest with a finger. "Anybody so much as farts in Northside, the pigs come knocking at my door. And now with this crazy kidnaping . . . Man, they're really gonna be after me. You know something, Doc? You come to the right place. I got to help you find those crazy sonsabitches *just to prove I had nothing to do with it!*"

Henry smiled. "Thanks, Colley." He reached across the table and shook Watson's outstretched hand. "Now I owe you one," he said.

"Forget it, Doc. The way I figure it, finding your son is probably gonna save my hide. If they're in Northside, we'll track 'em down. And about the clinic, we'll see. You and me may keep bumping heads, but in the end, I want you with me."

"Maybe we'll both have to give a little," Henry said.

Watson's smile was wide. "Maybe." He stood up and moved to the desk. "Meanwhile, let's get moving, huh?" Picking up the telephone, he made a series of calls, using half jive talk and half foreign phrases, punctuating his speech with exclamations like "Zonk!" and "Blip!" At one point, noticing Henry's curious expression, he explained: "Northside Swahili, Doc. Just in case J. Edgar is listening, which he usually is." He made four more telephone calls, then turned back to the table. "Put your coat on," he said, "we're leaving."

Henry followed Watson through the front room and out onto the street. They walked north for two blocks, then crossed Lenard Avenue and headed for the river.

Fifteen minutes later, they turned down a street of three-story brownstones. The block looked different from the others they had passed through. There was no garbage on the street, no abandoned cars. Watson said there weren't the usual number of prostitutes, pimps, and dope pushers either. The Simbas moved in last year and the word had gone out: this street must remain clean and free of crime. Those who transgressed would answer to the Simbas. "All I need is to have a cat house or a pusher living next door," Watson said. "Man, they'd never stop busting us. So we keep it clean." A sardonic look crossed his face. "Makes you think, don't it? Why I could round up every pusher, numbers writer, and pimp in the Northside. But what good would it do? You think the pigs would lock 'em up? Hell, no! They're on the take, same as everyone."

In the middle of the block Watson stopped and led Henry up to a brownstone door. Inside, a Simba in black turtleneck shirt, black trousers, and beret recognized Watson and opened the inner door. They went through and passed into a large apartment. The first room, facing the street, had large metal shutters covering the windows. The next room appeared to be a work area. Four metal desks and chairs were against the walls and, like the storefront, the walls were covered with posters. Beyond this was a living room where ten Simbas were waiting, sitting in straightback chairs. The group was very young, some boys not out of their teens, and they were all dressed like the guard outside. Most of them had mustaches and beards, like Watson, and a group of three, clustered on the near wall, stared balefully at Henry through reflecting sunglasses. A gun rack covering one of the long walls from floor to ceiling was filled with rifles and shotguns.

Watson ordered both connecting doors closed and motioned Henry to a chair. Then he addressed the waiting group (in his fire-and-ice television voice, Henry noted), explaining who Henry was and the circumstances of their meeting. The script was the one Henry had approved. Watson only said that they were to search for a car and for his son. The word "kidnapping" was not mentioned, although the message was implicit. If the boy or the car was in Northside, Watson was to be notified at once. The Simbas were not to take action of any kind, this was to be purely an intelligence operation. Some of the men listening asked questions and both the Simba leader and Henry answered. Later, Watson took out a city map and assigned each man a specific territory. Within an hour the meeting broke up. The men were on their way.

When they had gone, Watson turned to Henry. "End of phase one," he said. "Each one of those guys is a field marshal. They've got captains and lieutenants under them. Inside two hours we'll have a hundred Simbas on the street. By early afternoon we'll have covered every front stoop and bar in Northside." Noting Henry's look of concern, Watson added, "Don't worry, man. The only place them mothers could hide from us would be in the station house. And I don't think they'd exactly be to home down there."

10:15 A.M.

"Don't worry, man," Greer was saying, "by tonight it's gonna be all over and we'll be on our way. I got a good feeling."

Joyboy took another sip of coffee, his face impassive. "I ain't worried. I was just thinking about Sparrow."

"Yeah, Sparrow," Greer said sourly. "Look like he turned out to be a chicken. Well, fuck him. Wherever he run off we're probably safer without him. We got enough to think about without running scared."

"How about picking up the money?" Joyboy asked.

Greer smiled. "That's taped. No problem. It's after that, I'm still figuring."

Joyboy looked at Greer and shifted his eyes to the ceiling.

"Right." Greer glanced to see that Jimmy and Loretta were out of earshot, then leaned across the table. "We'll do them together, you and me, soon's I get back here with the bread. We'll send Jimmy and Loretta outside to keep watch. I wouldn't want them to see anyway."

"It's gonna be a goddamn shooting gallery," Joyboy said, keeping his voice down.

He saw Greer nod briefly, and lower his eyes. Hell, thought Joyboy, it's getting to Greer. Now that it's down to knocking them off, he don't like it.

"There's got to be another way," Greer said. "Easier than just gunning them down."

"Some trick, huh?" Joyboy said. His smile was inside, private and all for himself. Let Greer worry about the details. He was the great genius who was going to lead everyone out of the wilderness. Except that when he came back with the money he'd find out who was really the smart one. When that .38 was pointed at Greer's belly, it would take more than a fast brain, Joyboy thought, to keep him from walking out with a suitcase full of cash.

10:55 A.M.

"It's Jim Abernathy," Pauline DeBusschere said, and Carew took the call feeling the knot in his stomach beginning to unwind.

"It's confirmed, Charlie," said Abernathy. "The shipment should be unloaded and in our vault by one o'clock."

"Fine, Jim, that's wonderful news."

"You can pick up the money any time after that. I can give it to you in a Federal Reserve sack, or you can bring a suitcase, whichever you prefer."

"All taken care of, Jim," Carew said, and he thanked the banker once again before hanging up. The suitcase, purchased by the headmaster himself this morning after he had left the bank, stood behind his desk. It was a cheap affair, more cardboard than cloth, but large and strong enough to serve its purpose.

Carew sighed with relief. His insistence on handling the affair without the police had been vindicated. The money was confirmed. This afternoon he would have it in his hands; by this evening, in all likelihood, it would be turned over to the criminals, and the children would be safely back.

Then, and only then, would he inform the police. An event of this magnitude could never be kept completely quiet—and he knew what a sensational story this would make in the press—but at least the Sloane School would be shown in its proper light—as guardian and protector of its own who had skillfully handled a very difficult situation. There would be no cheap-jack journalism, either. No interviews with the press, no reporters and television crews swarming over the grounds, asking, "How did you feel, Dr. Carew, when you spoke to the kidnaper?" God, how incredibly stupid those reporters could be. As if anyone wanted to share such personal information so that the average viewer could have a cheap thrill.

He turned back to his desk and began to work, once again, on the budget for the following year. In the back of his mind, as he was adding the column of figures on the sheet before him, he realized he was actually looking forward to the next telephone conversation with the kidnapers.

11:15 A.M.

Hamp Norris pushed the cart down the alley and left it outside his door. He was tired and he was hungry, and a long morning's work had produced very little in the way of salable merchandise. He walked through the scraggly garden in the rear of the house and entered the cellar, passing through the boiler room and storage area to the small room he called home.

Before opening the door he paused and, turning around, found the broom he had left leaning against the wall. Cautiously, broom in hand, he thrust a hand inside the doorway and reached for the light switch. The rat was on top of the table, bold as brass. Hamp felt nauseated. He and the rat had been playing games like this for more than a week now. The little bastard acted as if he owned the place, coming and going as he pleased, brushing against Hamp's legs in the night as he slept on the cot against the wall.

Hamp stamped his foot hard on the floor and the rat jumped down off the table and ran under the sink. His heart sinking, Hamp stalked slowly inside the room and edged toward the sink, leaving plenty of room for the rat to run by him and out of the door. He extended the broom toward the leg of the sink and stamped his foot again, jumping back in terror as the rat came out of hiding. By the time he could swing the broom again the rat had scuttled outside and disappeared. Hamp walked to the door and slammed it, breathing hard.

Wearily, he went to the shelf and took down the can of dog food. A squad of fat brown roaches scattered as he opened the cabinet to secure a small enameled pot. He opened the beef chunks and dropped the lid into the garbage pail. With a hand towel he wiped the pot out carefully before putting the stew to heat on the stove. In another pot he ran some water for tea and put this on the stove beside the stew.

When it had heated he sugared the tea and sat down at the table to eat. He put a few chili flakes into the dog food and added salt. The meat was tough, but the flavor was good. Finishing the last drops of his tea, he made another half cup with the remains of the water and the old tea bag. The day stretched endlessly in front of him. How foolish he had been yesterday. A few dollars in his pocket and he had gone wild. Too much wine and nothing to eat. No wonder he felt pumped out.

Yawning, he took the cup to the sink and washed it, along with the stew pot and plate. The cot, rumpled as it was, looked inviting. Maybe he would nap for a while before going out again.

11:45 A.M.

Every time the telephone rang, it was like a fingernail scratching against a blackboard.

Henry Taylor found himself sweating, although it was far from warm in the Simbas' command post. His raincoat was folded neatly over a chair and he had taken off his jacket. Even his tie had inched down from his open shirt collar in these two maddeningly slow-moving hours.

Colley Watson worked at a desk in the center room, commanding the assault on Northside like a five-star general. The headquarters was alive with Simbas. Three young girls manned the other desks and a swarm of young boys milled about the room. Watson worked from a city map, crossing off streets as reports came in from the outside. From Adolphus Park in the South to the northern city line Simbas were on the move, but so far they had found no trace either of the car or of Junior.

The searching had started at the perimeters of the ghetto and were slowly converging on Northside's central business district. They would cover that important area inch by inch. Above all, Watson counseled patience. You had to track down every lead, run down every rumor, no matter how off target they might appear to be.

Despite all the activity, Henry worried on. He jumped at every call, and met each messenger at the door, reading the notes they carried before passing them on to Watson.

Some hours ago he had spoken to Roy Hart on the

telephone, explaining his absence from the clinic and describing the aid he had enlisted from the Simbas. He had also kept in close touch with Mildred. The Schwartzes had left for home. Not having slept all night, Norman wanted to lie down in his own bed for a few hours before going to meet Carew. Mildred thought that now she too might sleep, if Henry promised to call her should the Simbas turn up a lead. Her voice was weary and resigned. Trying to sound hopeful, Henry promised not to take any needless risks and to keep her posted.

As he stood looking over Watson's shoulder, the telephone rang again. Watson picked it up, listened intently, and turned to meet Henry's gaze. The doctor's heart began to pound as Watson scribbled a note on the scratch pad in front of him. It was an address on Fulton Street, just north of Adolphus Park.

Watson hung up and ripped the note from the pad. "That was Luke Jackson," he said. "There's a guy having lunch in the Haitian Bakery who says he knows something about a Cadillac limousine." He handed the note to Henry. "Maybe you ought to check it out, Doc."

"How about you?"

"I'd better stay here and keep the boys moving," Watson said. "But call me if it's for real."

In no time at all, Henry had his jacket and raincoat on and was out the door. He walked quickly to the corner and hailed a southbound taxi, only to have the driver point to the off-duty sign and speed off. He walked two more blocks and was refused by another off-duty taxi before a gypsy cab pulled to the curb. In ten minutes he was at the Fulton Street address.

The neighborhood was a strange mixture of shoddy

brownstones, small retail stores and industrial establishments. At this noon hour the street was crowded with men in work clothes who stood on the sidewalk or sat on doorsteps, eating huge sandwiches and drinking cans of beer wrapped in brown paper bags. As Henry pushed his way to the Haitian Bakery, he saw that it was nothing more than a small bakeshop that had taken to making sandwiches as a profitable sideline. Before he could make his way inside, a slim light-skinned youth wearing a Simba beret tapped Henry on the shoulder. "Dr. Taylor?"

"Luke Jackson?"

"Let's get out of here," the young man said. "The guy had to get back to work but it's just down the street."

Henry followed Jackson to a low cinderblock building. A sign over the door stated "FOAMRIGHT FURNITURE," and once inside they walked through aisles stacked with sleek foam-rubber couches and chairs in various stages of assembly. A smell of varnish hung in the air. "He's out back," Jackson said, leading the way to a shaded rear courtyard. A large pockmarked man in bib overalls was stenciling numbers on a packing case. "That's him, Cleavon Walker. And Doc"—Jackson held up a hand, rubbing his thumb across his fingers—"he's lookin' for a little something, you know?"

Jackson stayed by the door as Henry walked across the yard and introduced himself. The man looked at him briefly, then went back to stenciling. "My friend tells me you know something about a Cadillac limousine that was stolen yesterday morning."

Walker pursed his lips. "Could be." He lifted the stencil from the case and regarded his work with a critical eye.

"It's a black Fleetwood limousine with County plates."

"Watch out there," Walker mumbled. He slapped the stencil on the packing case directly behind Henry and drew a paint brush across it.

"It's worth ten dollars," Henry said.

"If it's worth anything, it's worth twenty." Walker's face was closed and hard.

"All right."

"You ain't the law now, are you?"

Henry forced a smile. "No."

"How do I know you ain't the law?"

As Henry started to answer, Jackson called out, "He's with me, man."

Walker thought this over for a moment, then nodded. "Twenty," he said. Henry counted the bills into Walker's hand. Walker stuffed them quickly into a pocket. "Remember," he said, "I didn't tell you nothing." He looked over his shoulder nervously. "They's a garage down the street, on the next block. Two fellas run it, repaintin' mostly. They's been known to do some fast work on cars that are hot. This morning, on my way here, I seen them working on a big black Caddy, resprayin' it a different color."

It could be, Henry thought, his pulse quickening. As he turned to go Walker shouted, "I never seen you before, remember?"

Henry walked down Fulton Street so fast that Jackson had to jog to keep up. He crossed the intersection and saw the garage a few doors down the block. Two gas pumps stood on an island on the sidewalk. Behind them loomed the open door.

As he walked past, Henry found his hand gripping

his small automatic. There it was, a big dark Cadillac covered with masking tape.

"I'm going in," he said to Jackson. "Stay behind me." Cautiously, he walked inside the garage and approached the car. They had taken off the license plates but the color had originally been black. He walked closer. "What you want?" a voice called, but Henry did not reply. Because he could see, scripted in metal letters on the rear fender, the words *El Dorado*, not *Fleetwood.* It was a Cadillac, all right, but the wrong Cadillac. And it wasn't a limousine. It was only a very expensive car.

12:50 P.M.

"It wasn't necessary, you know," Carew said as Carmine turned the limousine onto Claremont Avenue, not far from the County Bank. "I could have managed this quite handily by myself."

Norman Schwartz looked at the older man sitting across from him on the wide rear seat. "Of course," he said, "but I don't think I can take another day like yesterday. At least this way I feel I'm doing something." He looked out the window at the litter of run-down stores and buildings. "It's hard to just sit by and wait."

Both men looked up as Carmine swung into the parking area behind the bank and parked in a spot marked "Reserved: Officers Only." He grinned over his shoulder at the passengers as he turned off the ignition. "I think it's okay to park here today, don't you?"

Carew took the empty suitcase from the car and they went inside. Jim Abernathy was waiting at the entrance to the vault.

Inside the massive steel grille, three girls were working at a large desk lined with green currency. "So that's what six hundred grand looks like," Carmine said with a low whistle.

The money formed a platform of green, as thick as a mattress, on the long desktop. Neat packets of bills, one hundred to a stack, were bound with blue bands stamped Federal Reserve. Two of the girls looked up as Carmine exclaimed, then went back to their work, riffling through packets of bills and laboriously writing numbers down on yellow pads.

"We usually break the bundles in half and reband them with our own labels," Abernathy explained. "But today, I thought we might leave them intact."

Carew nodded. "What are they doing?" he asked.

Abernathy looked shrewdly at the headmaster. "We're taking down every serial number. We've got the new money registered already—it came on the load sheet. But about half of it is old, and that's what the girls are recording."

"I see," Carew said. "Will it take long?"

"About an hour, I would say. I've got three more girls coming down when they get back from lunch."

Carew glanced at his watch and thought of the telephone call that might be awaiting him back at Sloane. "Must we do this?"

Abernathy sighed and drew the headmaster aside. "Charlie, I've broken about every law in the book for you. If I don't protect myself now—well, I just might be working up at school after this, sweeping out the halls. It won't be finished when you hand over the money, you know. The FBI and the police will be all over us. They'll want to know what we did, and how, and why we didn't call them at once. Giving them the serial numbers is the least we can do to help catch those people afterwards."

Norman Schwartz edged into the conversation. "Is there anything I can do to help?"

Jim Abernathy pointed at the wide expanse of green. "I've got extra pads and pencils," he said.

Within a minute, even the headmaster was sitting at a large desk, recording the serial numbers of currency that would pay for seven lives.

1:25 P.M.

Mark Lockhart, called Chico, was hot and thirsty and getting tired. He was also disgusted, for just when he had finished his assignment near the river Colley sent a note sending him to a new area. Damn, his feet would be sore tonight. And for what? Tracking down a mysterious black Caddy that probably never was within ten miles of Northside anyway. Stupid.

But Chico, like the other Simbas, had long ago learned to do what he was told. They were together now, the Simbas and the people of Northside. The tide was beginning to turn. A year ago, when the other blacks saw a beret, they looked the other way, because the Simbas usually spelled trouble. But not now. Their success at the hospital, and with the breakfast program, had earned them respect. The people were no longer afraid of the Simbas. In fact, they admired their guts.

Chico questioned the two men lounging under a lamppost at the corner and moved down Rogers Avenue. Five more blocks and he'd have to call in again. And damn, they'd probably give him still another area.

Chico decided he needed a rest and when he saw the open door of the Paradise Club, he walked inside. The bar was cooler than the street, and ten minutes on a stool sipping a Bud wasn't going to hurt anyone. Aretha was shouting a funky blues behind him as he sat down, and the beer was cold. He poured down the middle of the glass and took a long slug.

"Here's to the Simbas," a voice said beside him, and Chico looked over his shoulder. A neatly dressed man in a gray fedora grinned at him from over a shot glass of scotch. "All you guys out on the street today," the man said. "What's up?"

"Looking for something," Chico said briefly.

"I already figured that."

Chico turned on the stool and downed the rest of his beer. "Maybe you seen it," he said. "A big black mother Cadillac. Disappeared down here yesterday morning."

Chico was walking toward the door when the man called out. "A black Cadillac you say, huh? Wait a minute."

Chico walked back. The man in the gray fedora pushed his hat back from his eyes with a finger. "Seems to me I heard somethin' about a Caddy yesterday," he said. "Now just lemme think."

"Take your time, man," Chico said. He sat down on the stool and signaled for another Bud.

1:45 P.M.

Greer vaulted the low fence and came through the back door at full speed. He took the stairs two at a time and announced his arrival with a fanfare, cupping his lips with a fist. The others looked at him with astonishment.

"They are down at the bank, getting the money! Wahoo!" He seized the smiling Loretta and danced a few steps around the table.

Jimmy danced too, shaking his fist. Only Joyboy, who watched from his seat at the table, was not smiling.

"Gimme some water," Greer hooted as he sat down. "My golden throat is gettin' dry. Oh, man, we are so close now, babe, so close."

"Beautiful, baby," Loretta said, rubbing the back of his neck.

"We gonna be rich, Greer?" asked Jimmy.

"Only temporary, fella," Greer chuckled. "That money's got to stretch a long ways." Joyboy's face was a blank, and Greer couldn't resist reaching across the table and punching him playfully on the arm. "Cheer up, man. Payday's almost here."

Joyboy's hooded eyes flickered. "Ain't there yet," he said.

"They're coughin' it up," said Greer. "Don't you see?"

"I ain't counted it yet."

Oh, baby chick, Greer thought, his mind suddenly on Sparrow, I could sure use you now. He met Joyboy's empty eyes and felt a chill. It was like falling down after an up. Reality always came back and caught you flatfooted. "In about an hour or so, I'll be leaving," he said. "When I get back, I'll let you do the counting."

2:20 P.M.

Business was quiet now, but it would pick up later. It was Friday, payday, and before the night was over the Red Apple would be jammed with people drinking and talking and dancing the blues away. There would probably be a fight, too, Floogie Williams was thinking. A Friday night wasn't complete without a hassle. He put down the glass he was polishing and looked underneath the polished mahogany counter for the sawed-off baseball bat. The old persuader was right where it ought to be.

He gave the hooker another whiskey sour and was lighting a cigarette when the two men came in. The guy with the beard and beret he recognized immediately. But what would Colley Watson want with him?

2:25 P.M.

"I was so afraid he'd be angry because you weren't here," Pauline said when Carew returned.

"And he definitely said he'd be calling back?" Carew asked.

"Oh, yes. Later, he said."

"And the children?"

"In good shape, I think he said. I remembered to ask about them, but really, I was so nervous I'm afraid I may not have written it all down exactly."

Carew leaned back in his chair, the suitcase right behind him near the window. "I'm sure you did as well as you could," he said. "It couldn't be helped. I had to get the money."

Carmine Mancuso cracked his knuckles loudly. "You did swell, Pauline. Stop worrying." When she left the room he turned to Norman and asked, "What d'you think?"

Before Schwartz could answer, Carew turned in his chair. "The ball is in their court now, Mr. Mancuso," he said. "What happens now is—we wait."

2:30 P.M.

"When did all this happen?" asked Floogie Williams.

"Yesterday sometime," said Henry Taylor. "In the afternoon."

"And this guy says I told him something about a Cadillac?"

"Right. A black Cadillac limousine, with County plates."

"Yeah, well . . . I don't remember nothing like that."

"Come on, man," said Colley Watson. "It was only yesterday."

Williams' face looked pained. "Hell, you think I remember everybody comes in here and every little thing they say? Shit." The bartender began wiping the counter with a wet rag. "What he look like, this guy?" he demanded.

Henry looked at Watson. Was this another false alarm? "Average height," said the doctor, "wearing a dark suit, blue shirt, yellow tie. And a pearl-gray fedora."

Williams straightened up, his eyes wide. "Oh, *him,*" he said. "He drinks scotch, right?"

"How the hell do I know what he drinks?"

"Well, if it's the guy I'm thinking of, he drinks scotch," Floogie said. "Lemme see now . . ." He walked a few paces down the bar. "He was here yesterday afternoon, wearing that pearl-gray fedora—never seen him without that hat—and . . . and . . . yeah! The old fella was sitting right where you are, by the taps."

"What old fella?" Henry asked quietly.

"Hold on, I'm trying to remember. It was the old

guy who told me about the car and I was telling it to the guy drinking scotch." Smiling now, Floogie walked the few steps back to Henry and Watson. "The old geezer was drinking wine. He always drinks wine."

"That's fine," Henry began, "but—"

"And he was laying his head on the bar, see. Like this." Floogie leaned over and put his head down on the dark wooden counter, right in front of Henry.

"I see." Henry ground his teeth silently. "About the car, now, what did he say?"

Floogie's head popped up. "Who?"

"The old man."

"Oh. Yeah, well, he said he was going crazy because he seen a big black Cadillac coming down this street. And then it just disappeared."

"Disappeared?"

"Right. One minute it was there and the next minute it was gone." Floogie's voice was soft and confiding. "But you know, the old guy's a wino. Can't take no stock of what he says."

"What do you think?" Watson asked Henry.

"I think it's probably nothing, but it's the only lead we've got." He turned back to Williams. "What's his name?"

"The guy in the fedora?"

"No," Henry said patiently, "the old man. Where does he live?"

"Don't know his name. He's a junkman. Pushes a cart, you know? He don't come in every day, only when he has a few bucks. Drinks burgundy, mostly, sometimes port." He paused, then added, "Sometimes he goes in that pawnshop across the street. Maybe they know where he lives."

"Thanks again," Henry called. "You've been a big help."

"Keep the change," said Floogie Williams.

2:35 P.M.

"I got good news for you," Greer told the children when Joyboy opened the door. They were grouped around Carter, their faces alert. "In a little while we're gonna get the money. By tonight you should be home."

"Terrific," Carter said flatly.

"The reason I'm telling you is I don't want no funny business like we had yesterday. You behave now, 'cause it's gonna be over real soon. Okay?"

"When I get home I'll believe you," Kathy said defiantly.

"Behave yourselves," said Greer again and left the room.

"Lock 'em in," he told Joyboy and when the lock snapped they shook hands. "I'm off to run Carew's ass all over Northside," Greer said. He started to give Joyboy the key, then changed his mind and pocketed it. There was no reason for Joyboy to open that door while he was gone. "See you later," he said, and went down the stairs.

Joyboy stood in the hallway for a moment and then followed him.

Carter's throat was dry and his heart was beating very fast. What luck, he thought, what incredible luck. He looked at his watch, for he had a good idea of when the critical moment would come. He leaned forward and ruffled Ralph Flood's shock of red hair. "Okay, kids," he began, "you'd better listen to me now. We have a lot of work to do and we must get started right away."

2:40 P.M.

The pawnshop door tinkled behind them as Watson and Dr. Taylor stepped back onto the pavement of Lenard Avenue. The sun had crested and now the shadows were beginning to lengthen. "Hamp Norris," Watson said, "he's our man."

"But where he lives, nobody knows." Henry sighed. He felt drained and weak. And if they caught up with the old man, he thought, what then?

"I'll have to send the guys out again," Watson said. "With the old geezer pushing a cart he shouldn't be too hard to find."

"No. I suppose not." Henry's voice was flat and discouraged, and Watson looked at him queerly.

"Hey, man, don't be so down. We're only getting started. Come on, let's get back to headquarters."

Henry hesitated. "You run along," he said finally, "I'll meet you there in a few minutes. I'm going to stop by the clinic." As Watson stared at him, Henry added: "I'm prescribing an amphetamine for myself before I fall flat on my face."

Watson grinned. "Speed kills, Doc," he said and started down the avenue.

3:15 P.M.

Traffic buzzed by on the parkway, heading north, as Greer dialed the phone in the parking area. The routine was familiar by now, and he waited while the secretary called Carew, shielding his eyes from the sun, which was topping the trees across the road. "You got it?" he asked quickly when he heard Carew's voice.

"Good. Now here's what you do. Get into your station wagon and head toward the city on the parkway. Alone. You got that?"

"Yes."

"If you got pigs or the FBI on your tail, I'm gonna know because we are watching you. So don't try to fool me. Okay. Now just after the city line as you come down the parkway there's a pull-off—a parking area. Drive in and get out of your car and go to the telephone."

"What about the children?" began Carew, but Greer cut him off.

"Later," he said. "Get moving right now. And when the phone rings in the parking area, it's for you." Before the headmaster could say more, Greer had put the phone down.

He walked quickly to the Volkswagen and pulled back into the traffic. The next exit came up fast and Greer swung off. At the first crossing he looped over the parkway and headed south again on the service road. Just north of the twin parking areas, a pedestrian footbridge spanned the parkway. He left the Volkswagen on a cross street and walked onto the bridge, stopping in the center of the span. From here he had an excellent view of the rest area and the telephone booth. When Carew arrived, he would be waiting. If Carew had got himself an escort, he would know.

3:20 P.M.

They might have been wishing him Godspeed before a long journey. Carew had just put the suitcase onto the front seat of the station wagon. Mancuso, his swarthy face grave, was shaking his hand. Norman Schwartz did the same, anxiously searching Carew's face.

"Don't worry," the older man said. His smile, forced though it was, betrayed no hint of his private doubts. "I'll just have a pleasant ride down the parkway, hand over the money, and find out where we can pick up the children."

Sure, thought Carmine, just like that. I hope to hell it's that easy. "Take care," he said, as Carew eased himself into the driver's seat. The headmaster turned the ignition key and the long green station wagon sparked to life. The car slid away across the lot and turned onto the drive that wound to the front gate. Slow and easy, Carew said to himself, but the muscles in his thighs and the pit of his stomach were tense and tight, and his mouth felt suddenly dry.

The policeman on duty held traffic for him and he swung left across School Avenue and began heading for the parkway. As he drove his hand strayed to the cheap brown suitcase. The amount of money had lost its meaning. The enormous sum was merely a chip in the game, and he realized how long ago yesterday had been.

Traffic heading toward the city was light now and he had no trouble moving into the right-hand lane. He passed the city line and slowed to the legal limit, watching carefully for the sign that marked the rest area. He spotted it just as he passed under a pedestrian overpass and he rolled off the parkway. The telephones were to the left. Two cars were parked near the split-rail fence that marked the lay-by's rear border. A youth was working on one of the cars, half buried inside its open hood. A man and a woman sat smoking cigarettes in the other. Satisfied, Carew walked to the phone and waited for the call.

Greer crossed the footbridge and checked the traffic. No tie-ups or police were visible. No cars that might have shadowed Carew were parked on the grassy shoulder. So far, so good. But he still intended to play it safe. He waited another three minutes, left the bridge, and walked across the service road. The gas station at the next corner south had an outdoor booth. He took the card from his pocket and dialed.

Although he had been waiting for it, Carew was startled when the telephone rang behind him. He picked it up before it could ring a second time. "Carew," said Greer, "you're doin' fine. Don't look around and just keep listening. There are three men tailing you but you won't know who they are. I want you to keep driving down the parkway and get off at the first Northside exit. You know it?"

"Chelsea Avenue?"

"Right. The place you're heading for is the White Hut." He gave the headmaster explicit directions and asked Carew to repeat them. "Fine," he said. "You pull in there and park. Take the suitcase and walk to the phone booths outside. Sit down in the middle booth and wait. Don't make no phone calls, hear? Don't touch the phone, 'cause we'll be watching. Just wait. You got it?"

"The middle phone booth at the White Hut," Carew repeated. "Yes, I understand. But what about the children?"

"I'll tell you later. Now I want you to hold that receiver off the hook for five minutes. Then you leave."

Greer left the booth and came back up the service road, being careful not to run. From the bridge he could see Carew leaning against the corner of the call-box with his head down and the telephone in his hand. Greer waited as the moments ticked by, looking away from time to time to see if others might be watching too. But it looked like he was home free. Carew was playing it straight.

4:10 P.M.

There were forty-eight shelves in all and Carter had started first with the ones on top. Now almost all of them were down, and Mike, Junior, and the Flood boys were stacking them against the wall.

Kathy stood with her ear to the door, listening for footsteps. To help cover the noise of transporting the shelves, Heidi Porter had turned up the volume of the television set, and cartoons and commercials blared out in a steady roar.

As he worked Carter was still planning. The shelves had to be stacked against the door. He had at first thought that he would lay them flat one upon the other. But he realized that with forty-eight shelves, each one inch thick, the barricade would only be four feet high. It wouldn't protect the children if they decided to shoot through the door.

By the time he had taken the last shelf down, Carter knew what he was going to do. He carried the first two shelves to the wall near the door and waited while

Mike and Junior brought over a third. Motioning Kathy to stand away, he placed these three shelves on end against the door, being careful not to make any noise. It was perfect! Standing on end, the shelves just covered the top of the door. And butted edge to edge, they projected an inch or so on either side of the entrance. With the shelves arranged this way, he saw with relief, there would be a barricade sixteen inches thick between the children and the men outside. He was pretty sure no bullet could pass through that.

When all the boards were in place, he turned to the boys and said, "Okay, now for the mattresses."

"What about the mattresses?" Mike Schwartz asked.

"We pile the mattresses against the shelves so they can't push open the door."

It took no more than fifteen minutes to get them into place. Five mattresses were piled against each other, leaning against the shelves that blocked the door. The other two were placed at the sides, blocking the door on a diagonal. It was a hell of a barricade, Carter thought.

But still, if the gang kept at it, in the end they would get through. And once they entered, his only chance would be to disarm them. After a minute's thought, Ben walked to the nearest shelving frame and wrestled with a support until it tore free. Now he had a two-by-four in his hands, about ten feet long. He angled it against the wall near the floor and smashed down with his foot, breaking the long beam into two pieces. He picked up the shorter piece and examined it. Not a hell of a weapon, Carter thought, but better than none at all. Hopefully it could be used to buy time while some of the children got away.

He went back to the barricade and showed the children how to position themselves when the time came. He and Kathy would lean shoulder to shoulder against the mattress. Mike and Junior would stand behind them, pushing, and the Flood boys would back them up. Heidi Porter would kneel and just try to make herself the smallest possible target.

Carter surveyed this line-up and winked at Kathy. They had a thin chance to survive now, but only if the barricade held, and the gang was afraid to wait around until they could break in.

He leaned his back against the mattress and closed his eyes. He felt very tired and his head ached. Deep in his belly a nerve twitched. Come on, Sergeant, he told himself, hang in there. You have done all you could.

He opened his eyes and looked at the children waiting in a circle at his feet.

4:35 P.M.

"The hell of it is," Roy Hart was saying to Henry as he paced the Simba headquarters, "I've probably seen that old junkman myself—"

"I know," groaned Henry, "but where?"

"Simmer down," said Colley Watson from the command desk. "All my boys are out looking. Hell, they should have found Norris already. An old gray-haired coot, raggedy clothes, pushing a cart. Man, that's easy."

"Then what's taking so long?"

"Take it easy, Henry," said Roy. "It's going to be all right."

"All right? For two days now, that's all I've been hearing. 'It's going to be all right.' Damn it, Roy—if I thought it was going to be all right I'd be home now, holding Mil's hand, waiting by the telephone. But it's not going to be all right. Not unless we find Junior very soon."

Henry took out his pipe and tobacco. But the mere effort of pinching a fingerful of tobacco into the bowl was too difficult and he laid it aside. "I just talked to her. Carew left the school with the money an hour ago. For all I know it's already in their hands. And once they get that money . . ."

His words trailed off, the look of pain on his face was more than Roy Hart could bear.

"Colley?" The girl at the desk in the corner held the telephone away from her ear. "It's for you."

Watson walked swiftly to her and took the phone. His eyes were very large and strangely bright. "Listen to me, hear?" he said very clearly into the phone. "You hold that old geezer by the scruff of the neck until we get there, understand? Don't let go. We'll be right there." He put the telephone down and headed for the door. "They got him across town," he said. "Let's get moving."

4:45 P.M.

Carew spotted the White Hut all the way down Van Sicklen Street. He pulled up onto the wide parking slot and turned off the engine.

There were no white faces anywhere, and he was suddenly afraid. That implacable voice on the telephone. All the way down the parkway it had been reverberating in his head. Yesterday he had been able to make the kidnaper back down, at least to the extent of letting him speak to one child. But today Carew felt there would be no concessions.

There were the telephone booths, across the parking lot. In front of the white building that looked like a frozen castle. Inside, he could see a row of black faces staring out of the window. Two men in work clothes were walking toward him, one carrying a cardboard tray of food and drinks. They moved past the hood of his car and into the cab of a small pickup truck parked two spaces away.

Northside . . . there were no white faces anywhere. . . .

He got out of the station wagon and pulled the suitcase after him. Walking stiffly, he crossed the parking lot. They were staring at him, he knew that. White eyes in black faces, staring at him. Across the street at the corner, in front of a row of seedy stores, a group of blacks lounged at a lamppost.

He pushed the suitcase into the middle phone booth and tucked it underneath the seat. Then Carew sat, closing the door. An odor of urine assailed his nostrils. Out of the corner of his eye he saw that someone had written on the door with black marker. Eyes swimming, Carew focused. "Free Angela," it said. "All power to the people!"

Carew looked at his watch. Beneath his shirt, rivulets of perspiration ran from his armpits. He swallowed hard. Behind him, a row of eyes was boring into the back of his head.

4:50 P.M.

Greer had picked up Carew just before the Chelsea exit. At the turn onto Van Sicklen Street, he was directly behind the green station wagon. Then, slowing, he had pulled into the same lot and gone into the restaurant.

He sat staring out of the window at the man in the telephone booth. Sweat, you bastard, Greer thought, enjoying it. Just sit there and sweat. Around him people munched on hamburgers and drank their coffee and behind him there was the sizzle of meat frying on an open grill. He took another sip of his orange drink and wet his lips with his tongue.

5:00 P.M.

"Don't wanna talk about it," Hamp Norris insisted. His eyes, hooded and withdrawn, stole glances at the crowd that surrounded him.

"Goddammit, man, you got to tell us about it," Colley Watson declared, his face no more than six inches away. A group of curious adults and children had gathered, listening to the debate and watching the participants with practiced eyes. The old man had stolen something, obviously, and these others, the ones who had come tearing up in the blue Oldsmobile, they meant to get it back. They would make the old guy talk, sooner or later, but it might take some time. Meanwhile, it was a good show.

Under his blue denim jacket, Hamp was cold. Why didn't they all go away and leave him alone? He wanted to forget that car. Who wants to remember he's going crazy?

"Man, I'm telling you," Watson said, "you don't open up I'm gonna hit you upside the head, hear?"

Hamp shivered, staring at the black pavement.

"That's enough," said Henry. He edged past Colley. The old man didn't want to tell them anything, that was plain. And the more Watson pressed him, the more obstinate he was becoming. Henry put a gentle hand on the old man's shoulder. "I'd like to buy you a drink," he said quietly.

Hamp considered. They had already pressed money into his hand, throwing questions at him until his head spun, particularly the man in the beret, who looked as mean as a man could look.

But this older man, he seemed kind. As if he understood that sometimes a man had to drink and that the drinking could make him see strange things. His nod was barely perceptible.

"Come on, then," Henry Taylor said. He put an arm around Hamp's shoulder.

"Stand back!" Colley cleared a path to the sidewalk. "Let 'em through!"

At the curb, the old man hesitated. "My cart . . ."

"My boys'll watch it," said Colley.

"Don't let 'em take nothing. I got things in that cart."

"Don't worry about your cart," Henry said as Hamp stood unmoving. "I'll buy you another cart."

"Don't want no other cart," Hamp insisted. He put a foot back into the gutter.

"Believe me," Henry said, "nothing's going to happen to your cart. These people will protect it all night if they have to. Now will you come along?"

He came, and they walked down the street to Henry's car. The crowd followed right along. Henry opened the front door and let the old peddler get in before swinging behind the wheel. Colley Watson and Roy Hart climbed into the rear seat and closed the door behind them.

"You sure you don't want to talk about it now?" Henry said mildly before starting the engine. The old man shook his head. "Not till I get a drink."

"All right," Henry said.

"And maybe not then," Hamp said abruptly.

Henry sighed. A dozen angry words sprang to his lips but he bit them back. In time, the old man would tell them what he had seen, but not before he was ready. "Where to?" Henry asked.

Hamp's face brightened. "The Red Apple is nice," he said. "The Red Apple will do fine."

5:10 P.M.

Greer left the White Hut by the front door and circled the corner. If there was someone watching Carew, he was sure they weren't in a car on the parking lot. All of the cars that had been there when Carew pulled in were gone. And almost all of the ones that had arrived shortly afterward had left too. The lot was safe.

As he waited for the traffic light to change, Greer stared at Carew. He hadn't moved in ten minutes. Greer crossed the street, looking back again when he reached the far corner. Somewhere in this corner that faced the White Hut the pigs could be waiting. Casually Greer walked up the street, looking into the row of parked cars that lined the curb. Empty, all of them. Midway down the block he crossed the street and turned back.

Outside a tenement a man sat in a beat-up Plymouth, his head bent under the dash. Greer slowed his pace and stepped up to the car, looking in. A kid stared, his eyes wide with fright. As Greer jumped back in alarm, the kid leaped out of the car and began to run away.

Greer wanted to run too, but he was frozen. From under the dash a jumble of wires protruded. Greer stared at them, realizing that he had surprised the kid in the act of stealing the car.

He stepped back and leaned against the front stoop of the tenement. Then he hustled down the street to the corner where he could see the phone booth.

Carew was still there, unmoving in the middle booth, the phone safely on the hook.

Giving Carew a final look, Greer stepped inside the candy store. He walked slowly past the counter, ignoring the hard stare of the scar-faced proprietor. Easing his way past the wire rack of potato chips and pretzels, he sat down in the phone booth at the rear of the store. The card was in his jacket pocket, the number of the telephone booth across the street plainly printed on it. Fishing a dime from his trouser pocket, he dialed.

5:20 P.M.

Carew picked up the phone on the first ring. That voice again, edged with steel.

"Welcome to Northside, Carew. How you like it?"

Silent, Carew stared out on the parking lot.

"We been watching you all the way down here, and there's more of us lookin' at you right now. So don't try anything funny. Now, here's what you gotta do—"

"Just a moment," Carew interrupted, "the children. When will you release them?"

"Keep your pants on, Carew, you're getting ahead of yourself. First you're gonna drop off the money. Then I'm gonna pick it up. Then I'm gonna count it. Then I'm gonna make myself very scarce. And when I get to where I'm going, then I'm gonna call you and tell you where to find the kids."

"Before I turn the money over to you I want to talk to one of the children again," said Carew.

"Uh-uh."

"Why not? Why can't I make sure the children are still safe?"

Carew heard a quick intake of breath. "Listen, you, if you don't do what I say I'm gonna call the whole deal off and go blow their little fucking heads off."

Carew closed his eyes. There were no options any more. "All right," he said quietly. "I'll do as you say. But please, don't hurt the children."

There was a short laugh. "Why would we do that? We ain't crazy. And by tonight, if you play it straight, they gonna be home. Now just listen to me."

A heavy sigh escaped Carew. A cab would come for him in fifteen minutes. He would use the name "Mr. Charles." He was to give the driver a certain address. Carew repeated it carefully.

"It's an empty lot, but don't worry about that," said Greer. "Pay off the cabbie and let him drive away. Make sure he's gone, you hear?" Greer went on, giving Carew explicit instructions on where to walk, what to look for, where the money was to be placed. Afterward, Carew was to come back to his car on the parking lot of the White Hut and sit in it for exactly one hour. Then he was to drive back to the school. About midnight, Carew would receive a call telling him where the children were to be found.

"Don't mess it up," Greer said at last. "If you call the pigs, the kids are dead."

"Hello, Black Diamond," Greer said when the cab dispatcher picked up the phone. "I'm at the White Hut on Van Sicklen, sitting in the phone booth out back. How long?"

"Fifteen minutes, maybe less," the dispatcher said.

"Okay," Greer said. He spoke very distinctly. "My name is Mr. Charles and I got a suitcase. Tell your man to drive onto the parking lot."

"Right."

"Oh, and by the way," Greer added, "he won't have any trouble knowing me. I'm the only white man in the place."

5:25 P.M.

At the Red Apple, Floogie uncapped a bottle of muscatel, but before he could pour Hamp stopped him. "Not that." Hamp jerked his head at the doctor. "My friend's paying. Bring the burgundy."

"We're waiting, Norris," Colley growled, but Henry waved him to silence.

Hamp took another sip.

"Any time you're ready," Henry Taylor said quietly.

Hamp sighed, and drained the glass. "You don't suppose," he began, rolling his eyes toward heaven.

"You can take the bottle home if you tell us what we want to know," Henry said.

Hamp poured the glass half full. "I seen it, then it went away," he said. "A big black Cadillac, one of them limousines. I seen it plain as day, just a-comin' down the street."

"County plates?" Henry held his breath.

Hamp shrugged. "Couldn't say." He eyed the wine.

"You said it went away. Where did it go?"

"That was the crazy part. First it was there, big and black. And then, when I give it another look-see, it wasn't. Simple as that."

Colley Watson made a noise with his lips and looked toward the door.

This is what it has come down to, Roy Hart thought, the drunken daydream of an old wino who was probably half out of his tree. He felt sick.

Henry Taylor stared at the junkman. As much as he wanted to believe the old man, Hamp Norris's words had filled him with despair. "I see," he said at last.

"Honked the horn, too," Hamp said. "Leastways, I think I heard it."

A whole day of searching and this is all we've found, Henry Taylor thought. He remembered Junior's face and a muscle began twitching in his leg. "Hamp," he said huskily, "I believe you. You and me, we know you saw that limousine. Now, Hamp, I want you to tell me *where* it disappeared."

Hamp nodded, his lips pursed. A gnarled hand scratched at the stubble on his cheek. "That's just it," he said, his voice no more than a whisper. "Damned if I can remember . . ."

5:45 P.M.

Sitting in the Volkswagen at the rear of the parking lot, Greer saw the bright-red gypsy cab swing onto the blacktop. It rolled to a stop alongside the telephone booths.

Carew approached the car. It didn't look much like any taxi he had ever seen. A diamond-shaped black panel on the door proclaimed, "Black Diamond—you call, we haul!" Stenciled on the rear fender was a slogan: "WE'RE NOT YELLOW—WE GO ANYWHERE." But there was no sign on the cab's roof.

The driver leaned his head out of the front window. "You Mr. Charles?"

Carew hesitated. "Are you a taxi?"

The driver expectorated onto the blacktop. "No, I'm a fire engine," he scowled. "You call for a cab, buddy?"

"Yes . . . yes, I did." Turning, Carew retrieved the suitcase and climbed in. The smell of exhaust fumes filled the cab. The driver had a clipboard and pencil in his hand. "We goin' somewhere?" he said. "Or are we sitting?"

"Oh," Carew said. He quoted the address and was jerked back as the taxi shot forward. Unconsciously, his hand clenched the handle of the suitcase.

They drove past streets he had never before seen, through avenues that might have existed only in his mind. Once, long ago, he had served on a federal commission charged with finding art treasures hidden away in postwar Germany. The center of Dresden . . . the Tiergarten in Berlin . . . that was what these mounds of rubble and half-gutted buildings reminded him of.

Greer was far ahead, zipping through the traffic and heading west toward the river. He felt confident. The turf he had selected was his own. There would be no hangups.

It was almost dark when he reached the empty lot. The street light he had smashed had not been replaced. There was not a soul around, for people no longer lived in the district. Someday, proclaimed a sign, the city would construct a low-cost housing unit on the block. Hang by your thumbs, Greer thought, as he swung around the corner and came down the block behind the empty lot.

Sterling Place . . . He brought the car to a halt before number 1719. Five years ago he had lived there. The year Mama died. For ten years he had played on these streets, running the back alleys and hiding in cellars. No one could know this place better. Home . . .

Greer pulled the car halfway across the street, then backed cautiously onto the sidewalk. He steered the little car down the alley as far as the side cellar entrance. Cutting the engine, he took the flashlight from the glove compartment, then stepped out.

He entered the cellar and moved swiftly along the passage. In the room to his left he had shot craps for the first time. On the roof of 1741, down the block, he had had his first woman.

He emerged from the cellar into a rear courtyard strewn with rubble. To his right was a brick wall just higher than the top of his head. Behind the wall was the empty lot. Greer stepped carefully to the wall, his shoes crunching on broken glass. He stepped up onto a small window ledge and peeked over the wall. It was very dark now, and his head was deep in shadow. Standing here, he could look out onto the lot and the street beyond. Soon Carew would come. And the money would be in his hands.

"You sure you got the right address?" the cabbie said. The taxi rolled slowly down the street, the driver noting the house numbers.

Behind him, Carew sat tense on the edge of his seat.

"This is it," said the driver, stopping just beyond the empty lot. "Got to be a mistake somewhere," he said. "Ain't nobody lives here any more."

"How much do I owe you?" Carew asked.

The driver looked at him curiously, then turned on the overhead light. For the first time Carew noticed that there was no meter. "What does this trip usually cost?" the driver said.

Carew looked at him and shrugged. "I've never come here before."

"Oh," the driver said. He looked away for a moment. "Call it a buck and a half then."

Carew took his wallet from his breast pocket and withdrew two dollars. He opened the door and stepped out onto the pavement, pulling the suitcase after him.

"Maybe I better wait for you," the driver said.

"Thank you, no. I'll be all right."

The driver put the cab in gear. "Watch yourself. This ain't a good place to go walking around at night."

Carew looked across the empty lot. He couldn't ever remember being so afraid before. Behind him, the cab rolled away, the sound of its engine receding as it picked up speed.

Carew stepped across the sidewalk and onto the path that led across the lot. He walked by the bare frame of a chair through which weeds sprouted. Beer cans and broken bricks were everywhere. Far away, traffic hummed. Carew found the turning and passed between a broken packing crate and a pile of automobile tires. In a few more steps he was at the wall. Behind it, Greer stood, his senses tuned and alert.

Carew put the suitcase on the ground beside him. "I'm here," he said. He hesitated for a moment, waiting for a reply, then took the suitcase in both hands and, struggling with its weight, placed it on top of the wall. He looked up as two black hands flashed in the twilight. The suitcase was no longer on the wall.

"Whoever you are," Carew shouted, hearing Greer's footsteps recede, "please . . . don't hurt the children. Please . . . let them go. . . ."

6:03 P.M.

Henry rolled the Oldsmobile to a stop and looked across the front seat at the old man. As if he could anticipate the question, Hamp Norris spoke: "That's the truth of it, honest. I just can't remember."

"Henry, we're getting nowhere," Roy Hart whispered from the back seat.

"Look, Hamp," Henry began, his voice open and friendly, "don't let it all crowd together in your mind. Relax for a minute. Let's take it one step at a time, okay?"

The doctor was right, thought Hamp. When you try to remember everything at once you can't think of nothing.

"Was the sun shining when you saw the car?" Henry said.

Hamp considered. "Yep," he said. "I remember how the sun was low in the sky . . . and when I looked at the car it was a-shinin' in my eyes."

"That's fine, Hamp." Henry turned to look at Watson and Roy Hart. "The car was coming from east to west. That would make it an odd-numbered street."

"If he's right it would," Colley Watson said.

"That only leaves half the streets in the Northside to cover," said Roy.

Henry turned back to the old peddler. "Before or after the car disappeared, did you see anything that you can recall?"

"Let me think."

"Take your time."

"Wait a minute now," Hamp said. "I do recall somethin' . . . but what was it?" His seamed face was wrinkled with concentration. Then his eyes flickered for just an instant and his head bobbed up and down. "Yes, sir, I'm sure of it. Just after the car went away I started walkin' toward Lenard Avenue. And the sun warn't in my eyes no more, it was to my back."

"East of Lenard Avenue," Henry said, his voice rising slightly. "That's where you were then, on an odd-numbered street east of Lenard Avenue."

"I reckon, yep."

"Hey now, we're getting warm," Colley Watson said.

"You're sure now, Hamp?" Henry said.

"Hell, yes," the old man replied, nodding his head. His jaw was set. "Why I could see Lenard Avenue plain as day ahead of me. No more than five or six blocks ahead of me."

"*You could see it?*" Henry said sharply.

Hamp Norris smiled. "Sure could. It was all downhill from where I was standin'. Lenard Avenue, straight ahead."

"The Hill!" Colley Watson and Roy Hart said at once, before Henry shot the Oldsmobile away from the curb.

"East of Lenard Avenue, up on the Hill," Henry said, "on an odd-numbered street. Hold on to your hats, we're on our way!"

6:05 P.M.

When the footsteps had gone, Carew backed slowly away from the wall. Turning, he walked back across the path and made his way to the sidewalk. Somewhere nearby, a small motor kicked over and began to throb. Far away, he heard heavy traffic. He walked slowly to the corner, feeling the coldness next to his skin where perspiration had run.

The next street was as deserted as the one he had left. A cat walked out of a cellar and crossed ten feet in front of him. Behind him there was a sudden noise, as if an empty can had been kicked. Whirling, he looked back and saw nothing. He began to walk faster.

He crossed the next street. In the gloom the empty tenements stared at him. Behind him, the sound of a shoe striking pavement. And then another footstep. Now he was afraid to look back. He walked still faster, hearing steps speeding up even as he did. He ran.

Civilization lay ahead, a blur of lights, stores and buildings occupied by human beings. But still blocks away. He was breathing hard, but more fearful than tired he kept on. At the corner he ran almost directly into a tall black man. Carew stopped short. "Please," he gasped, "help! I'm being chased."

The black man looked at him strangely. "By who?"

When Carew turned and stared back down the street there wasn't a soul to be seen.

6:15 P.M.

Everything was coming true, thought Greer, all of it. In other cities he would find other men. More Joyboys and Sparrows, men with nothing to lose. And now he could offer them more than a dream. The beginning of it all was right in his hand.

Jimmy was on the landing when Greer came up the stairs. Spotting the suitcase, he shouted, "He got it! He got it!"

"Yeah!" shouted Greer, bounding up the last three steps. "We done it, by God!"

Loretta danced with him, trying to take him in her arms. Only Joyboy was silent.

"It was nothing, you hear?" Greer said. "It all worked, everything." He put the suitcase on the table.

"Ain't we gonna open it?" said Jimmy.

Greer nodded and the boy's hands flew to the locks, snapping them open in an instant. The lid came up and he gasped.

"Oh, man," Joyboy murmured.

"It ain't real," Loretta said. "Pinch me, I don't believe it's real."

"Better be real," said Greer. Moving forward, he picked a banded stack of twenties from the case, weighing it in his hand.

"Shit," he said, "this stuff is brand-new." He put the stack down and began riffling through the rest. "A lot of it's new," he said. "Maybe half."

"Maybe you oughtta take it back," said Loretta.

Greer laughed. "Yeah," he said, "maybe. Hey, Joyboy, you think we should give it back?"

"Greer," Joyboy said, his voice very strange.

Slowly, Greer turned. Joyboy had backed away from the table, halfway across the room. The gun was in his hand.

"Greer," Joyboy said again. His lips were trembling.

Greer blinked in the dim light, a sickness rising inside him. His mouth moved, but he could say nothing. What a stupid joke, he thought, but he knew, even as he thought it, that this was not a joke.

"Greer," Joyboy started again, but he couldn't get the rest of it out. "Hey, man," he said. "Greer . . ."

Greer swallowed the lump that rose in his throat. "No," he said low, "you can't. I won't let you."

The hand holding the gun wavered for just an instant. It was Greer's eyes. He couldn't do it now. His nerve was gone.

"Put the gun down," said Greer.

"Greer," Joyboy said, but it was so hard to talk. "Hey . . . just a split, man."

"No." Greer's face was hard as stone.

"Oh, man," Joyboy pleaded, "just give me a split and let me out. Please . . . Greer. I don't want no more."

"Joyboy," Greer rasped, his voice growing stronger, "you owe me your life. You're mine, Joyboy, I saved you, remember? Picked you off the junkheap and made you a man again."

"Oh, man . . . please."

"Together, Joyboy. We put it together, remember? We don't quit now. Not you, not none of us."

Those eyes were burning into him. Joyboy felt tears. So weak, so weak. He couldn't do it. He would not get the money. There would be no Paris, no long trip, no life of his own. Greer would win again, and they would go on and on and then they would be dead, all dead, caught and killed because of Greer. "Please," he moaned.

But Greer wouldn't yield. He took a step toward Joyboy. And another step.

"No," Joyboy said, looking into those eyes.

"Give me the gun," said Greer, advancing slowly.

"Please," Joyboy begged as the gun roared and jerked in his hand and Greer's forehead was blown apart, a mist of pink filling the air as blood and brains and bits of bone flew onto Jimmy and Loretta, and Greer's body careened backward. There was smoke from the gun and the smell of blood and iron and fire as the screaming began.

Inside his head Joyboy still heard the sound of the explosion. Staggering back, he leaned against the refrigerator, crying out himself as he looked at the crumpled and bleeding body on the floor, seeing Loretta throw herself upon it to grasp that lifeless head to her breast, and hearing as if from a distance the cries of pain that came from deep within her. The boy had fallen to the floor beside her, his thin fists pounding the floor in a useless tattoo as over and over again he called Greer's name.

Retching, Joyboy leaned his head over the sink. Dead, he thought, I shot him dead. Looking stupidly at the gun, he tucked it back into the waistband of his trousers. With no thought or plan he moved forward, circling around the screaming figures on the floor and reaching the other side of the table. He stood there looking into the open suitcase, wondering what should he do now that he had done what he dared not think about before. Jimmy and Loretta were divorced from him now, strangers mourning over a stranger on the floor. My God, I killed him. I killed Greer. He closed the lid and snapped the lock. He had killed Greer and now the money was his. All of it.

His mouth moved, but he said nothing. Loretta's sobs

crushed the air. Joyboy moved to the landing, walking very slowly. A voice in his head told him to run, to go down the stairs and run. But that was not the way.

He put the suitcase down and sat heavily on the top step. He had to think it out now. On his own.

He lit a cigarette and tried to bring his thoughts under control. He could not just walk away. Upstairs were the children and the driver. The witnesses. If they lived, he would never be safe.

He dropped the cigarette on the step and ground it under his foot. For a moment he looked at his hand, then used it to wipe at his eyes. He began to feel better. He had to get rid of the bunch of them upstairs, that was the first thing to do. After that, he would figure out the rest.

He took a step toward the upstairs landing when he remembered the lock. The key. Greer had it in his pocket. He turned around and walked back into the room, no longer hearing Loretta's cries. Circling, he knelt beside the body. Greer's head was in Loretta's lap and she was talking to him, rocking back and forward. Feeling nothing, he searched in Greer's trousers pocket, bringing out car keys, a few loose bills, and the small key to the lock on the door upstairs. He put the key in his own pocket and he walked to the cabinet by the sink. Opening a drawer, he took out the box of ammunition. A handful of shells went into his jacket pocket, the rest of the box he put down on the sink. It was going to be a shooting gallery, but it couldn't be helped. He'd hit the driver first, then the older girl, blocking the doorway so the little kids couldn't get past him.

Without thinking he grasped the handle of the suitcase and took it with him upstairs. Easy, he thought, go slow now. Still, his hands were shaking as he opened the lock. The gun in his right fist, he turned the doorknob and pushed. Nothing happened.

He pushed again, then put his shoulder to the door. "Hey, open up," he said, before realizing why it would not move. They were blocking it from inside.

"Hey," he shouted. "Open the door."

No one inside answered. Charging across the narrow hall, Joyboy rammed the door with all his force, rubbing his shoulder with shock as he rebounded away. The goddamn door was blocked solid.

"Come on now," he shouted. From downstairs he heard Loretta scream.

He put his ear to the door and listened. He thought again of running, but he knew if he did he would never stop.

"Don't you want to go home?" he shouted. "Hey? Don't you want out?"

A laugh floated from inside the door, deep and rich; it hung in the hallway. The driver.

"Hey, man—we got the money, you hear? Time for you cats to go home."

"Beat it, buster!" the driver's voice called.

Joyboy thrummed a fist against the door. "Come on . . . time to go home. Open up!"

Still no answer.

"Motherfucker! Open the fuckin' door!" Shaking with fury, Joyboy brought the gun up and fired a shot into the door. He pushed again but the door would not move."

"Go away!" Carter called. "We're not coming out."

Joyboy tasted bile. Somehow, he had to get inside to finish the job. He could not leave them alive.

He sat down on the suitcase and lit a cigarette. In the

dim light a trail of blue smoke curled up. He took a short drag, coughing when the idea struck. He'd smoke them out. Burn the fucking place down. Downstairs, in the Caddy, was a tankful of gasoline. He'd splash it on the door and set it afire. When they felt that heat they'd run out fast enough.

He locked the door again, smiling. And if they didn't open up they'd die where they were. The fire would get them. The fire would get the whole damn fucking garage when it started.

Now it was clear again in his mind. He took the suitcase and went down the stairs.

"It worked," Kathy said as they heard Joyboy go back down the stairs.

"So far," said Ben, deciding Joyboy must have gone downstairs to get the others. They'll be back very soon and who knows if the barricade will hold. "Stay where you are, kids," he said. "Big Ben is going to even up the odds a little." Moving away from the mattress, he walked to the rear of the room and smashed the hanging light bulb. Then he broke the one that hung over the television set, and the room was black. "It's only me," he called, groping back to the door in the dark. His hands found a small head and he heard Heidi sniffle. "Be brave now," he whispered, holding her for a moment, "very brave."

The hand that guided him to his place was Kathy's. He put his back against the mattress. "When they try again," he said, "everybody do the same as before. Only this time let's push even harder."

The children were very quiet. The sound of their breathing was soft and even. Leaning his club against his leg, Ben wiped his sweating hand against his shirt.

He wondered briefly about the noise he had heard from below just a few minutes before. It had been a shot, of that he was certain. But what did it mean? Had they been fighting among themselves? Or were they merely cleaning their weapons? In either case, it promised nothing.

6:28 P.M.

Below them the lights of Lenard Avenue glittered in the dark. Henry Taylor looked at the old man. "This street?"

Hamp coughed, covering his mouth with a hand. "Could be. It's hard to know." He coughed again. "Could you ride a little slower?"

Henry braked to a crawl. Behind him, Roy and Colley leaned forward on the edge of the back seat, peering through the windshield.

"Hey now," Hamp Norris said. "Just a minute here."

Henry Taylor held his breath.

"You know," the old man said, "it just could be this here street. Can't be sure." He scratched his head. "I'm just a tryin' to remember which one of these cellars I was comin' out of when I seen it." He turned to face Henry. "Doctor, maybe if I gets out and walks a while, maybe then I'll know."

Henry pulled to the curb. Hamp opened the door and stepped to the sidewalk, his head tilted up, sniffing the air. As he turned and headed for Lenard Avenue, the other men got out and followed.

"It's familiar," Hamp said, "but it don't look right." He pointed toward the corner ahead. "Maybe that next block there . . ."

Roy's huge strides made the others walk faster.

Hamp and Henry Taylor crossed the intersection at a dogtrot. On the other side of the street the old man paused, looking ahead. "I think"—he began, then pointed ahead—"down by the next corner. I was by that old house down there, the one that's lit up."

"The limousine, then," Henry Taylor said, "it disappeared right here. Before it got to you."

The old man's nod set everyone running. "Look, Henry!" Roy Hart shouted, pointing ahead, "there's a cut in the sidewalk up there!" Henry could see it now, not fifty yards away. A driveway that led to a three-story building with a large door facing the street. It looked like a garage.

Joyboy put the suitcase down in the small office on the ground floor and began looking around for a container that would hold the gasoline. In the darkness outside the back door Joyboy saw a patch of white. Stooping, he picked up a can marked Valvoline, an oil can, with a triangular hole already punched in its crown. He came back inside the garage and walked across to the Cadillac.

On his hands and knees at the left rear tire, he looked underneath the massive automobile. The rounded belly of the fuel tank was within his reach, but just barely. He took the switchblade from his pocket and snapped it open. With a few downward strokes he widened the opening in the top of the oil can.

Lying on the greasy concrete floor, he saw he would have to crawl underneath the car to get at the fuel tank. Cursing under his breath, he wriggled underneath until it was almost directly over his head. He held the point of the knife to the tank and pounded its butt with his right fist. The point penetrated and immediately a thin rivulet of gasoline began to run down the blade onto his hand, then up his sleeve. He reached for the oil can and placed it directly under the knife. When he pulled the knife out of the tank a rush of gas streamed down, splashing into the can and on the floor, making a small pool that lapped at his shoulders. Joyboy began wriggling away, coming half out from under the car and turning onto his stomach. The smell of gasoline was everywhere.

Just as he was about to pull the can out, he heard someone trying to open the garage door.

Roy Hart was tugging at the handle when Henry ran up. Putting his hands on top of Roy's, the two men heaved together. The door creaked and then shot upward.

"Look!" Henry shouted. The limousine was clearly outlined against the rear wall. He reached for his pistol. From underneath the rear wheels of the limousine there was a flash and a bullet whined off the concrete under his feet. And just as suddenly there was a muffled explosion, a ball of red-orange flame under the wheels of the car that stopped Henry in his tracks. Then a loud and crushing *whoomp* as the fuel tank exploded in a blast of heat and flame that threw Henry back to the street. He watched in horror as Joyboy rolled screaming in agony from under the car.

Henry dashed forward, stripping off his raincoat. Like an avenging angle he swooped down on the body, covering the flaming torso with his coat, dropping onto his knees to beat at the licking flames. His arms windmilled, hitting coat and arms and shoulders. And then his hands balled into fists and now he beat still harder, smashing down with clenched fists, striking down with all his force with a rage that he could not control.

Two arms circled him roughly and pulled him away. "Enough," Hart said. "The fire is out."

Henry shuddered. He drew himself to his feet and looked down at the badly burned man who lay, barely breathing, at his feet. Suddenly he shouted "Junior!" Roy had already turned away and was running up the narrow staircase, Henry's pistol in his hand.

On the second floor, both men stared into the dimly lit room, looking in horror at the girl who sat quietly on the floor, crooning to the body in her arms that could no longer hear her voice.

"Where are they?" Henry demanded, but the girl did not even look up.

Both men ran up the next flight of stairs, Henry still screaming his son's name. From behind the locked door at the top of the stairs, wary and guarded, came a voice: "Hello. Who are you?"

And behind that, first in wonder then in joy, a child said, "Daddy? *Hey, it's my Dad*!"

SATURDAY

8:00 P.M.

Stuffed with dinner, and having been pampered outrageously all day, the two boys were now upstairs in Junior's room watching the basketball game on television. In the dining room below, Mildred Taylor and Irene Schwartz lingered over coffee. The night was clear, unseasonably warm, and Henry and Norman Schwartz were standing in the garden.

Mildred's irises were in full flower, and the first of the tulips were sprouting green shoots near the budding hedge. Henry's pipe glowed red in the dark, casting pale light on his drawn face. He looked up as Norman said, "I thought Carew was going to have apoplexy when that guy interviewed him on television. Did you see that look on his face?"

"Yes," Henry said. "Lost his dignity, didn't he?"

"Well, the police had just given him a hard time, I understand."

"Yes," said Henry. "Which reminds me, I'll have to give them another statement myself on Monday."

"Colley Watson?" Norman asked softly.

"I hope not. No, I don't want to involve Watson if I can help it. Strange, how he just faded away when Roy and I broke in. Not that I blame him."

"No, I suppose not," Norman said.

"Colley Watson," Henry said, shaking his head. "I wonder how it's going to feel, working at the Young Simbas Medical Center, if that's what we decide to call it. Of course," he added, "I have my own ideas on that."

"Such as?"

"Malcolm X wouldn't be a bad name, would it? He was someone both Colley and I admired. Anyway, now that Colley and I are going to be colleagues, I imagine there'll be many things we'll be disagreeing about. I'm looking forward to teaching him some things . . . and learning some, too."

"Sad about Mrs. Barnett, isn't it?" Norman said.

Henry nodded in the dark. "Didn't even recognize her daughter, I understand, when Carmine took her home last night."

"People react strangely to things like this. My phone didn't stop ringing all day long."

"Your phone?" Henry said, laughing. "My answering service is giving me hell for not taking any calls. And some of my patients, too, I imagine."

"My mother called this morning," Norman said, "when the story broke on TV. God, it was a good thing she didn't know about it until it was over." He looked thoughtful for a moment. "You know my mother lives in the city . . . in the house where I grew up. All she could talk about this morning was how she had to sell the house and move away. Get out of the neighborhood. Because . . . well, she said the neighborhood was turning black."

Henry sighed.

"Of course we argued," Norman continued. "I told her she was foolish, but something she said struck me, Henry. It wasn't Negroes, *per se*, she was worried about. The family next door to her is black—lovely people—and there have been quite a few black families living on the block for years. So it wasn't that, she said, which worried her. But around the corner, near the supermarket, there've been a couple of muggings and a woman had her purse snatched not two weeks ago. And her beauty parlor, she said, where she goes every week, that's about five blocks away and now she's afraid to walk there by herself. There are men standing on street corners, she says, and drug addicts."

"Street crime," Henry said, "the curse of the ghetto. Did you tell her, Norman, that black people are afraid of muggers, too?"

"No, but I should have," Norman said. "The beauty parlor and the supermarket. Taking a walk to buy a newspaper. Being afraid to go to a movie at night. Stupid little things you never stop to think about. And for those things, not from hate, she's going to move away. And because of her fear, another good street that was beginning to be integrated will turn black."

"And where does it end, Norman?"

"I don't know."

"Ah, Norman," Henry began, "I wonder sometimes if

it's ever going to work. This marvelous idea that black and white should live side by side.

"Look at us, you and me. You know what we are? The high point of integration in the United States. That's right, Norman, you and me. Two people who've come to know and respect each other because our ideas are the same. We think alike."

"And we're lousy golfers," Norman said.

"That, too. Yes," Henry said. "But where are the rest of us? *Where the hell are the rest of us?*"

Henry turned and looked back at the amber spill of light that came from the windows of his home. He heard a gust of laughter from the boys in Junior's room upstairs. A breeze fanned the leaves of the maple tree above his head. The two men walked back into the house.

8:15 P.M.

When the diesel cleared the toll station, Jimmy climbed down from the cab. "Thanks for the lift," he called. The driver waved and swung south toward Lancaster.

Jimmy crossed the highway and walked against the traffic up the long hill. Harrisburg. It had changed since he'd been away. There were new motels and diners. And the highway had been widened. To his left, the slag heap of the Bethlehem plant glowed red in the night.

It was cold now, and he shivered in his thin denim jacket.

Pictures flashed in Jimmy's mind as he walked. Loretta and Greer, hugging and laughing in the old days. Greer, reading to him from those books upstairs. Greer, alive and tall and strong, teaching him about so many things. And now dead. And somewhere, maybe today or tomorrow, the police would be out searching for a kid named Jimmy Little.

He reached the top of the hill and looked at the valley spread like a map before him. The lights made the capitol dome shine like gold against the black Susquehanna. In the streets behind that building, he thought, is where I'll find them. If Mama is still there. If the rest of them are still living here.

He began walking down the hill toward the city. If they were still here, he would find them. And he would make them take him in and keep him safe.

He wondered if they would know him now, and if they had changed.